# A SHOCKING ASSASSINATION

*Selection of Recent Titles by Cora Harrison
from Severn House*

The Reverend Mother Mysteries

A SHAMEFUL MURDER
A SHOCKING ASSASSINATION


*The Burren Mysteries*

WRIT IN STONE
EYE OF THE LAW
SCALES OF RETRIBUTION
DEED OF MURDER
LAWS IN CONFLICT
CHAIN OF EVIDENCE
CROSS OF VENGEANCE
VERDICT OF THE COURT
CONDEMNED TO DEATH
A FATAL INHERITANCE

# A SHOCKING ASSASSINATION

## Cora Harrison

severn
House

This first world edition published 2016
in Great Britain and the USA by
SEVERN HOUSE PUBLISHERS LTD of
19 Cedar Road, Sutton, Surrey, England, SM2 5DA.
Trade paperback edition first published
in Great Britain and the USA 2016 by
SEVERN HOUSE PUBLISHERS LTD

British Library Cataloguing in Publication Data
A CIP catalogue record for this title is available from the British Library.

ISBN-13: 978-0-7278-8596-8 (cased)
ISBN-13: 978-1-84751-727-2 (trade paper)
ISBN-13: 978-1-78010-788-2 (e-book)

Typeset by Palimpsest Book Production Ltd.,
Falkirk, Stirlingshire, Scotland.

This book is dedicated to my dear brother, James, my friend and companion in the Cork of the 1940s and 1950s. It is also dedicated to the memory of my father and mother who told me many tales of events that occurred in the early 1920s in that deeply divided city. As the one was a young solicitor with 'west Briton' leanings and the other was a convent schoolgirl with Republican connections, I hope that I have correctly remembered both sides of the story.

# ACKNOWLEDGEMENTS

Thanks, as always, are due to my wonderful agent, Peter Buckman, as hard-working and shrewd as he is humorous and entertaining; to my editor Anna Telfer, who still, after so many books, manages to say nice things about my writing and to be perceptive as well as enthusiastic. And also to the team at Severn House who choose such wonderful covers and make my books a joy to behold.

Thanks to fellow author, Peter Beresford Ellis (Peter Tremayne), who has given me permission to quote from the writings of his father, Allan Ellis, a journalist on the *Cork Examiner* during the burning down of the city of Cork. I owe a debt of gratitude, also, to the authors of *The Burning of Cork*, Gerry White and Brendan O'Shea; and to Diarmuid and Donal O'Drisceoil for their fascinating book, *Serving a City*, the story of Cork's unique 'English Market'.

# ONE

St Thomas Aquinas:
*Sustinare est difficillius quam aggredi.*
(To endure is more difficult than to attack.)

Reverend Mother Aquinas was buying buttered eggs in the English Market on the Friday morning when the city engineer was assassinated.

No one screamed. She remembered that afterwards. They just moved away.

The gas lamps in the gallery above the stalls had been extinguished, quite suddenly. Seconds later the shot rang out. Her heart thudded, just a single stroke, and her breath quickened as she was swept back by the moving bodies all around her. The thick darkness intensified the smell of blood, of raw meat, of wet clothes, stale sweat, dung and the pungency of damp sawdust, mixed in with the almost palpable odours of fear. There was an uncanny silence for a moment after the shot when, like a well-drilled platoon of soldiers, the crowd of people all stepped back from the centre of the market, back behind the stalls, crowding into the shadows, huddling against the walls on either side. The woman beside the Reverend Mother sucked in a great gulp of air and sobbed audibly. There was a rattle of rosary beads as though someone had started to pray and she herself sent up a quick appeal to God that she might be spared, not for her own sake, but for the work that she would leave unfinished. And, like everyone else, she held her breath waiting for the next shot.

Gun shots were an almost daily occurrence in Cork city – had been for years. Even now, even in the April of 1923, when the War of Independence was drawing to a close and Liam Lynch, chief of staff of the Republican Army, had been assassinated over a fortnight ago; yet in this rebel city the guns still rang out. At the sound of an explosion no Cork person hesitated. Even the youngest of the children instantly dived for cover.

A few more moments' hush, but no more shots exploded. Michael Skiddy lit a candle from his own stall and one by one the stallholders followed his example. The gas system at the market was notoriously unreliable and everyone was prepared with a candle by the till or money box. Michael Skiddy, the Reverend Mother suddenly remembered, had a candle lit even before the gas lamps went out. She remembered seeing on the tiled wall the shadow of a man who had been leaning over the stall talking earnestly in his ear. It had been a man in a belted raincoat with a slouch hat pulled well over his face. A member of the Republican Army, she had thought when she had seen him first – they were notorious for this unofficial uniform. She noticed that others avoided the stall, that they hesitated and then passed on. *The Shadow of a Gunman*, she said to herself remembering reading the review in the *Irish Times* of the Seán O'Casey play now showing in the Abbey Theatre in Dublin. We live our lives in the shadow of the gunmen, she was thinking now, as the superintendent of the market shouted, 'Patsy', handed the keys to the gallery to the woman and then, a few minutes later, one by one the gas lamps on the overhead gallery popped into life again.

But it had only needed one lamp to illuminate the body on the ground. Black coat, black trousers, top hat a yard away leaving the bald scalp with its fringe of grey hair exposed to view and the face hidden in the sawdust on the floor. No sign of an injury, but the people of Cork were used to dead bodies, used to the smell of death and this body looked undoubtedly dead. No one moved forward. It was best not to interfere with public assassinations.

In any case, the assassin was still there, still standing, still holding the gun in his hand. Only two minutes ago, James Doyle, the city engineer, surrounded by colleagues and market shoppers, had been halfway through a well-rehearsed speech about the wisdom of waiting to rebuild the whole market instead of just repairing the two stalls burned down over two years ago and the next minute he was lying dead on the ground and his audience had rapidly distanced themselves. All except for that one man. For a moment all that the Reverend Mother had seen, left exposed in the centre space, was the slumped figure of James Doyle, City Engineer, but then she recognized the other figure. Young Sam O'Mahony was standing a few yards from the body, standing very still and holding a small pistol in his hand. No one moved, but the Reverend Mother noticed that every head had turned to look at him. There was a long minute of silence, almost as though all were frozen and she wondered why he had not taken advantage of it in order to escape. Then Sam started violently, gave an inarticulate cry and flung the gun from him towards the stone fountain in the centre of the stalls. It hit the scalloped top basin, bounced against the beak of an elegantly carved long-legged heron, missed the second basin and fell with an audible splash into the murky waters of the curved stone bowl at the base. That seemed to break the spell; a low buzz of voices began. One or two people emerged from the shadows and went hesitantly towards the body. Mrs O'Mahony from behind her drisheen and tripe stall screamed, 'Sam!' and then stopped abruptly as though the sound was choked off.

In the frightened silence that followed, fifteen-year-old Lizzie Carlton dropped a box of onions. They rolled across the tiled floor and Lizzie hastily retrieved one from under the nose of the dead man. The two Murphy brothers, both butchers, came out from behind their stall, red-stained choppers and saws in hands, almost as though the chief engineer of Cork city was a mere carcass dragged in from the nearby lane and lying ready to be carved into neat joints.

The superintendent of the market shouted, 'Everyone stand still! Stay right where you are!'

The town planner, Robert Newenham, came forward, bent down and put a hand on the man's heart and Thomas Browne, the city engineer's assistant, followed him, looked back at the market superintendent and then said hesitantly, 'Shouldn't someone get the civic guards?'

At those words the two beadles, dressed in their official uniform, leaped forward and each grabbed one of Sam O'Mahony's arms. For a moment he looked stunned and then realisation dawned. His face was contorted as he struggled violently, shouting, 'I didn't do it! I didn't do it, I tell you. That gun landed on my foot. I just picked it up! I flung it away in case it would go off. I know nothing about guns! I've never touched a gun in my life.' He looked across the heads of the crowd over towards his mother's stall and yelled at the top of his voice, 'I didn't do it, ask my mother. She'll tell you that I've never owned a gun, never handled a gun. I don't believe in violence. I'm not a Republican or a Free Stater. I wouldn't do a thing like that.'

There was an inarticulate, choking sound from Mrs O'Mahony, and all heads turned towards her as she came forward, red, swollen hands extended in front of her, held out towards her son. Her mouth opened, but no words came, just a sound of dry retching followed by a great gush of blood that spurted from her nose and dripped down her chin, soaking the rough apron of pale brown sacking that covered her dress. She mopped her nose impatiently with the edge of her black shawl, but her eyes never left her son.

There had been times during the last fifty years when the Reverend Mother had wondered whether she had missed something from her life by not bearing children, but the anguished expression on Mrs O'Mahony's face made her feel that no joy could compensate such agony. Sam, she knew, was an only child, a good-looking young man, dark hair sleeked back, a slight build, not tall, but an intelligent face. He struggled violently in the grip of the beadles, but they overpowered him after a minute, twisting his arms behind his back. One placed a heavy boot on the young man's foot and Mrs O'Mahony took another step forward, her hands still outstretched in a passion of protectiveness while blood still haemorrhaged from her nose. Patsy emerged from the door to the gallery, offering the corner of a threadbare towel, but Mrs O'Mahony ignored her.

'Sam!' She choked over the word and another flow of blood came from her nose. Once again she put the shawl to her face.

Patsy put a compassionate arm around her and the market superintendent shifted his feet uncomfortably.

'Poor woman,' said the owner of the buttered eggs stall and then said no more as all heads turned to look at her before swivelling back to look at the man who had held the gun.

The Reverend Mother knew about Sam, although he was not one of her former pupils. His widowed mother worked for twelve hours a day with her tripe and drisheen stall and had managed to make enough money out of her sales of these two Cork specialities to send her only child to a fee-paying school from where he had gone on to become a journalist and, by all accounts, the pride and joy of his mother's heart. But then Sam, she had heard, had lost his job after his outspoken article in the *Cork Examiner* about waste and corruption on the city council and now, she had been told by one of the lay sisters who normally did the marketing for the convent, Sam worked with his mother at the market. Perhaps he had got another reporting job; he certainly had been holding a notepad and pencil poised ready to take down the words of the great man. She had noticed that, just before the shot rang out.

'Take it easy, Sam. Take it easy, lad,' said the superintendent and the Reverend Mother wondered whether she was the only one to notice a slight tremble in his voice. Mr O'Donnell had been superintendent at the English Market for over twenty years and dealt efficiently with cases of drunkenness, fights, dirty stalls and disposal of refuse, but a murder was something new for him. And yesterday's paper had announced that the city engineer, Mr James Doyle, had been tried in a secret Republican court and found guilty of embezzlement of the money to reconstruct the city. If this were an assassination, it would not be unknown for the Republicans to stage a rescue of their gunman.

It took him an anxious minute of looking up and down the shadowy passageways before he turned to one of the messenger boys from the butcher's stall. 'On your bike, lad,' he barked. 'Get to the barracks as fast as you can and tell Inspector Cashman what happened. Tell him that the city engineer has been assassinated. Go on, Georgy. Fast as you can. Nobody is to move until the civic guards come. I'm shutting the Princes Street gate now and Jeremiah and John, you put up the barrier between your two stalls and don't let none of the traders or the shoppers from the Grand Parade side of the market get through.'

'I didn't do it,' said Sam loudly and hoarsely. He struggled again for a moment, but the beadles were solid, squarely-built men, used to dealing with tough and sometimes drunken traders and they held him grimly.

'Now take it easy, Sam,' said the superintendent again. 'Look, you're upsetting your mother. 'Take it easy, now. The inspector will be along in five minutes. Won't take him more than that. He'll sort everything out.'

'It must have been somebody else. I never saw that gun in my life.' Sam was sweating heavily now. Patsy had lit the gas lamp just beside Mrs O'Mahony's stall and it showed the perspiration beaded on his forehead and cheeks. His voice was hoarse and cracked but he held himself very straight. 'It must have been one of the Republicans,' he said and there was a note of desperation in his voice as Patsy Mullane in a dazed fashion went methodically along the line of stalls beyond the tripe and drisheen stall, lighting each gas lamp as she went, until the superintendent made a signal to her and then she stopped, standing hesitantly with the taper in her hand and the old bloodied towel still draped over one arm.

Poor Patsy. She had been an excellent children's librarian, but the Black and Tans had burned down the Carnegie Library as well as the city hall beside it and Patsy was given a week's notice. That was a couple of years ago and still the library had not been rebuilt. *Waiting to make a palace out of it; that Mr Doyle has big ideas.* Patsy had answered her query earlier with a sour grimace and the Reverend Mother did not blame her. Patsy, so good, she had heard, at her job in finding the right book for a child, was fairly poor as a sweeper in the market and she would be earning less than ten shillings for long hours spent sweeping soiled sawdust from under the feet of the shoppers.

'That's better,' said the superintendent with a false heartiness. 'Now we can all see what we are doing.' Like everyone else he now averted his eyes from the despairing face of the young man held so securely by the two officials and looked all around him.

A spectacular building, thought the Reverend Mother, built when the British Empire was at its height and able to spare some money for its far-flung outposts – wonderfully tiled floors and walls in warm colours of red, orange, green and yellow with striped awnings over each individual stall. The stalls, though, could certainly do with being better lit during the dark days of fog and rain which happened nine days out of ten for three seasons of the year in this marsh city. The money to run the market properly was lacking in 1923. Prices and wages had stagnated during the last few years. The stallholders could not afford higher rents and the place could not be run properly unless extra revenues were generated.

There was still a heavy silence over the normally noisy market. The gas lamps cast light down but left many shadows. Several of the stallholders had lit candles and were fiddling with goods on their stalls by the feeble light. Michael Skiddy lit a second candle, illuminating his wares. He had been another one of the many victims of the Black and Tans' burning of the centre of Cork city two years ago, when a prosperous men's clothing shop had been set on fire and Michael Skiddy's soap and candle shop in a nearby lane had been unlucky enough to be in the path of the flying embers. Candles and soap had all gone up in flames; though the Skiddy family had managed to rescue some of their machinery and candle moulds to set up a new business in one of the stalls at the English Market.

She must purchase some candles from him before she left, was her thought and then she looked back at Sam O'Mahony. What could have possessed the boy to choose such a public place for this so-called execution? She supposed that his masters in the Republican Army had wanted this to be an example to all other municipal officers who might abuse their position.

'Better get that gun,' said Captain Robert Newenham, the town planner. 'Would you like me to take charge of it, super-intendent? I was in the army, you know. Spent four years in France fighting Fritz! Not much I don't know about guns.' He moved forward towards the fountain with an air of authority and then, as the Reverend Mother stepped into his pathway, he stopped abruptly.

'Oh, Reverend Mother,' he stammered. 'I didn't know that you were here.' His eyes went to her basket and widened slightly. They met from time to time at the bishop's gatherings and he always made a big fuss about them being cousins – second cousins, once removed, in fact, but she allowed him to claim the relationship. He was visibly astounded at the sight of her doing her own shopping, but he recovered after a minute. 'I've got my car here. Let me drive you home, take you out of here.'

'I would be most grateful, once the inspector allows us to leave, of course,' said the Reverend Mother, primly, wondering how he would like taking his expensive car through the mud along the quays. 'I think, Captain Newenham,' she murmured in his ear, as he stretched out his hand towards the fountain, 'I do think that the gun should be left until the inspector arrives, don't you? But, of course, you would know more about those things than I.'

He looked annoyed, but she stayed there, smiling blandly at him. 'I suppose that the gun will be quite safe in the fountain until the civic guards arrive, isn't that right, Mr O'Donnell?' she said as the superintendent approached.

'Quite safe, Reverend Mother, don't you worry. Nothing for you to worry about.'

The Reverend Mother looked across at the white, blood-smeared face of the woman now clinging on to the edge of her stall and then at the angry, terrified face of her son and thought that there was very definitely something to worry about. Sam O'Mahony was a talented young man who had made a bad mistake when he attacked, by name, a prominent citizen, like the city engineer, in his newspaper column. That had been stupid, but it was a mistake that was easily made in the arrogance of youth and hopefully he would get another job, or, like many others, get the boat to England or America. He was clever and well-educated and could be expected to make a success of his life.

But if he were found guilty of this killing he would be hanged. The Reverend Mother stirred from her position, took the piece of ragged towelling from Patsy's limp hand, dipped it into the icy cold water of the fountain and handed it to Sam's mother.

'Just hold that to your nose for a few minutes,' she said

authoritatively. It was, she thought, the only practical thing that she could do at the moment.

Ten minutes later, the inspector and his team arrived. Inspector Patrick Cashman was newly promoted from the position of sergeant, but already he had begun to look older, thought the Reverend Mother, noting his gravity and self-possession as he arrived at the English Market flanked by a group of civic guards. He had been one of her pupils, one of the few successes amongst the many who were lost to emigration, prostitution, unemployment, chronic illness and death, either from disease or from suicide. She was proud of him, but did not underestimate the difficulties and dangers of his position.

Patrick came in very quietly, spoke softly to the superintendent, noticed the Reverend Mother with a quick glance, looked sharply at Sam O'Mahony, at the two beadles who still held his arms, at the white-faced, dry-eyed woman beside them and then turned his attention to the body, kneeling down in the sawdust and touching the dead face momentarily. After less than a minute he rose to his feet.

'It's Mr James Doyle, the city engineer,' said the superintendent and Patrick nodded gravely.

'God have mercy on him,' added the superintendent.

'Wasn't he a Protestant?' asked one beadle to the other in a loud whisper, over the top of Sam's head.

The superintendent glared and everyone else politely pretended not to hear.

'Does anyone know what happened to Mr Doyle?' asked Patrick. There was enough emphasis on the word 'know' to inhibit the normally vociferous market stallholders and their customers. Only the town planner, Captain Newenham, stepped forward.

'This young man, so competently secured by the good superintendent of the market and his beadles, was found standing over the body with a gun in his hand,' he said. 'That gun is now in the fountain; he deliberately threw it in there. I'm a witness to that. I thought it best to leave it there until you arrived.' His voice, clipped, assured and the accent sounding English to Cork ears, made everyone look at each other silently but no one else spoke.

'And your name, sir? And your business here at the market this morning?' Patrick nodded at his assistant, Joe, who produced a shorthand notebook and a pencil. It took only a minute for the details to be written down but it was long enough for Mrs O'Mahony to find her courage.

'Sam had nothing at all to do with this, inspector, sir,' she said. Her voice raw and hoarse from shouting her wares at the market was now broken with suppressed sobs. 'He was nowhere near Mr Doyle. He was over beside my stall, standing there as quiet as anything. And then the shot went off, just after the lights failed. He had a notebook and a pencil in his hand, just like the guard there. Look, here they are, just where he dropped them. You saw him, Patsy, didn't you?' She whirled around to confront Patsy Mullane and her broom and Patsy cleared her throat and muttered something nervously, looking sideways at Sam.

Patrick was kind, the Reverend Mother was glad to see. He nodded gravely, made no pretence of not knowing Mrs O'Mahony – he would often have been sent to the market for tripe, the mainstay of the poor, by his mother when he was a boy – and he waited until Joe's pencil had stopped before thanking her and then he turned to Sam.

'Your name, sir?' he asked formally and Sam gave it without a tremor in his voice. Anger was still holding him up and he glared across at the town planner as though blaming Robert Newenham for everything.

'Would you like to tell me what happened, sir?' invited Patrick. 'Or would you prefer to wait and to tell me in private?'

Away from his mother, perhaps. But she came across and stood beside her son.

'Tell the truth, Sam, tell them what happened. Where did you get the gun?' She gazed up pleadingly at him, but he looked away, embarrassed, perhaps. Patrick nodded to his assistant, Joe, who approached with notebook and pencil in hand.

'I wasn't anywhere near him, inspector. I was taking down James Doyle's speech to the stallholders, hoping I could sell it to some newspaper,' said Sam, speaking rapidly. 'I was purposely keeping away from him. He'd lost me my job on the *Cork Examiner* before and I knew that he'd get me thrown out of here if he saw me writing, so I stayed over there beside my mother's stall, beside the tripe and drisheen stall. The lights went out; they're always going out and I was waiting for the superintendent to get them lit again.' Sam pointed towards the door to the gallery stairs and Patrick nodded.

'Go on,' he said quietly.

'Then I heard the shot, like everyone else. They were all pushing and shoving to get back against the wall and then someone dropped the gun, right on top of my foot. I didn't know what it was. I picked it up automatically, but I didn't even look at it. I pushed my way forward to see if there could be anything done for the man. I was taught how to stop bleeding when I was a boy, when I was in the Fianna Scouts; I have a certificate from the St Patrick's Ambulance Association. That was my first thought, to give first aid; I've seen lots of gunshot wounds over the last few years, working there in the centre of the city.'

'And the gun, sir?' asked Patrick, his eyes on the young man's face. They would be about the same age, thought the Reverend Mother. Probably may not have known each other, though. Patrick was from the slums on the south parish side of the city and the O'Mahony family, thanks to Mrs O'Mahony's hard work, lived, she thought, somewhere near St Luke's Cross to the east of the city and, of course, Patrick was a scholarship boy at the North Monastery while Sam had been sent to a fee-paying school.

'I told you,' said Sam impatiently, 'someone dropped it at my feet; it hit my toe. I just stooped down, picked it up and held on to it, I don't know why. Perhaps to stop it being fired at someone else, to keep it safe, I just can't tell you. It was an impulse of the moment. Wish to God I had never touched the wretched thing. I wish I had done like everyone else and stood back and looked out for myself.'

'Did anyone else see where this gun came from?' Patrick faced the cluster of people huddled around. There were about twenty stalls in this section of the English Market, not all of them occupied, but with the customers and including the city planners and engineers, there must be about fifty people present. No one spoke though, and the Reverend Mother was not surprised. After four years of turmoil and street fighting, everyone was wary. A near neighbour, a cousin, or even a brother or a sister could be a spy for some party or other.

'Perhaps everyone would go to where they were standing when the shot was fired, or when the lights went out? How long between the two things?' He looked across at the superintendent.

'Not more than a minute or so between them,' said the superintendent. 'The lights went out and I was just taking my keys out of my pocket to send Patsy up to switch them on again when the shot went off.'

'They are always going off. It's a terrible system,' said the woman who had taken her place back behind the chicken stall.

'Dreadful unreliable,' said Michael Skiddy removing the wax from the side of his candle.

There was no one in front of his stall, now, noticed the Reverend Mother and yet she had seen that figure there, just a minute before the lights had gone out, a man in a belted raincoat with a slouch hat pulled well down over his face. She looked all around at the people standing in front of the stalls and the group awkwardly reassembling around the dead body of the city engineer, but there was no man dressed like that in this part of the market. Now that her mind was focused, she remembered quite clearly that she had seen him bend over the counter and blow out the candle that was probably kept lit by Michael Skiddy in order to advertise the wares. The man had blown out the candle; it had been he, not Michael Skiddy; she was sure of that, and then she had seen no more of him. This must have been a few minutes before the lights went out because she could clearly remember Michael Skiddy's face looking anxious; angry and anxious, she thought. Once again she scanned the crowd, but there was no sign of that figure in a raincoat, no sign of that over-large hat pulled down to obscure a face.

She looked back at Michael Skiddy's soap and candle stall. Who had been the man in the belted coat and slouch hat who had blown out the candle just before the lights failed, or were extinguished, and who had then melted away? Michael Skiddy himself, now standing beneath one of the gas lamps, had a scared look on his face, but then so did others. No one would be keen to volunteer information if there was any suspicion that the Republican Army might be involved.

Patrick gave Sam a long considering look and then turned his attention back to the huddled group.

'Who was standing beside Mr Doyle when the shot was fired?'

'I was. I am his assistant, Thomas Browne, Assistant City Engineer.' A man moved forward. That would be one of the Brownes from Sundays Well. He had the family looks, that long nose, the full-lipped sensual mouth, the cleft chin, the very black hair with one long lock falling down over his fore-head, looked rather like the poet Yeats as a young man, she thought, examining his face with interest. It was, she decided, the face of a dreamer rather than a man of action. She had heard that one of the Brownes had become an engineer, though most of the others were stock market traders or had gone into banking, like their grandfather before them. He wouldn't be as monied as the other members of his family, she thought and then chided herself for thinking of gossip when a man lay dead on the floor in front of her.

Doyle, now, the dead city engineer, he came up from nowhere. It was not a name that the Reverend Mother knew, and she knew all the names of the merchant princes of Cork. He, she thought, would have come from one of those families like Sam O'Mahony, some family where either the mother or father was self-sacrificing enough to pay for a good education for a bright child and to encourage them along the path of a lucrative profession. She had heard that he had been an apprentice and had worked his way up. Like Sam O'Mahony his brains had helped him to move out of his class.

There might have been a difference, though. Sam, judging by an article of his that she remembered reading in the *Cork Examiner*, had been high-minded and very sincere. James Doyle's meteoric rise in the power structure of the city seemed to hint at something else. She had heard rumours about his ruthlessness and there were reports that he was feared and hated. Dr Scher, she thought, had hinted about this and she wondered whether the doctor would be conducting an autopsy on the body of the city engineer. And just at the very moment when she had thought of the doctor, he appeared at the Princes Street gate to the market, dressed in overalls and accompanied by two hospital orderlies carrying a stretcher. He gave an annoyed look around at the crowd of people and whispered something to Patrick who nodded, but made no move to clear the crowd. He was looking from side to side, picturing the scene just before the shot rang out, while Dr Scher kneeled beside the body.

'What about the gallery?' he asked the superintendent. 'Was there anyone there?'

Mr O'Donnell shook his head firmly. 'Not possible, inspector, I keep the keys and that place is locked unless I go up there myself and even then I lock the door behind me. We keep all the money up there so I am very, very careful about locking that door and keeping the keys in my own pocket all day long.'

'So it was not possible that anyone could have been up there?'

'Not a chance, inspector. I hadn't even gone up there myself this morning. When the lights went out, I was just going to send Patsy up there to get them working again, but that very moment the shot rang out and of course we were all in a bit of bother . . .' He tailed off, feeling, no doubt that this was an inadequate comment on a man's murder. 'Am I right, Patsy?' he said turning to where she stood, awkwardly clasping her broom as if wishing to sweep all unpleasantness away.

'You're right, Mr O'Donnell,' she said, but the superintendent ignored her, fishing his keys from his pocket and inviting Patrick to see for himself. One of the guards was despatched upstairs to make a cursory search. All eyes went back to Sam.

'Bless us and save us,' said Cornelius O'Flynn from the egg stall audibly. 'What possessed the *langer* to wait there like a goldfish in a bowl?'

# TWO

St Thomas Aquinas:
*Pro patria ad Deum*
(For the fatherland to God)

'Let me carry your basket, Reverend Mother,' said Robert Newenham. His tone was deferential, though his expression was slightly dubious as he gazed from his immense height down at the eggs and the drisheen sausage and the crusty loaf of bread. The crowd was thinning out as all names and addresses had been taken. Sam had been escorted to a police car, but Mrs O'Mahony had resolutely refused to go home and had taken her place once more behind her stall. The Reverend Mother found herself rather bored at the prospect of making conversation with this pompous man and had meant to make an excuse saying that she had another errand in the town as they walked out together, but one glimpse of his splendid car made her resolve to get him to drive her to the very gates of her school. It would be around the time of the dinner-time break and all of the small boys would be fascinated by the appearance of a Rolls Royce.

'Thank you, but no,' she said briskly, keeping a firm hold of her basket. 'I'm sure you are at home with guns, Captain Newenham, but I venture to think that you may not have much experience with carrying a basket of eggs. I must continue to be responsible for them. If I may, I will place them in the footwell of your back seat and I will sit in the front.'

'Very nice eggs at the English Market,' he said after a minute's silence. He had opened the door to the back of the car obediently, but still eyed the basket dubiously as if suspecting it of containing a bomb.

'Very,' agreed the Reverend Mother, but then she took mercy on him. It would, after all, be far more interesting for the two of them to discuss the terrible events of the morning rather than him to spend time silently speculating on any possible reason why the Reverend Mother might have popped out of the convent in order to buy buttered eggs.

'They are for my gardener,' she explained. 'He's been looking very unwell and has lost a lot of weight. Sister Bernadette tells me that he eats very little. He lived in the country when he was young and his mother used to keep hens. He was talking about them one day, telling me that his mother used to produce them for the English Market and how once he had one for his birthday. Since Dr Scher thinks he should try to eat as well as possible, I decided to get him some buttered eggs from the market.'

'Very kind of you,' he said. There was still a note of astonishment in his voice.

Not particularly kind, she thought wryly. She was still quite shocked at herself for ignoring that incessant hard, dry cough that could be heard every time anyone went into the garden. It had taken Dr Scher on a visit to an elderly sister to take action and to insist on examining the man. Nothing to be done, he had said afterwards. 'There's no real cure for TB, just a faint hope that if he stays in the open air and eats well that his life might be prolonged a little. He'll go quite suddenly, you know. I'd say that he is in remission now, wants to get his potatoes planted, but then he'll probably sink.'

'An old retainer of yours, is he?' he added with a smile when she made no response. 'Someone from a cousin's estate, perhaps?' There was something so falsely snobbish about this that she felt herself getting annoyed.

'Mr Cotter has only been a gardener with us for a short time. He used to have a bicycle shop in a lane off Patrick Street until the night when it was burned down when the Black and Tans set fire to the city,' she said aloud. 'He and his son had run it together for years before the son's death.'

'Very kind of you to take him in,' he said politely.

'He's a good gardener,' she said. He had always liked growing things better than tinkering with a screwdriver and oiling cogs, he had told her, on one of the few occasions when he had volunteered any information. His son, she had thought, might have been the one more interested in bicycles, might have been the driving force in setting up the small shop for the repair of brakes and gears and the replacement of damaged saddles and handlebars.

'That was an extraordinary business this morning, wasn't it?' said Captain Newenham, dismissing the subject of the gardener.

Not interested in people, she thought, unlike Dr Scher who had offered his condolences before examining the man. Robert Newenham was interested only in events which had a significance for him personally.

'Not the assassination,' he continued as he took out the starting handle from the back of his opulent car. 'Lord, no, we're all used to that sort of thing. I often say that this place is like being back in Flanders again, just as dangerous; no, not that so much, but the fact that the man didn't run for it. He could easily have done so, couldn't he? If I took advantage of the lights going out and aimed a pot shot at a fellow, I'd make jolly sure that I was nowhere to be seen when the lights were switched on. I'd fly before anyone noticed me. There was time enough before the lights were switched on, even before the first candle was lit.'

'You don't think that it would cause a certain amount of talk if a prominent person like you were missing and a dead body was lying there on the pathway?' queried the Reverend Mother. She cast a quick glance at him from under her wimple and then nodded her thanks as he held the door open for her. He had looked slightly taken aback at her sentence as if perhaps he thought that she had implied that there was a possibility that he could have done the deed and stayed on the scene. She would leave it at that.

It was, though she was very sorry for his mother, a most unlikely idea that anyone other than Sam O'Mahony had fired the fatal shot.

But, still, Robert Newenham had a point. Why just stand there? Why not run? It was a valid question and it did cast a slight doubt on the identity of the gunman. Moreover, there had been a look of genuine disbelief on Sam's face.

A very comfortable car, she thought, as she sank into the softly padded leather seat, arranged the folds of her black habit

and straightened her veil and waited for him to crank up the
engine. It started almost instantly. Of course, Rolls Royce had
a great reputation. Even nuns in a convent knew that. How
had he managed to buy as expensive a car as that? He was
the youngest of a long line of sons and she had a notion that
there had not been much money in that family. I must talk to
Lucy, she said to herself as he swung himself into the driving
seat. Her cousin usually knew all the ins and outs of the
members of Cork society, especially those who were related
to them.

'Which regiment were you in during the war, Captain
Newenham?' she asked when he had pulled out into the road.
She probably had known this at some stage, but she was
anxious not to discuss Sam O'Mahony and his motivation at
the moment. His despairing face as he was taken away by the
city guards had upset her. All appearances were against him
and there would be calls for vengeance against the killer of
an important person such as the city engineer. And, of course,
the town planner, Captain Robert Newenham, would be one
of the first to call for the death penalty. His evidence would
be taken very seriously by the court that tried the young man.
A good-looking man, spoke well, and his height and broad
shoulders gave him an air of authority.

He wasn't as pleased by her question as she had thought
that he would be. There was a noticeable hesitation, almost
as though he wondered how to avoid a straight answer.
Eventually he said, rather abruptly, 'The Dorsetshires,' and
then went straight on to remarking, 'What a terrible thing that
was to witness. That unfortunate man, James Doyle! Who
would have thought such a thing would happen. That must
have been a dreadful shock for you. Perhaps I should have
got you a glass of brandy. Are you going back to the convent
now? I hope you aren't thinking of visiting your sick gardener
first; surely one of your lay sisters can undertake that errand
for you.'

'No, I'm perfectly well,' said the Reverend Mother. 'No
one gets to my age without witnessing many deaths.' She
didn't mention the fact that her sick gardener had, without her
knowledge, set up home in the shed at the back of the convent

gardens and was probably now working among the vegetables. 'As, of course,' she continued, 'you, yourself, must have, doubtless, witnessed many deaths when you were in the Dorsetshires Regiment.' *The Dorsetshires. For some reason that is familiar to me. Perhaps a member of my family mentioned it, some other cousin, perhaps.* But no, she was fairly sure that she had heard of that regiment in some different context.

She relaxed as he competently turned his car in the wide space of the Grand Parade, drove down Washington Street and along Lancaster Quay and then crossed over the bridge that spanned the south arm of the River Lee and led across to St Mary's of the Isle, that ancient island that had been the first settlement place on the great marsh of Munster, the beginning of the city of Cork when the monks had settled there, centuries before the invasion of the Vikings and then of the Normans.

The Dorsetshires, she said in her mind as he pulled up in front of the convent and its school. She could hear a voice pronouncing that name. Now she remembered. It had definitely been Sister Bernadette, the lay sister who attended the door and welcomed visitors to the convent, who had mentioned that regiment, not recently, quite some time ago, and had mentioned them in terms of loathing and anger, also. But why?

'Did the Dorsetshires serve here in Ireland some time?' she asked, making her voice sound indifferent.

'Good lord, no.'

She saw his moustache stretch across his face as he grinned and she watched his face with interest.

'No, no, Reverend Mother,' he said. 'Ireland was the poisoned chalice. No, we served just in France; and after that we went out to India. I had just signed up for the war; I was barely eighteen then, lots of others also. Once 1918 came the regiment was reduced to its original size. I was lucky to get this job here in my native city. Lots of poor fellows were on the streets afterwards and had to pick up any work that was going. Selling bootlaces and kitchen brooms and worse. Taking any job that was offered to them.'

That was it. The Reverend Mother now knew why Sister Bernadette had mentioned that English regiment. During the

War of Independence when the Republicans had threatened and assassinated many of the police, the Royal Irish Constabulary, appointed by England to regulate Ireland, had trouble recruiting men, recruitment had fallen rapidly and resignations were on a daily basis. The English had supplemented the police force with 'auxiliaries', known locally as the 'Black & Tans' because of their black jackets and their tan trousers. Many of them had been in the British army during the war. Were some of the ex-soldiers from the Dorsetshires Regiment employed as Black and Tans? Making a resolution to talk to Sister Bernadette, the Reverend Mother turned her attention to directing Robert Newenham where to find the convent.

'Good thing that you are not walking along here, alone,' he said looking through the window with disdain at some of the shawl-covered women and the shabby men who walked aimlessly around the streets and quays, spitting on the pavement from time to time. The Reverend Mother could not be bothered to argue with him, to tell him that she often walked along the quays in perfect safety and that the dock workers always stood back courteously to allow her to pass. As she had hoped the children were in the playground when the big car purred to a halt by the pavement. Her appearance from this magnificent machine caused a sudden rush to the railings.

'It's the Reverend Mother.'

'In a Roller!'

'Would ya take a sconce at that?' Willie O'Sullivan's voice was shrill with admiration.

'PI 645. It's two years old; Father O'Donnell's car is 649 and he bought it in June. He told me that the 600 numbers started in January. The Father said that he never thought he'd see the day that six hundred cars would have been sold in the city of Cork. The city cars allus have PI on them, before their number. The country cars just have IF.' Paddy Maloney was an altar boy and had once had the excitement of a lift in the parish priest's car after a funeral and was now an authority on cars.

'D'ya see the yoke on the bonnet, that's on all them Rolls Royce cars,' said Francie Murphy knowledgeably.

The Reverend Mother decided that they needed longer to admire this rare apparition. 'Do come in, Captain Newenham,' she said hospitably. 'You will allow me to offer you a cup of tea after your kindness in driving me home.'

He looked slightly reluctant, but she did not wait for an answer. Sister Philomena, who was on playground duty, advanced, keys in hand, and unlocked the gate with a beaming smile.

'They won't touch the car, will they?' he asked, lifting his top hat politely to the nun, but looking anxiously at the ragged and dirty-faced crew whose faces were stuck between the bars.

The Reverend Mother could have told him that it was one of the strict rules of the convent that gates were kept locked while the children were under their care because Cork was not a safe place for the young and vulnerable, but decided that he was more interested in the safety of his immaculately clean car. 'Perhaps you could tell Francie the name of the emblem on the bonnet,' she suggested, concealing a smile as she saw him surveying the iron bars of the railings and watching anxiously until Sister Philomena had relocked the gate.

He started and looked at the skinny, barefooted child almost as though he were some sort of strange animal with whom the Reverend Mother had eccentrically ordered him to engage in conversation.

'It is called The Spirit of Ecstasy,' he said awkwardly and then with a glance at the puzzled face, he added, 'some people call it The Flying Lady.'

'Ecstasy means excitement, wonder, delight – all sorts of things like that,' explained the Reverend Mother. 'And there might be a sweet for someone who can remember that word in a few days' time when I pop into your classroom and ask you to tell me the grand name for the statue on the bonnet of the Rolls Royce car. Come and see our gardens, Captain Newenham. Sister Philomena, could you choose some sensible person to tell Sister Bernadette that we have a visitor and he would like a cup of tea.'

'You believe in bribery,' he said as she escorted him through the gate into the convent gardens, leaving the children excitedly memorizing the word 'ecstasy'.

'I believe in education,' she said tartly.

'Is it worth it, do you think, with children like those? What's the use of knowing a word like *ecstasy*?'

The Reverend Mother compressed her lips and made no reply. She thought of saying that she believed in children knowing and using words, she thought of saying that Inspector Cashman, to whom Captain Newenham had been obsequiously polite, had been a little ragged boy, with a thirst for information, in this same playground fifteen years ago, but she suppressed the words. The man was too stupid. In any case, Patrick would have a difficult job with this enquiry and she should be careful to preserve his dignity and his status while he had the task of cross-questioning many of the prominent citizens who had been present in the English Market this morning. And then she remembered her basket and diverted him away from the shrubbery and the ugly contorted monkey tree and the beds filled with ragged ornamental grasses and steered him towards the vegetable garden from where she could hear the sound of a dry cough.

'Oh, Mr Cotter,' she said. 'Should you be out in the damp and cold planting those potatoes? Surely they could wait for a few days until your cough is a little better?'

He straightened himself and looked at her reproachfully. 'There's a time for planting, Reverend Mother, and the potatoes won't wait anyone's convenience. See the little shoots coming out; they need to be got into the ground now while they are fresh and then someone will have to earth them up and then they'll have to be picked in July or perhaps the beginning of August. Don't let everyone forget about my potatoes, Reverend Mother, will you? These are good ones, they . . .' And then he stopped talking and bent down to place another tuber in the ground with the little white shoot, the hope for the future, pointing upwards towards the cloudy sky.

He is thinking about the fact that he won't be here to see these potatoes through to maturity, thought the Reverend Mother. Her mind went to the quotation from Ecclesiastes: 'A time to be born, and a time to die; a time to plant, and a time to pluck up that which is planted.' Mr Cotter's time to be 'plucked up' was, according to Dr Scher, fast approaching.

'I'll make sure about that, Mr Cotter,' she assured him. 'Look at those splendid cabbages, Captain Newenham; the convent never lacks for fresh vegetables. Ah, there is Sister Bernadette. I'm sure that she has a nice hot cup of tea for you. Don't stay out in this damp air, too long, Mr Cotter, will you? You need to take care of yourself.'

He made no reply and she did not press the point. Fresh air as well as good food were important for him, according to Dr Scher, and that reminded her of her errand so she handed over the basket.

'And here is something for your midday meal,' she said. 'I remembered you telling me about the buttered eggs that your mother used to sell at the market and I got you some when I was in the market this morning.'

He was taken aback by this and he stared at her. He would be shocked that she, in person, had done the shopping and she hastened to change the subject so that he was not embarrassed. She wouldn't, she thought, mention the events of the morning. There would be enough talk about this later on and she disliked idle gossip. Better to focus his mind on eating a good lunch.

'Tell Captain Newenham about how your mother used to prepare her eggs and about you and your brother going to the English Market to sell things from the farm. You used to bring in vegetables as well, didn't you?'

He made a poor effort at the story which he had told her a week ago with such animation, even imitating the sound of a hen laying an egg which had been the signal for one of the children to dash in and bring it straight to his mother so that it could be buttered while still piping hot. He muttered a few words awkwardly and he was as relieved as Captain Newenham when Sister Bernadette came out of the door and down the path with the news that tea was ready in the Reverend Mother's room.

'I mustn't stay long,' said the captain once he swallowed the tea and declined the cake. 'I really need to get back to the office. There will be all sorts of things to be done. We will need to issue a statement for the *Cork Examiner* about this terrible affair and then I suppose that there will be a funeral to arrange after the police release the body. There should not be too much delay about that, I suppose. It doesn't need a doctor to tell that the man died of a gunshot wound, but I suppose they have to go through the formalities.'

'Yes, of course,' she said rising to her feet instantly and handing him his hat from the windowsill where he had placed it. She was as glad to be rid of him as he was to go. The bell had sounded for the children to return to their classrooms so the small boys and girls would have had their fill of looking at the splendid car. 'I'll show you out,' she said, but was not surprised to see that Sister Bernadette, alert for the opening of the Reverend Mother's door, was already in the hallway. He took off his hat courteously to her once again when she accompanied him to the doorstep and pressed her hand, hoping that the morning's events had not been too much for her and then hurried off down the path.

'Sister Bernadette . . .?' said the Reverend Mother once the door was closed behind him and then stopped. It would not do to blurt out her query straight away. Sister Bernadette was a kindly woman, but a terrible gossip and traded pieces of information with the local postman and lamp lighter. 'Something terrible happened this morning,' she substituted.

'I know, I know! It's shocking, isn't it?' Sister Bernadette was excited by the news. 'The city engineer assassinated! And Sam O'Mahony to do a thing like that! After all that his poor mother has done for him! The messenger boy who brought the fish told me all about it. Said you were quite safe. He saw you go off in a gentleman's car, that's what he said.'

'That's right,' said the Reverend Mother. 'Captain Newenham is a distant relation of mine. We had a nice chat. He was telling me that he fought in the war against Germany. He was in some British regiment. Something to do with Cornwall, was it? No, I'm wrong, it was the Dorsetshires, that's what it was.' She waited, her eyes on a vase of pallid daffodils in front of a statue of the Blessed Mother, but very aware of the sudden intake of breath from the lay sister. And then, in as casual a way as she could manage, she said, 'Sister, you were telling me something about the Dorsetshire Regiment here in Cork city, weren't you? Was that when you were a girl?' She aimed the questions at the departing figure and Sister Bernadette turned around with her face full of interest.

'No, not that, not that at all, Reverend Mother, you're getting things mixed up and no wonder, with all that you have to do. No, I was telling you that the fellow in charge of those Black and Tans was an officer in the Dorsetshire Regiment. That's what I was telling you. His name was Charles something, a German name, Schulze, that's what it was, Charles Schulze, he was the captain in charge of those hooligans that burned down the city. And he used to be in the British army during the war against Germany and they turned him out of that. I'm not surprised. A more wicked man never walked the earth. They say that he was the one that fired the shots at those two poor lads in Luke's Cross, sitting up in their beds without a stitch on them.'

'I see,' said the Reverend Mother storing the name into her memory. An unusual name; Sister Bernadette was right. It did sound German. There would be little chance that a fellow officer would have forgotten it. Cork, she thought, was a very small city. Did these two men from the Dorsetshire Regiment meet and recognize each other? She thought that it was almost certain that they would have done so. Sister Bernadette, she noticed with amusement, was looking slightly embarrassed. She opened her mouth a few times, gave a perfunctory dust of the shining wood around the statue and then turned back to the Reverend Mother.

'The Dorsetshires,' she said hesitantly. 'The Dorsetshires. Perhaps, I've got the name wrong, Reverend Mother, I was thinking that it was the regiment of the captain of those Black and Tans that burned down Patrick Street. At least that was what the postman told me. Perhaps he got it wrong. I only know what he told me. Captain Charles Schulze; that was his name, bad luck to him; he was the man in charge that night. He was the one telling the men where to throw the cans of petrol and which buildings were to be burned and which ones were to be left untouched.' Sister Bernadette gave a guilty look at the Reverend Mother and added hastily, 'Still, I suppose that there are all sorts of men in a regiment, like everywhere else in life. I'm sure your cousin is a very nice man and would have nothing at all to do with that Captain Schulze. And it was probably a different regiment entirely.' She gave an uncertain smile and then sidled off, back to the kitchen, but her kind face looked troubled and the Reverend Mother understood. That night when Cork city burned on the 11th of December 1920 was engraved into the memories of all Cork people. The anger would be there for many generations to come. And anyone who had any connection with the outrage would be anathema to the citizens. Sister Bernadette could not bear to think that the cousin of the Reverend Mother might have been connected with that terrible time.

# THREE

W.B. Yeats:
Hearts with one purpose alone,
Through summer and winter seem
Enchanted to a stone.
To trouble the living stream.

The grass on Gogginshill, near Ballinhassig, was very green; Eileen always noticed that. It was five miles south of Cork city and the air was very pure. Mists did occur, but smoke-laden fogs were infrequent on the high ground there. On that Friday afternoon when the city was shrouded in murk and moisture, the air was fresh and the April sun was warm, illuminating the cowslips and the primroses on the steep fields. She and Aoife picked a few. They, like all members of the Republican Army, were always careful to give their actions an air of innocence and what could be more casual than two seventeen-year-old girls picking a bunch of spring flowers.

In fact, of course, they were checking their line of escape in case the hideout was raided by the army or by the civic guards.

Beneath the patchwork of fields that covered the steep hill ran the Cork to Bandon railway tunnel. One of its ventilation shafts came up in the centre of this very field, marked by the presence of a lone blackthorn bush, saved by superstition from the attention of the railway staff. It was one of Aoife's duties to check the entrance daily, to make sure that the metal ladder that led down into the tunnel was in good order, that the blackthorn screened, but would not impede, desperate men from the Number One Brigade of the Republican Army if the Free State Army discovered their hideout in a deserted farmhouse. Casually they rubbed some new buds from the black twigs so that the entrance was kept free.

'Have you thought about something to write for your column in the *Cork Examiner* this week, Eileen?' The words were only just out of Aoife's mouth when there was a noise of a motorcycle driving slowly and cautiously along the lane nearby.

'Tom Hurley,' said Aoife. 'We'd better go back. Everything seems to be fine here.' She shone her torch for the last time down into the tunnel and then they turned and went back. 'Should we throw the flowers away? He'll be saying something sarcastic about women, if I know Tom Hurley,' she said.

'Let him,' said Eileen indifferently. 'The trouble with him is that he is stupid and narrow-minded. Hang onto the flowers; we'll put them in a jam jar when we get back. Don't hurry yourself, Aoife, why should we run to him? He's never got a civil word to say. You're doing the duty assigned to you.'

Nevertheless when Aoife started to run, Eileen followed her. No sense in putting him in a bad mood when he found that the farmhouse was empty and if he was rude to Aoife she wanted to be around to pay him back with his own coin.

As they expected, his face was dark with anger. He had a habit of flicking his middle finger against his thumb when he was impatient and the sound of the loud crack always made Aoife feel jittery.

'Is anything the matter, Tom?' Aoife was asking nervously as soon as she climbed the wall and Eileen could hear the note of anxiety in her voice. 'Have you any news for us?'

'News? Well, I suppose I have some news. James Doyle, the city engineer, copped it in the English Market this morning. That's what the news is. Shot, girl, shot. Dead as a doornail. This morning he was James Doyle, City Engineer and now he is James Doyle R.I.P.' Tom Hurley's temper was never good, but he was increasingly on edge these days. Ever since the death of their leader, Liam Lynch, defeat was staring them in the face. Some Republicans had slipped off on the boat to England but this unit, safe for the moment in their headquarters in Ballinhassig, had remained fairly intact and Tom Hurley was determined to be effective. Their orders from the chief were to continue the fight and their immediate aim was to expose the corruption of officials who were supposed to be rebuilding the city centre and to prove to the people of Cork that the Republicans would form a better government. Warnings would be sent out and if they did not heed the warning, then they would be shot. James Doyle, the City Engineer who was busy lining his pockets, was due to be warned. She had written out the notice herself and intended to pop it into the office of the *Cork Examiner* newspaper later in the day.

'Do you mean that he's dead?' asked Aoife. 'Did you shoot him?' She sounded a little uncertain, thought Eileen, Aoife was squeamish about assassinations.

'He was a legitimate target,' she said quickly, trying to sound as tough as Tom Hurley himself. The French Revolution, she told herself sternly, would never have been achieved without the spilling of blood. Her thoughts went to her schooling at St Mary's of the Isle and to the discussion that she had held with the Reverend Mother after the sixth form class had read Dickens' *A Tale of Two Cities*. Eileen had attacked the great man, saying that he had changed his mind about the revolution halfway through the book and that had weakened the book. The Reverend Mother had defended her favourite author, saying that was what made him great. The more he wrote, she said, the more real his characters and their experiences became and in the book he had centred on the experiences of Dr Manette and his daughter Lucie, so as the book went on his sympathies turned away from the ideals and more and more towards the victims of the French Revolution. It had been a good discussion and when the bell went for the end of school, Eileen was still finding arguments and only Sister Bernadette, summoning the Reverend Mother to a phone call from the bishop, had put an end to it.

Someday, thought Eileen, I'll write a book about Cork called *The Tale of a Rebel City* and everything will be in it: the fear, the blood, the suffering, the betrayals, the mistrust between allies and at the same time the fun and the excitement, the camaraderie and, above all, the shining hopes for a great future where there would be equal rights and equal opportunities for all citizens. In the meantime, she had to learn to take the unpleasant aspects of the present as well as looking forward to a glorious future.

'What happened?' she asked, doing her best to sound harsh and experienced.

Tom Hurley gave a half-smile. 'The man fell dead in front of a crowd of Cork's foremost citizens, town planners, the bishop's secretary, builders, Reverend Mother Aquinas from St Mary's of the Isle, old Uncle Tom Cobley and all,' he said and turned his back, beginning to walk towards the house which a sympathetic farmer had given them – an ideal bolt-hole, lost in a network of small lanes and with that wonderful escape hole, the west Cork railway tunnel which ran underneath one of the fields, only 150 yards from the farmhouse. Tom had not answered any of their questions, noticed Eileen. He was an old-fashioned type who regarded the woman's organisation, the *Cumann na mBan*, as fit only to make sandwiches and endless cups of tea for the men.

'How did you get away?' she called after him and he turned on her, his face dark with temper.

'Keep your voice down,' he said harshly. 'Who knows who might be listening? You're not calling the cows home, you know.'

'We were practising firing in the barn this morning, that made a lot more noise,' said Eileen. He's not going to intimidate me, she told herself as she stared defiantly at him. I'm as good as he is any day. I've got more brains, more idealism. There was a brief staring match and then Tom Hurley shrugged.

'It's Friday,' he said. 'Easy enough to get away; the world and his wife were buying fish and I just walked straight for the nearest fish stall and pushed my way through the crowd, all making sure that they obey the bishop and don't eat meat on Friday. I was out on the Grand Parade before you could say Jack Robinson. In any case, no one was looking in my direction. They were looking at the man with the gun in his hand, and why wouldn't they?'

'The man with the gun!' Aoife sounded puzzled.

'The old trick,' said Tom Hurley with a sarcastic grin. 'Fire the gun, drop it on another fellow's foot, he picks it up – they all do. Everyone stares, starts shouting, you walk away quickly, get on your motorbike, put a few miles between yourself and the scene.'

Eileen giggled. She was not too keen on Tom Hurley. He seemed to despise her because she was a seventeen-year-old girl, not a tough thirty-year-old man, but there was no doubt but that he could be quite funny.

'Who picked it up? The bishop, I hope,' she said.

'No, actually it was that young fellow. You know the chap who used to work for the *Cork Examiner* – what's his name? Yes, I know, Sam O'Mahony.'

'Sam O'Mahony!' Eileen felt her lips grow cold. She sensed that Aoife had turned to look at her, but she kept her own eyes fixed on Tom Hurley.

'You walked off and left Sam O'Mahony holding the gun.' Her voice did not sound like her own.

Tom shrugged – it was his most frequent gesture. 'Why not? Who is Sam O'Mahony, anyway? Not one of us, is he? He'll keep them busy for a while. James Doyle was the cause of Sam being sacked from the *Cork Examiner* so the gun couldn't have been picked up by a better person. Yes, he's ideal. They'll take him seriously. The bishop would have been no good. No one would have believed that he did it, even if they saw him with their own eyes.' And then Tom deliberately turned his back on her and walked off with the long-loped stride and the furtive glances from side to side that were now second nature for most of the Republicans.

Eileen went after him. Fury was almost choking her. She grabbed his arm. He jerked it away with a force that almost overbalanced her. She grasped it again and hung on. On the perimeter of her vision she saw Aoife move slowly towards them and then stop. Aoife was a little scared of Tom. He wasn't like the rest of the carefree bunch who laughed and joked, played music, talked seriously about the future of Ireland and then ended the session with a an improvised *ceilidh*. Tom Hurley came and went on secret missions, snapped out orders, eyed all with suspicion and then disappeared again. No one quite knew where he went or what he did. He never quoted the idealistic writings of Connolly or of Pearse. He dealt in the harsh currency of guns, of explosives, of the necessity for tit-for-tat killings.

'You're letting Sam suffer for something that you did, is that right?' Eileen heard her voice tremble with anger.

'Why not? What's he to you?'

'He's her . . .' Aoife stopped. Tom Hurley's views on emotional attachments were well-known and frequently expressed. No one on active service was to form an attachment to anyone, especially not to anyone outside their own brigade. Engagements or marriage were to be put on hold until after the war was won and Ireland in its entirety – its thirty-two counties, not just twenty-six – were free from Britain. It was well known that the relationship between Florrie O'Donoghue, Head of Intelligence for the Republican Army, and Josephine Marchment, his future wife, was only tolerated because her job as a clerk in the army barracks during the War of Independence meant that she could bring valuable information to her future husband. Josephine had excellent shorthand skills and could, sitting on a lavatory seat, manage to take down the essence of any document in the time that another woman would take for a bathroom break. Eileen knew what Tom was implying and it roused her temper.

'That's nothing to do with it,' she raged. 'I'm talking about ordinary common decency. If you killed the man, then we must put a notice in the *Cork Examiner* to say that it was an execution carried out by the Republican Army who had judged James Doyle to be guilty of corruption and of misuse of money meant to house the people of Cork city. We must say that Sam O'Mahony had nothing to do with it, that he just happened to pick up the gun.'

Tom Hurley had been walking towards the house that sheltered them, but now he turned back and swung his leg over his motorbike. His face was still averted from her.

'Well, if you won't do it, then I will,' said Eileen resolutely and at that he turned and looked at her. His face was white with anger.

'Who told you that I killed him?' he snapped. 'I never said such a thing. You keep your tongue to yourself, girl, and obey orders or you might find yourself shot for disobedience.' He looked at her steadily and her tongue faltered and she knew that her face betrayed her fear. There had been too many shootings, too many bodies buried in bogs for a threat like that to go unheeded. Rumours could often be untrue, but it would be naïve to imagine that they always lied.

'Sam should not be left to bear the burden of a killing that was not of his doing.' She managed, eventually, to force the words out.

His only answer to that was a contemptuous glance. He revved up his engine and sped off in a mist of smoke and petrol fumes. Eileen stood, resolutely not looking back at Aoife, but following with her eyes the motorcycle as it went hurtling along between the hedges. The sound seemed to fill the hills and one part of her commentated on the security shield which they all tried to maintain. Tom, in normal times, would be first to condemn anyone who would draw attention to himself by driving like that. She knew why he did it, of course. Her questions had angered him, but they had also made him feel uneasy. She did not, however, deceive herself with the thought that he would wish to extricate Sam O'Mahony from the danger into which he had been pitched. She stood irresolute for a few minutes and then her ear picked up another sound, a heavier deeper sound. It was the Crossley tender, a vehicle which they had stolen a few years ago and which had proved its worth time after time. She stood and waited, feeling that she needed some friendly support and when the big vehicle appeared at the gates she went forward and threw open the second gate so that it could come into the farmyard.

'Was that Tom Hurley, driving as though the demons of hell were after him?' Eamonn parked the Crossley tender outside the front door and jumped down out of the driving seat. For once he was alone. The others must have stayed in the city. She nodded dumbly and he looked enquiringly at her.

'What's the matter with him?' he asked in puzzled tones. 'He's driving like a lunatic. And he's the one who is always lecturing the rest of us about keeping our speed down and not drawing attention to ourselves.'

'There's been a shooting,' said Eileen. She could hear how flat her voice sounded. 'There's been a shooting. James Doyle, the city engineer, was assassinated in the English Market. Tom Hurley shot him and then dropped the gun on Sam O'Mahony's foot and now Sam has been arrested by the guards.'

'Sam O'Mahony?'

'The fellow that she's been doing a line with,' hissed Aoife and Eileen stared across the hedge into the spring-like fields where the snowy whiteness of the blossom softened the harsh blackthorn. It was a funny expression, 'doing a line'. She didn't know whether the rest of the world said that, but certainly Cork people did. Probably originated, her mother thought, when a newly engaged couple would be allowed to walk out along a lane from the city together and after them came the matchmaker, then the parents of both and probably most of the children of the neighbourhood, all forming one long line behind the happy pair.

Things were different nowadays. Nowadays things were less permanent, more private. She and Sam met at the steps of the Pavilion cinema, cuddled together in the warm, cigarette-smoke-filled darkness while they watched a Charlie Chaplin film, or walked hand-in-hand up through the dark lanes of the marsh and alongside the bank of the river. They never really talked of marriage or the future. Life was too uncertain. And, of course, once Sam lost his job on the *Cork Examiner*, the only sensible future for him was to get the boat to England.

And to there, Eileen would not follow him.

She felt tears prick at her eyes. Why had she kept him back? If only he had been out of this misfortunate, strife-torn city before that fatal shot was fired. She knew Tom Hurley well enough to know that he would deny firing that shot and would go on denying it, even to his colleagues. Aoife had said enough for a man as astute as Tom Hurley to guess how matters lay. He would not trust her, or any of the other young members of the group now.

# FOUR

St Thomas Aquinas:
*Lex mala; lex nulla*
(Bad law is no law)

'Well, I've been to see your gardener, again,' said Dr Scher as soon as Sister Bernadette closed the door behind her, promising to bring some tea and fruitcake. Sister Bernadette was devoted to Dr Scher and made sure that there was always fruitcake available when he called.

'And?' queried the Reverend Mother. Then she added hastily, 'That was good of you to come in so late, especially with all that you will have to do today. I suppose you have had to conduct the autopsy on the dead man?'

'I'll be doing that tomorrow. We had to wait for the coroner to authorize it. The usual business; he was in court for most of the afternoon. Imposing fines on men who can't feed their own families just because they obstructed the pavement. That's the law for you! Couldn't expect him to exert himself any more, of course, could we? Talk to him in the morning; that was the message. Anyway, there shouldn't be too much to do. Won't be much to find out if all the witnesses, including yourself, are telling the truth. I'll find a bullet in his chest, somewhere in the ribs, perhaps, dig it out, present it to the police, turn up in court and tell the judge that the man was shot and died of his wound. Strange business, wasn't it? I suppose they will hang that boy. What possessed him? I know he lost his job because of James Doyle, but that's months ago. Why suddenly shoot him now? Though perhaps he was getting more desperate and he couldn't resist the opportunity. He could be a very unpleasant fellow, Doyle. Might have said something to the lad, sneered at him, what do you think? You were there.'

The Reverend Mother thought about the matter. 'Personally, I didn't see him approach, but I wasn't taking much notice.

I did see Sam with a notebook in his hand, but he seemed to be writing, not asking any questions.'

'Could have said something to him beforehand, though, couldn't he? The late, lamented James Doyle could be a fairly unpleasant sort of person. Tried a few sneers at me, to be frank with you; though I don't take too much notice of that sort of thing, learned how to ignore it when I was a lad in Manchester. By the way,' he said hurriedly, 'what took you to the English Market this morning? Got a surprise when I saw you. You didn't bring a pistol concealed in your basket, did you?'

'I was buying buttered eggs for our gardener,' said the Reverend Mother. 'And how is he?'

'Nothing much that I can do for him,' said Dr Scher bluntly. 'He has tuberculosis and I would reckon that he is in the final stages of it. The lungs are very bad. There's nothing really that I, or any other doctor, can do for him. I brought him a bottle of a new kind of cough mixture this evening – they always like to have something – but it'll do no more than soothe his throat. A pity I didn't see him months ago, sometimes it works if you get them at the first few coughs, depends on the state of health.'

'I see.' The fault was hers more than others, she thought. She had been listening to the gardener coughing for months. It had been usually the first sound that came to her ears when she walked from the convent to the street gate or through the gardens to the chapel. She should have done more about him, should have asked Dr Scher to have a look at the man a couple of months ago. She had not even enquired as to where he was living, believing that, as the poor did, he had found refuge in one of those crumbling tenement houses in the lanes as his bicycle shop and home had been burned down. The convent had given him a job as a gardener after that. They paid him a small wage, enough to feed him and pay his rent. But she should have thought about his health. She had noticed that he was getting thinner and thinner, but had done nothing about it until today when she had gone to buy him a small present. A ridiculous errand, buying buttered eggs for a dying man, she thought angrily.

'Don't blame yourself,' said Dr Scher, reading her mind as

usual. 'I'd say that you couldn't have saved him, even a few months ago, and how were you to know what was wrong with him? Three quarters of people in this city are suffering from tuberculosis. It's in the air that we all breathe. Nothing to be done for that poor man; I'd give him only a few weeks, Reverend Mother,' he added. There was an unusual degree of brutal frankness about him – his nature was a cheerful one and usually he smoothed out the bad news as much as possible. She sensed his unhappiness. She could understand his frustration and anger, though. The deadly disease was permeating the wet, fog-ridden city of Cork, wiping out scores of men, women and children every month, most of them from the slums.

'He must be moved into hospital; we must make arrangements for him. He can't go on living in that shed. I never realized that he was doing that.' She was ironically conscious of the energy in her voice. What good would it do the poor man, she thought? It would have to be the Union – the renamed workhouse – and most people hated that.

Dr Scher shook his head. 'I mentioned the possibility to him and he took fright. As I said to you, he's no risk to anyone out there in the fresh air and that shed with its stove is a better place to live in than many others that I've seen. Anyway, he was dead against hospital, said it wasn't worth his while. One place was as good as another, he said. He didn't want to move, just to end his days peacefully.'

'So you told him – told him that he was dying. I thought that you had done so.' She thought back to the man's words about caring for his potatoes.

'Best to tell the truth; he took it well. Said he had guessed, that he had thought for the last few months that he was going the way of his brother. Didn't seem to mind too much!'

'He had been a countryman; he told me that once,' said the Reverend Mother to fill in the minute. She wanted to talk about Sam, but that subject could wait until Dr Scher had received his tea. She could do nothing for poor Mr Cotter, but perhaps she might be able to do something for Sam. And for his mother. Soon she would hear the shuffle of the lay sister's feet in their large slippers that helped to polish the convent's shining wooden floors. And then in another minute the tea would appear. There would be scones, fruitcake, sugar and cream, all for one overweight, middle-aged man, while outside the walls of her convent the poor starved and died of wasting diseases.

'Is that right?' Dr Scher sounded animated and interested in this. The people of Cork city loved gossip and had an inexhaustible curiosity about fellow Corkonians and the doctor was no exception. 'He's quite a big tall fellow, isn't he, big shoulders and chest? You could see that he might have been brought up in the country,' he went on before adding, 'the son, too, the one that was hanged for the murder of the R.I.C. man; Frank was his name, wasn't it? Frank Cotter. That's right. I remember thinking that he had a big frame. Terrible waste of a young life! These Republicans have a lot to answer for. Well, here comes Sister Bernadette.' He leaped to the door and opened it with a flourish and exclaimed loudly about the delicious and tempting morsels, neatly arranged on doily-covered plates.

Dr Scher would probably have attended the hanging of Frank Cotter, she thought as she watched him go to the door to help Sister Bernadette with the tea trolley. He would have been there to pronounce the body dead when it was cut down. Once again she thought about Sam and about his mother's tragic face as she stood there with blood haemorrhaging from her nose. There was an awful finality about the death sentence. No mistaken verdict could ever be remedied. A law that judicially murdered people could not, she thought, with a sudden memory of Thomas Aquinas' words, be a good law.

'Pity he didn't stay in the country; himself and his son. Keep the young fellow of his out of mischief.' Dr Scher opened the door and stood there beaming.

'Oh, Sister Bernadette is that all for me! You spoil me, you know. I won't be able to eat a bite for my supper and then my housekeeper will be furious. Look at that fruitcake! Makes my mouth water! Let me push the trolley. And I can just smell that tea! Lovely! Some people make tea so weak – might as well be coloured water.'

'Tea isn't tea unless the spoon can stand up in it, my mother used to say that. She was a great woman for her cup of tea. Lived until she was ninety years of age and never sick, either.' Sister Bernadette took the lid from the teapot and gave the tea a quick stir.

'Well, there you are. What better proof could you have of the good medicine in a strong cup of tea? Still, Sister Bernadette, we'd better keep that to ourselves or we doctors would starve for lack of patients.'

They bantered together in the customary way while the Reverend Mother brooded on Sam and wondered whether there was anything that she could do. It was none of her business, of course, but it was hard to keep his face and the face of his mother out of her mind's eye. Once Sister Bernadette, pink with pleasure, had backed herself out of the room, she turned an expectant face towards Dr Scher as he poured himself a cup of tea and cut a generous slice from the moist fruitcake.

'Well, what about this business this morning, what did you make of it?' she asked.

'That young fellow, Sam O'Mahony, don't you think that he assassinated James Doyle, then?' he enquired and she knew from the sharpening of his gaze that he had realized how many doubts she had. 'You were there, weren't you, when the shot was fired? What do you think, yourself? Was it Sam? Or did someone "pull a fast one on him", as they say in Cork?'

'He looked shocked,' said the Reverend Mother after a moment's thought. 'Shocked and bewildered,' she added.

'Hmm, doesn't necessarily mean that he's innocent. It must be a bit of a shock to kill a man for the first time.'

'That is correct, but if the intention was to kill, if he had been chosen as the assassin by the Republicans, then I would imagine that he, or someone else, would have worked out an escape route.' Once again the Reverend Mother thought about the man in the belted raincoat. He had slipped away almost as quickly as though he had already assessed his escape route. Who was that man, she wondered.

'True for you. Making martyrs went out once they hanged Connolly and Pearse in 1916. Nowadays they look after their assassins, keep them safe for another day's work. He surely

could have slipped away in the crowd.' Dr Scher sipped his
dark orange tea with a thoughtful air.

'Perhaps that was what happened. Perhaps the real assassin
escaped and dropped the pistol on Sam's foot. There's no
doubt in my mind that Sam had a notebook and pencil in his
hand when I last noticed him, just before the lights went out.'

'Odd thing to do, though,' argued Dr Scher. 'It would be
different if the assassin had just picked a knife from the stall.
He'd want to get rid of something like that quickly, but a pistol
is a valuable thing to the Republicans. I've heard that they are
very short of weapons. Most of the ambushes these days are
to get supplies of bullets and guns. I can't see one of them,
or one of their agents, throwing a pistol away. Still, I suppose
that the fellow could have lost his nerve. That's always possible.
I don't suppose it's easy to kill someone. It's bad enough to
stand by their bed and know that you can do nothing to save
their life.' He waited for a moment, frowning slightly at his
tea cup, and then when she didn't reply, he looked up and
said, 'There's something troubling you, isn't there, Reverend
Mother? Not just the waste of a young life – you think it
might not have been Sam, that it might have been somebody
else, don't you?'

She could see him studying her face, but she took her time
before replying. She had always prided herself on having a
detached and an unemotional approach to life's problems.
When she spoke she was glad to hear that her voice sounded
calm and dispassionate. After all, if Sam O'Mahony did, in
reality, kill James Doyle, if he were guilty of taking a life, it
was perhaps only just that his own life should be forfeit.
Although everything within her cried out in protest, she could
not deny that was the teaching of the church and was the law
of the country in which she lived.

But did he do it?

'I saw a man,' she said evenly. 'He was at Michael Skiddy's
soap and candle stall. I saw him about five minutes before the
shooting took place. I noticed him because he had his hat
pulled down to one side of his face, the brim completely
covered his face; he had his head tilted to one side – the brim
cast a shadow from the candlelight and it hid him; he could

have been anyone. At some stage, I'm not sure whether it was before, or after the lights above in the gallery went out, but at some stage the man blew out a candle and when I looked for him as the superintendent was telling everyone to stand still, well, there was no trace of him. I suppose he melted into the crowd at some point when I was not looking in that direction. I don't even know whether he blew out the candle, or whether it was Michael Skiddy himself. But somehow, I fancy that it was not Michael. He probably keeps that candle lit in order to draw attention to his stock.'

Dr Scher nodded. 'Could be a Republican from your description,' he said. 'Doesn't necessarily mean that he had anything to do with the murder, though, does it? He might have been there for quite an innocent purpose. The Republicans have to buy their groceries like the rest of the world. I've heard that they are holed up in some empty cottages in west Cork. They would need candles out there in the countryside. Or he may have been there to make sure that the assassination was carried out and then he just melted away when he saw that young Sam was frozen with terror. They have to learn to be ruthless, you know.'

The Reverend Mother nodded sadly and he gave her an understanding look.

'You're thinking about your young Eileen, your star pupil, aren't you? You're afraid that she might be mixed up in this. Have you heard from her recently?'

The Reverend Mother shook her head. 'No,' she said. She didn't add that she prayed nightly that Eileen would extricate herself from the dangerous way of life that she had chosen. It was probably unnecessary to say this. Dr Scher had shared her secret when the girl, wounded in the arm, had come to seek refuge in the convent chapel. He knew the dangers and guessed her anguish.

'Well, I suppose the man with the raincoat and the slouched hat is safely back in some place in west Cork now,' he said. 'And I suppose it is possible that he is someone that your girl Eileen knows. She would be out there in west Cork, wouldn't she?'

He didn't wait for an answer to his question, just told her

that Sam O'Mahony would come before the court in a week's time. By then the police would have had time to gather the evidence against him.

'I'm afraid,' he said soberly, 'that there is no chance that one of the Republicans will come out with their hands up, saying, "It wasn't him; it was me". They get hard, even the most idealistic ones of them. No, these lads will probably keep their distance. There's a pretty good case against Sam O'Mahony, you know. He had the motive; James Doyle had insisted that he be sacked from the *Cork Examiner*, threatened to sue them if they didn't get rid of that impudent reporter, so I've heard. And of course, he had opportunity, was standing near, would you say near?'

The Reverend Mother thought back. 'About twenty feet, I'd say.'

'Near enough for an accurate shot. So he had opportunity, but of course the thing that will damn him will be the fact that a crowd of Cork citizens, including Reverend Mother Aquinas, actually saw him standing there with the pistol in his hand and the body on the ground with a bullet through his back.'

'His poor mother,' said the Reverend Mother sadly as Dr Scher rose to leave.

# FIVE

St Thomas Aquinas:
*Bonum est integra causa, maulum ex quocunque defectu*
(An action is good only if each element in it is good; it is
bad if any one of those elements is bad)

'**M**rs O'Mahony to see you, Reverend Mother.' Sister
Bernadette looked apologetic. 'I told her that it was
fierce early in the morning and that you'd only just
swallowed your breakfast, but she just stood there and said
that she would wait.'

The Reverend Mother raised her head from her account book
and looked through the window. It was raining in that dreary
way that it did in Cork, almost as though it would never stop,
water falling from the sky, mist rising up from the river trap-
ping the smells from the drains and from the nearby gasometer
beneath the low clouds. She could guess that Mrs O'Mahony
had had a sleepless night, listening to the patter of raindrops
hitting the slated roof of the attic where she and her son lived.
She would probably have waited as long as she could possibly
endure the inaction before coming to see her.

She would have to see her.

'Show Mrs O'Mahony in, Sister Bernadette,' she said aloud.
'Oh, and bring in some tea and cake. She's probably had
nothing to eat this morning.'

Mrs O'Mahony had rehearsed her apologies and started on
them almost before the door was closed behind her. She was
still apologising as she obediently sat on the armchair by the
fire. And then she broke down, hiding her face in her hands,
her head bending lower and lower until her forehead was
touching the old black handbag on her lap. The Reverend
Mother allowed her to weep. She would be strong and tearless
later on when she went to see her son and it would be best
for her to let her feelings of despair and terror surface now.

She went to the door when she heard the sound of Sister
Bernadette's slippers and took the tray from her and carried
it over to the table, firmly shutting the door behind her with
a practised jerk of the elbow. She waited for a few minutes
and then fished out a large clean soft cotton handkerchief and
pressed it into Mrs O'Mahony's hand.

'Come, come, this is not like you, Mrs O'Mahony,' she said
briskly. 'We need to discuss this matter, now. Sam has only
you to rely on, you know. Drink your tea and eat some cake
and then we'll talk.'

Mrs O'Mahony mopped her face vigorously and gulped a
few times. Her fingers were tightly clenched and she struggled
visibly to control her sobs. The Reverend Mother stood over
her, pouring out the strong tea, adding milk and a spoonful
of sugar and watched her drink it before cutting a slice of
fruitcake.

'I couldn't,' she said when it came to the slice of cake and
the Reverend Mother did not press her. Some troubles were
just too bad even for Sister Bernadette's fruitcake. Later,
perhaps, when she had unburdened her soul of a little of its
anguish.

'Have you seen Sam?' she enquired.

'No, not yet,' said Mrs O'Mahony wearily. 'I was told that
I could see him on Monday. Visiting hours are from three to
four every afternoon except on Saturdays and Sundays. I'll be
there, but I don't know how much that will help. I just don't
know what to say to him.'

'Did he shoot the city engineer?' asked the Reverend Mother
mildly and was pleased to see the flush of anger coming over
the woman's face.

'My Sam wouldn't shoot a stray tomcat,' she said indig-
nantly. 'He's against violence. It's not made him popular. The
Free State fellows don't like him. He's too inclined to write
articles asking what they are doing now that they have power
in their hands. He's been against murder, been against all of
this fighting. He wrote an article that would bring tears to your
eyes about the last hours of that man who was killed last year,
the R.I.C. man who was shot after bicycling out to do a bit
of fishing by the side of the Lee Road. And then when that

fellow who calls himself a patriot wrote a piece about what the Republicans would do if they were in charge of the country, well Sam just tore it to pieces, said that raids and shooting were the only things they knew about and that they hadn't the slightest idea how to manage the economy of the country. They sent him a death threat after that. Well, at least Sam thought it was a death threat. It was a piece of paper with a black spot in the middle of it.'

The Reverend Mother thought about that and guessed that she knew the person who had delivered the black spot to Sam O'Mahony. She had a pupil once who had loved the Robert Louis Stevenson novel, *Treasure Island*, and had been so absorbed in the account of blind Pew that she had been found with her head stuck in the book by Sister Bernadette, crouching over the remains of the fire, in an almost dark classroom, hours after the others had gone. For a moment she thought about Eileen in the classroom, her bright face, her absorption in a novel or a poem, her quick wit and love of argument. Once one of her star pupils and now a fugitive, part of the banned Republican army, holed up in some derelict cottage out in the countryside! Perhaps teaching these girls to think and to reason, to look to a better future might have been a mistake. A clever girl like Eileen got to thinking that she might make a difference to the future. But there was little use in regrets, so the Reverend Mother reverted to practicalities, bending over and cutting the thick slice of cake into manageable bite-sized morsels.

'Well, if I were you, Mrs O'Mahony,' she said, holding the plate in front of the woman and waiting until she took a cube before going on, 'if I were you, I would remind him that he didn't shoot the man, therefore someone else did. I would encourage Sam to think hard about that morning. He is an intelligent young man and he has plenty of time to reflect. Let him try to remember any movement, any sense that there was someone missing after the lights were switched on. Tell him to report any suspicions to the police. Both you and he know that he is innocent, so Sam should firmly keep in his mind that he has not done this murder. Make him stick to that. No one who was present yesterday morning at the market seemed

anxious to say that they saw him fire the shot. No one seemed
to know what happened. It was all so bewildering; the lights
went out and the crowd so thick, that it was hard to see anything.
The evidence against him is only that he was holding the gun.
And his explanation for that was quite reasonable, I thought.
He must just keep very calm, and keep asserting his innocence,' wound up the Reverend Mother, conscious of the fact
that Mrs O'Mahony was hardly listening but was absent-
mindedly pushing a few crumbs of cake around the plate in
front of her.

She looked up and then looked back down again, picked
up the cup of tea and drained the last few mouthfuls. They
seemed to give her courage because when she looked up again
she met the Reverend Mother's eye and kept her gaze steady
as she said, 'There's something else that you can do for me,
and for Sam.'

She's going to ask for a loan to engage a lawyer for Sam,
thought the Reverend Mother and she felt if that was true that
she would be uncertain as to whether she could justify it. The
school, run without charging fees for any of the children,
required a huge amount of fundraising in order to keep it
functioning efficiently. And then she had the work unit for the
girls who had passed school leaving age, and no longer wanted
to engage in book learning, but were willing to learn cookery
and typing and other skills that might help them to get a job
in a city that was full of unemployment. From time to time,
she had squeezed out some money from one fund or other for
a past pupil in dire straits, but Sam O'Mahony was not a past
pupil and to hire a lawyer to conduct his defence would be
an enormous expense. Not one that she could justify, she
thought. The bishop's secretary scrutinised her accounts and
this really would be an unjustified use of charitable donations.

'If it's within my power, I will do my best to help,' she said
cautiously.

'Well, it is within your power and it will help,' said Mrs
O'Mahony. There was a sudden change in her. The woman,
who had wept so piteously five minutes ago, was now sitting
up very straight, her eyes dry, her mouth a tough firm line.
This was the woman who had, single-handed, built up a

prosperous business in her stall at the English Market, who, when deserted by her husband, had managed to feed, clothe and expensively educate her son. 'There is something that you can do for Sam and you will save his life if you do it,' she said firmly. 'You can tell Inspector Patrick Cashman that you were standing just beside Mrs O'Donovan's buttered egg stall, and you saw Sam, over there beside my stall and he had a notebook in one hand and a pen in the other and you could still see him at the very moment the shot rang out.'

The Reverend Mother kept silent. The room seemed very still, the flames flickered over the burning coals, the rain pattered against the window and the clock struck the half hour. Eventually it was Mrs O'Mahony who broke the silence.

'It would not be a lie,' she said. 'Sam was standing just in front of my stall and I saw the pencil in one hand and the notebook in the other. I saw him a second before I heard the gun. There was enough light coming through from the archways to see him. There is no way that he could have fired that shot.'

'Then that is what you must tell the inspector,' said the Reverend Mother and heard her own voice lay a noticeable emphasis on the word *you*.

'As if he'd believe me!'

'What does the superintendent of the market think? Perhaps he, also, noticed Sam.'

'He's no friend of mine.' Her voice was harsh and aggressive. The Reverend Mother remembered talk of some sort of fight at the market. Wasn't Mrs O'Mahony convicted of assaulting the weighing scales man? She seemed to remember something about that in the *Cork Examiner*. She eyed her visitor narrowly, but said nothing.

'They'd believe you,' said Mrs O'Mahony after a minute. 'If you said that you saw Sam with the notebook in one hand and the pencil in the other, if you said that you saw his two hands occupied just at the very moment that the shot was fired. If you said that, Reverend Mother, there would be no one in the city who would call you a liar. Sam would probably be released straightaway. The inspector wouldn't go against your evidence.'

'But I didn't see him,' said the Reverend Mother after a pause. 'I was looking in another direction completely. I was looking down towards the fountain.'

'But you could say it. After all, what's a small lie compared to a human life?'

What, indeed? thought the Reverend Mother. Put like that, the question was a hard one to answer. And yet she had no doubt in her mind as to what the answer must be.

'I could not tell a lie,' she said firmly.

'A lie,' the woman shrugged. 'We all tell lies all the time. Haven't you ever told someone that they were looking good, when you knew that they were at death's door? I have. We all have. Haven't you ever said something like, "it's so kind of you to come to visit me," when you were wishing them gone?'

It was possible. And the small lies of social intercourse, the praise of a cake that she had hardly tasted; the thanks for an unwanted cup of tea; the bracing and completely insincere declared belief in a girl's ability to understand a difficult poem; the assurance that all was well to a classroom of terrified children as guns roared in the streets outside the school and at any moment a shot could come through the window and kill one of them; of course, she had told lies, had allowed a false impression to go uncorrected. And the worst of it all was that she knew Mrs O'Mahony was right. Patrick would believe her, the barracks' superintendent would believe her and if it came to a trial, the judge in the court would believe her.

But she would have to swear to her evidence. Call upon God to be her witness.

'I cannot do it,' she said again. 'Anything else that I can do, any influence that I have, I will bring to bear. But to tell a lie like that is not something I could do. My conscience would not allow me.'

Mrs O'Mahony put back her tea cup, centring it carefully on its matching saucer. She stood up, the broken veins in her weather-beaten face showing a dark red tracery across cheeks and nose. Her eyes were full of anger and when she spoke, she seemed almost to spit out the words.

'Then I hope that your conscience will not trouble you, Reverend Mother, when you have a death, perhaps two deaths – I can't see myself wanting to live if Sam is taken from me – so you will have my death, also, on your head. Have you ever seen a hanging, Reverend Mother? I haven't, not until now. But all of last night I could see what it would be like, I stood there and watched it happen time after time. I wouldn't wish a night like that on my worst enemy and there'll be worse to come, won't there?'

The Reverend Mother touched the bell to summon Sister Bernadette, then rose to her feet also. There was a certain menace coming from the woman but she refused to be intimidated.

'I shall pray for Sam, and for the truth to be uncovered,' she said quietly as the door opened and Sister Bernadette came in.

'Oh, prayer,' said Mrs O'Mahony loudly and bitterly. 'I've given up believing in that for a long time. Prayer will do no good; don't imagine that it will be of the slightest use to poor Sam down there in the gaol, knowing that he may be dancing on the end of the rope before the summer is here.' She pushed past Sister Bernadette, saying harshly, 'Don't bother showing me out. I can find my own way. You can clear away the tea and cake. The Reverend Mother will tell you that I loved it.' And then she was gone, leaving Sister Bernadette staring open-mouthed after her.

'What . . .?' she began and then fell silent.

'I must make a phone call,' said the Reverend Mother in what she hoped was her normal voice. 'Perhaps you would be kind enough to make up the fire, Sister Bernadette? I have some letters to write before I have my ten o'clock lesson with the older girls.'

It would be nice, she thought, to have a telephone in her own room, rather than having to stand in a draughty corridor, not sure of who might overhear her words. However, she did not feel that she could justify the expense. Charity collections during these last few months had not yielded the usual generous contributions from the city merchants. Ireland's independence from England had resulted in a fall-off in the export business and she was fiercely determined not to cut back on any of her schemes.

'Montenotte two-three, please,' she said into the phone and

then smiled with amusement as the woman at the exchange said promptly, 'Yes, of course, Reverend Mother. I'll put you straight through to Mrs Murphy.' It was a timely reminder that nothing private should be said to her cousin on the phone. Still, she and Lucy usually understood each other very quickly. They had been best of friends for almost seventy years and both knew every nuance in each other's voice.

'Good morning, Reverend Mother,' came Lucy's musical voice after a minute. 'I hear that you were centre stage in that shocking assassination. Buying eggs, I believe, when the shot rang out. Rupert said everyone was gossiping about it at the Chamber of Commerce meeting last night. Poor Mr Doyle! And they say that the man with the gun was a member of the Republican Volunteers.' Her voice purred on, delivering the normal platitudes, but there was an undercurrent of curiosity in it. Lucy would know all the gossip about the city engineer. Her husband, from one of the foremost merchant families in the city, was a prominent solicitor and usually knew everything that Lucy had not managed to pick up at her tea parties. She would be wondering now what would be her cousin's interest in this murder.

'I'm very well, thank you. I was driven back from the market by Captain Newenham; a distant cousin of ours, isn't he?' said the Reverend Mother and then she stopped and waited. The statement, she knew, would sound inconsequential to a listener, but Lucy was very sharp.

'Ah, yes. Yes, of course, you're right,' she said and then almost without missing a beat, she added, 'I must pop in and see you, this afternoon, make sure that you are all right. It must have been a terrible shock to an elderly lady like yourself.'

'And, of course, I don't use Pond's Cream, so I look even more elderly than others of my age,' murmured the Reverend Mother. By now, she thought, no one at the exchange would still be listening in to the conversation, but it would be safest to wait for Lucy's visit. She arranged a time briskly and then put down the phone, dragging out her round silver watch from her pocket and angling it towards the light of the corridor window. Another half hour before she was due in class.

'Inspector Cashman to see you, Reverend Mother,' said

Sister Bernadette coming down the dark corridor towards her. 'I've put him in your room,' she went on, fully confident that after the dramatic murder of the city engineer yesterday evening, that the Reverend Mother would be interested in talking with Patrick Cashman.

# SIX

St Thomas Aquinas:
*Quia parvus error in principio magnus est in fine*
(Because a small mistake in the beginning is a big one at
the end)

P atrick Cashman had always, even at the age of seven,
been a serious young man – a good scholar, not perhaps
the brightest or cleverest in that class, but tenacious and
hard-working. There were times, these days, thought the
Reverend Mother, when he had reminded her of a Scottie terrier
which she had owned in her youth. He had the same bright,
alert eyes, the same bushy eyebrows and the same capacity to
worry away at something for hours, allowing nothing to distract
him. She remembered him as a small child puzzling over a
long division sum, continually checking his arithmetic by multi-
plying back, rubbing his eyebrows and then with a sigh and
a squaring of his narrow shoulders, starting back on it again,
ignoring his teacher's exasperation and commands to put away
his copy book. Her patron saint, Thomas Aquinas, had recognized the importance of being meticulous, she often reminded
herself when her quick brain impatiently sought for an immediate solution.

Today the bushy eyebrows were knitted when he came into
her parlour and greeted her with a mixture of anxiety and of
hope. His manners were always very good and he spent the
first few minutes enquiring about her health and hoping that
she had not been upset by events in the English Market the
day before.

'Funny the way that we all still call it the English Market,
even after the English have left Ireland,' mused the Reverend
Mother. She had assured him of her good health, but he seemed
reluctant to come to the point so she chatted idly for a minute
on the various legends that surrounded the setting up of the

English Market and where its name came from – that it contrasted with the Irish Market on the Coal Quay, that it serviced the English ships moored in the great harbour of Cork during the Napoleonic Wars or that English was always spoken there when it was set up first and that the use of the Irish language had been banned within its walls. Eventually she ran out of her stock of potted history of this city built on the marsh under whose main streets still ran the rivers which had once seamed that swampy land, and she looked at him enquiringly.

'You look worried, Patrick,' she said bluntly. 'Not surprising, of course, with this murder, or was it an assassination, on your hands.'

'Assassination, in all probability,' said Patrick. 'James Doyle was the organizer of the Anti-Sinn Féin party, did you know that, Reverend Mother?'

'No,' she said, feeling, to her shame, an irrational spark of annoyance. Mostly she did know things. Facts, rumours, arcane pieces of knowledge floated to her every day, borne on the sheer crowd of people with whom she came in contact. She was meticulous about not passing them on; nevertheless, she had to admit that she did like to know. The name *Sinn Féin*, meaning *'ourselves alone'* had now become slightly discredited so the party preferred to be called Republicans, or even Volunteers. Nevertheless, the name of the opposition to them remained firmly 'Anti-Sinn Féin'. 'No,' she repeated. 'Well, I suppose it does look like an assassination with Sam O'Mahony as the executioner, or do you doubt that?'

He gave a wry smile. 'I'm annoying the superintendent,' he said. '"Don't know what else you can ask for, lad, you caught the feller red-handed. Had the gun in his hand, didn't he?" He even mentioned your name – "and you have fifty good citizens of Cork city to bear witness to that fact, including Reverend Mother Aquinas." And, of course, he is right. I've been through all the statements. Everyone says that. First the lights went out, then they heard a shot and then the lights were turned on and then they saw Sam O'Mahony standing over the body with a pistol in his hand. Unfortunately he was able to throw the gun into the fountain so we can't swear in court that a bullet was fired from that gun minutes earlier, but we can assume that it was the gun which killed James Doyle.'

'What if the Republicans deny that he was their agent?'

'Well, then, according to the superintendent, Sam did it because he was angry at the role James Doyle played in getting him the sack from his job at the *Cork Examiner*.'

'And in that case,' said the Reverend Mother feeling rather as though she were the lawyer for the defence, 'in that case, you must account for the pistol, where did Sam O'Mahony get a pistol unless he was agent of the Volunteers, or the Republicans?'

'Could have been stolen,' said Patrick briefly. 'It's British army issue. Probably picked up on the night that Cork was burned down by the Black and Tans. I was there myself, that night, a few of the lads from school were with me and we were ducking in and out of the lanes, daring each other to get closer. We saw them set fire to Grant's and then to Cash's and then the Munster Arcade went. They were going mad. They were all drunk as lords that night, lobbing cans of petrol into shops, shooting the fire brigade men, cutting hoses. A lot of guns were rumoured to have been lost that night. These fellows had no discipline. They fired off all their bullets, dropped the gun, couldn't find it in the dark, and then went for another one. They had fresh supplies of guns and ammunition in their lorries and just helped themselves, so I've heard. Sam was a junior reporter on the *Cork Examiner* at the time and some of them were out on Patrick Street that night. He might have picked it up out of the embers.'

The Reverend Mother thought about it. It did seem plausible, although more likely that the guns were picked up by the Volunteers as they were known then. That reminded her of something. The image of the man in the belted trench coat and slouched hat was still in her mind. There had been something very professional about the way that he had melted away before anyone else had moved. And surely he had been responsible for the blowing out of the candle on Michael Skiddy's stall.

'I suppose it seems likely that there is a Republican involvement in this killing, is there, Patrick?' she asked.

He frowned and after a moment said heavily, 'Most of the killings in this city have something to do with them, one way or the other. Either the Republicans or the Anti-Sinn Féin party trying to incriminate them. There's a lot of that going on these days. I'm not sure really. Sometimes I think that if the Republican Party was involved, more than one man would have been shot. After all there was the assistant city engineer, Mr Browne, and the town planner, Captain Newenham, there also. If they had decided to shoot, they would have taken them out, too. But the word is that the volunteers are very short of weapons and of ammunition. It will be just a matter of weeks before they give in and ask for a peace treaty, from what I've heard.'

It was a good point. And yet the Reverend Mother was fairly sure that the figure in a trench coat and hat well pulled down over his face was, in all probability, a Republican. Since uniforms for civilians were banned, these garments had been adopted as an unofficial uniform. Still, the fact that he had disappeared quickly did not mean that he was guilty. Any member of the Republicans would be used to quick action to avoid suspicion. She put the thought aside, therefore, and turned her attention towards Patrick.

'You look worried,' she said. 'What is it that bothers you?'

'I think that Sam is telling the truth,' blurted out Patrick. 'Goodness knows, I have enough experience of people telling me tall stories. I feel that I doubt everything by now, even if someone tells me that there's going to be a shower, I think that they are probably lying.'

'That, indeed, must be the height of scepticism,' murmured the Reverend Mother with a glance out at the everlasting drizzle trickling down the window glass.

Patrick's worried expression didn't lighten. 'And yet, somehow, I think that I have the wrong man. It probably was an assassination. A man shot out there in public before a crowd of people. It's just the sort of thing that the Republicans would do – it makes them popular, gets them new recruits, makes everyone think that they are on the side of the general public. People who want their jobs and their living quarters back would like to hear of the death of James Doyle, who was reputed to be quite corrupt, and was in the game for as much as he could get out of it, they'd have been glad to hear that he got his comeuppance. But, I just don't think that Sam was one of the Republicans. He denies it, and I must say that I've never heard that he was, when usually I hear things like that. That's why I came to see you, this morning, Reverend Mother. I hope you don't mind, but you were there, weren't you? You saw him with the gun in his hand, didn't you? What was your impression?'

The Reverend Mother shut her eyes for a second, though the vision of that scene yesterday morning was still quite clear on her inner eye.

'He looked startled,' she said slowly, 'incredulous.' She opened her eyes again, waited for a moment, still turning over the events of the morning within her mind. 'He didn't act like a guilty person,' she continued. 'He didn't make any attempt to run, or even to hide the gun. The light was very poor there, yesterday morning, Patrick. There was a heavy wet fog. Sam could have just allowed the gun to slip down onto the ground, kicked it into the sawdust around the stalls and then disappeared. And, of course, one would have expected that the assassin would have moved away instantly, there was enough of a crowd around the entrance to the Grand Parade side of the market. He could have lost himself amongst them and been out on the street before people had recovered from the shock, but Sam didn't do that. He just stood there, looking dazed. It was a couple of minutes, at least, before the beadles grabbed his arms. He had time to get away.'

Just as the man in the belted raincoat and slouch hat had done, she thought, and then wondered whether Michael Skiddy had anything to do with the murder. He was a man who might have expected that the compensation paid for the burning of Cork would have given him his shop back a year ago. James Doyle, with his grandiose plans for personal fame and fortune, had scuppered the hopes of a lot of small businessmen. 'Any useful witnesses?' she asked aloud.

Patrick shook his head. 'That's the extraordinary thing. I have statements from everyone there and they are all the same. Everyone heard the shot, moved back to the wall; goodness knows that's not surprising. There's been enough shooting in Cork over the last few years. You can see the same thing out in the streets if a car backfires. The instinct is to get your back to the wall, to get away from the line of fire.'

'And no one saw anything?'

'And no one saw anything except, of course, a minute or so later, Sam O'Mahony standing there with the gun in his hand. We have to hold onto him. He's our only suspect at the moment. He had a motive, too, you know. He was sacked from his job because James Doyle made such a fuss over the article he wrote in the *Cork Examiner*, threatened to bring the paper to court unless the journalist was turned off instantly. And, of course, if we could prove that he was a member of the Republicans, well then any jury would probably convict him.'

'So he had motive, opportunity, and, if you're right about guns going missing on the night that Cork burned, well then he would have had the means, also.'

'As you can imagine, my superintendent thinks that the case is shut. "We have our man!" that's what he's been saying. He's applied for a court hearing already.'

'But you're not happy, Patrick, are you? And I agree with you. Sam O'Mahony didn't act like or have the look of a man who had just committed a murder, but you have interviewed all present and got no satisfactory answers to your questions. Perhaps it is time to start asking other questions.'

'Other questions?' He had a half-startled, half-enquiring look on his face.

'That's right,' said the Reverend Mother firmly. 'If Sam O'Mahony did not murder James Doyle, then someone else did, and it has to be someone who was there at that Princes Street Market, between the fountain and the Grand Parade archway. So you start asking, was there anyone else there who would want to kill James Doyle.'

'Do you mean that it wasn't an assassination? A private murder?'

The Reverend Mother ignored that question. 'It would be easy enough,' she mused. 'It would be easy enough to drop the gun and melt away through the crowd if you were quick-witted and alert. Or perhaps not run away, but just move back

with the rest of the people and counterfeit that same expression
of shock and horror. No matter how used everyone is to gunfire,
there is probably an initial few seconds when you freeze and
then you move. In my case I was beside the buttered eggs
stall when I heard the shot, and I was hardly aware of my
movements but found myself flat against the wall a few seconds
later. And the crowd that had been gathered around James
Doyle in the centre of the aisle seemed to sweep me along.
Others, of course, would be quicker on their feet than I would
have been.'

'So nobody was looking to see who fired the shot.'

'Self-preservation seems to come first for us all – it's
instinctive, isn't it? Do you know that the minute baby lizards
are born, they immediately run away from their mother as
otherwise she would eat them. Something I learned by sad
experience in my youth,' added the Reverend Mother as she
noticed his startled expression.

'Well, Sam's mother is not like those lizard mothers,' said
Patrick ruefully. 'I thought that she would eat me.'

'He's her whole life.' The Reverend Mother thought about
Mrs O'Mahony's request to her. Was her conscience or a sense
of righteousness worth two lives? What would she feel if she
had to stand at the foot of a gallows and watch a young man
die a terrible death from strangulation and a broken neck?
Heart rending and almost unbearable for anyone; for a mother
it would be worse than any torture. And she, Reverend Mother
Aquinas, could prevent this event just by one small lie. Put
like that, it seemed a trivial matter. And yet, she thought, once
a sacred oath means nothing then the fabric of civilisation is
torn down, the veil of the temple is rent. Somehow, she had
to save Sam without flouting the laws of God and of man.
She turned with a sudden energy to Patrick.

'I don't think that Sam is the murderer of James Doyle,' she
said decisively. 'Let's look at the others who were there, standing
there, either around him, or by the stalls on either side of the
corridor. Let's consider their possible motives.'

'Someone else who wanted to be revenged on James Doyle.'
Patrick's eyes were thoughtful, reviewing the names of those
present. 'I suppose Sam wasn't the only one who bore a grudge

against him. I could start working on that, dig around a little, though I don't think that the superintendent will be too happy.'

'He didn't have the reputation of being a very kind man, James Doyle, I mean,' said the Reverend Mother. 'Perhaps you might find someone that he sacked from a job, someone who had been sent to prison on his evidence, some builder who knew that he would not be employed by him. Or, perhaps even more important, someone who felt threatened by him. I suppose that anger and greed are motives, but fear may be an even greater one. Some people collect guilty secrets and hold them as a threat over the heads of their victims. There have been a lot of foul deeds done in this city over the last five or six years. People have disappeared; murdered, one presumes. It seems to me that respect for human life is very low these days. Public assassinations can lead to private murders.'

'I suppose of the people who were standing around that morning, the only ones who would have known him well would have been Mr Browne, who was his assistant, and is now acting city engineer . . .' Patrick left a pause, waiting for her reaction, but she said nothing, just waited, so he went on. 'And then there was the town planner, Captain Newenham. You know him, Reverend Mother, don't you?'

'I know him,' she admitted, 'but not well,' she added. She would, she thought, keep her thoughts to herself for the moment about Captain Newenham. She would wait to see what Lucy thought.

'And the bishop's secretary, Father de Courcy, he was there, too, of course. And then there's Michael Skiddy, the man who has the soap and candles stall. He was fined a few months ago at the district court for lobbing a stone at the car window when James Doyle was driving down the Grand Parade. I had to arrest the man, caution him, bring the case to court, though I'd have preferred just to warn him. There was no real damage to the car, Michael Skiddy was just letting off steam, but James Doyle insisted on him being prosecuted.'

'And his anger could have festered during these few months.' The Reverend Mother made up her mind. She had to do her best for Sam. If nothing else, multiple suspects could muddy the waters. She would give Patrick other suspects to investigate.

'It may be nothing, Patrick,' she said, 'but I did notice a man at Mr Skiddy's stall, wearing a belted raincoat and with his hat pulled down over his face. I saw him there before the lights went out, but when I looked afterwards, when the super-intendent was telling everyone to stay still, well, he was no longer there. It may be, of course,' she said after a minute when she tried to recall the scene exactly, 'it may be that while everyone was looking at Sam, he made his way to the Grand Parade entrance. This was before the superintendent told everyone to stand still, so it could be that the man just did not want to be involved.'

Patrick nodded and made a note. 'I'll have a word with Michael,' he said. 'I wouldn't be surprised if there were a few others who moved off quickly. A lot of people in this city have learned to get out of the way fast once trouble starts. I'll get Joe on to questioning the stallholders on the Grand Parade side, near to the Princes Street entrance. They would have been busy at the fish stalls since it was a Friday, but you'd never know. Some of those stallholders are very sharp. They learn to keep an eye on what is going on around them or else they start losing stock. And, of course, there's young John Murphy, the butcher. He's working with his brother now, but he owned one of the stalls that was burned out at the Patrick Street end of the market. He's had no compensation; the stall was supposed to be rebuilt, but James Doyle was delaying the matter, hoping to get a bigger commission to redesign and rebuild the whole market.'

'Yes, I saw him,' said the Reverend Mother. 'He had a cleaver in his hand, though, not a gun.' Her mind visualized a map of the English Market, built in the centre of a space between Patrick's Street, the Grand Parade and Princes Street; it had entrances from all three of these places.

'Could have dropped the one and picked up the other,' said Patrick. He was pacing up and down energetically, only pausing now and then to make a note. 'Well, Reverend Mother, you've given me lots of ideas. I'll be off now. I'll have a word with Michael Skiddy before I go back to the barracks. It will be interesting to see whether he knows the man with the hat pulled down over his face and whether he can explain why he suddenly blew out the candle and then disappeared. And, of course, if he went towards the Grand Parade side of the market, well then he would have passed the place where Sam O'Mahony was standing and he could well have dropped the gun there at his feet.'

The Reverend Mother said her farewells. Patrick would do all the good police work, would survey the scene, take statements, painstakingly match accounts of what happened.

As for her, she thought that a gossip with her cousin Lucy might be fruitful.

# SEVEN

'**T**he superintendent told me to give you the *Cork Examiner*, inspector,' said Tommy, the duty constable. 'He's marked a page for you.'

The *Cork Examiner* had been opened at the advertisement page and was folded in half. A thick blue line from a nib that leaked ink into the paper had been drawn around one of the advertisements. It read:

> **Our City Engineer was assassinated by the Sinn Féin party because of his religion. We call for the immediate arrest and execution of all those who planned and executed this deed.**
> **Signed: The Anti-Sinn Féin Party**

Patrick stared at it with annoyance. 'As if things weren't bad enough,' he muttered. 'I thought the Anti-Sinn Féin Party had gone quiet, these days.'

'They say that they have a membership of 2000,' said Tommy helpfully.

'I wish the *Cork Examiner* would stop printing these things,' muttered Patrick under his breath. The *Cork Examiner* had declared itself to be impartial, would print anything from either party, or, as Patrick thought privately, any advertisement that was paid for, no matter what trouble it caused. 'Was he a Protestant, then, James Doyle?' he asked aloud. The words of the beadle at the English Market came back to him suddenly.

Tommy would know. He knew everything that was to be known about the inhabitants of Cork city.

'Yes, he was, inspector,' said Tommy. 'Used to go to that big square church at the end of Anglesea Street, just opposite to the Blind Asylum. They say that he got a new roof put on the church with money that should have been used for the rebuilding of the library. Well, they'll bury him there now, I suppose. I've seen him on a Sunday, with his shiny top hat and his polished boots. Used to look the real gentleman. You'd be surprised to know that his father was nothing but a poor tailor who worked in a cellar down in South Terrace.'

'That is interesting that he was a Protestant.' Patrick felt exasperated with himself. He had started the wrong way around. He needed to find out some more about the dead man before he began to see whether anyone other than Sam O'Mahony had killed him. But if he was a Protestant, and what's more a Protestant who was suspected of diverting money to his own ends, money that should be used to rebuild shops, offices and a library in order to give jobs and accommodation back to the people of Cork, well, then the Sinn Féin Republicans could certainly have targeted the man for assassination. In fact it was beginning to look like a much more likely motive than a revenge killing for Sam O'Mahony losing his job from the *Cork Examiner*. But was Sam the agent of the Republicans? That would have to be found out.

'Is Joe in?' he asked and received a sour nod. Tommy would have preferred to have gone on imparting knowledge, but he was a terrible old gossip who would be eager to report any unguarded word. Joe, Patrick's assistant, lived with his parents in a terraced house next door to the church that Tommy had mentioned. He would be a safer person to discuss the matter with.

'Hear any rumours about James Doyle and the repair to the church roof next to your place, Joe?' he asked once the door was closed behind him.

Joe gave a grin. 'Funny you should mention that, I was thinking, as I came to work this morning, that I must bring it up. It happened about six months ago. Apparently they had been appealing for funds for ages, had been having collections, having bazaars, all that sort of thing, but, of course, ever since

the troubles lots of the Protestants in Cork have left the city
so their congregation is getting smaller and smaller and smaller.
You'd see them of a Sunday, a dozen of them, if that, going
into the church, not like our churches where you have to fight
for a space if you don't get there dead early.'

'And so the roof was repaired,' said Patrick. 'And there was
talk about it, is that right?'

'Well, there are eight houses on the terrace – seven of them
Catholics but the people in number one are Protestants – people
of the name of Good – and the eldest boy there told my
youngest brother that Mr Doyle paid to have the roof done
himself, or at least gave the labour free. There was a lot of
talk about that, people saying that the builders that were
employed should have been doing other work, such as repairing
the houses at the top of Maylor Street. I don't know whether
you know those houses in Maylor Street, inspector, but their
roof timbers were burned when Cash's Department Store was
destroyed in Patrick Street. These houses could have been
saved but the rain has got in and the plaster has crumbled off
the walls and now they have a notice up saying: "Unsafe to
enter. In danger of collapse." And, all the poor people who
lived there have had to find somewhere else.'

'So it could be a political assassination,' mused Patrick. It
would certainly be a better and an easier solution, but these
political killings often brought revenge killings in their wake.
'Well, we'll see soon,' he said. 'If it was done by the
Republicans, they will probably claim it tomorrow.' An assassination of a corrupt public official would, he thought, be a
popular move, and might gain them some support. There must
be many people in the city who were still homeless, or who
had a relative or friend homeless because of corruption in high
places. James Doyle must have had many enemies.

'The word on the street last night, when I was strolling
down Patrick Street, was that Tom Hurley of the Ballinhassig
crowd had something to do with it. Some of Battalion One
are hiding out somewhere there, so they say,' added Joe hastily
disclaiming any real knowledge of the Republican Army. 'And
Tom Hurley was seen going real fast down the Grand Parade
yesterday morning.'

'I see,' said Patrick. If he were going to interview Tom Hurley, he would have to take a battalion of soldiers with him, and the likelihood would be that either he would be shot from behind a hedge, or that Tom would be impossible to track down – or both could happen. It would be easier to explore other avenues first of all.

And, of course, the easiest thing of all was to go along with the evidence from fifty people, with the strong conviction of the superintendent of the barracks, and build the case against Sam O'Mahony.

He thought back to the Reverend Mother and realized that the easy option was not available to him.

'Are we going to start the book of evidence against Sam?' asked Joe, watching his face.

'Certainly not,' snapped Patrick. 'You'll never get anywhere if you act in that sort of sloppy way, Joe. We take it step by step. The first thing is find out a bit more about the victim. I think that we'll take a trip to the city engineer's office. I'd like to have a word with the assistant – that's Mr Browne, isn't it? Was he a Protestant, too, do you happen to know?'

Joe shook his head emphatically. 'Not a chance. He's some sort of relation to the bishop. He'll get the job as sure as eggs are eggs. Just you wait and see.' He gave a quick glance at the clock and then a slight cough. 'And the superintendent is due in here in half an hour. He's gone to have a word with the Lord Mayor about all of this.'

That was interesting, thought Patrick. Mr O'Callaghan, the mayor of Cork, was a member of the Sinn Féin party. If he had summoned the superintendent, it may well have been either to confirm or to deny that the Republicans were involved. He would be subtle about it, of course, but he would leave the superintendent in no doubt as to his meaning. He wondered whether to wait, but then decided against it. If the word was that there was no political involvement, then a motive could be found to say that this, though not an assassination, was a revenge killing. A case could be made that Sam had been unemployed for six months now and had brooded on the man who had caused him to lose his job and then had decided to kill him. Sam might not be able to afford a lawyer, but even if he had one, the lawyer for the state could easily demolish any arguments about the unlikelihood of the guilty man just standing there, holding the gun. However, it could be urged that he had been discovered too quickly and had decided to brazen the matter out. No, Sam, if brought to trial even with no more evidence than they had at the moment would, in all probability, be condemned to death.

When Patrick and Joe were shown into the office labelled 'City Engineer', Thomas Browne was seated at the dead man's desk marking in some lines on a drawing of an enormous building with what looked like almost sixty windows placed along its frontage. He was so immersed in it that he seemed to have difficulty in dragging his eyes away and Patrick waited quietly for a couple of minutes, but still the man did not look up. He had not spoken a word, just nodded at Patrick's greeting when his visitors were announced and did not appear as though he was going to acknowledge their presence. Patrick felt a surge of anger. He suspected that if his accent had been different that he would not be treated like this. Joe looked uneasy and this added to his annoyance. It should be the man behind the desk who was showing signs of uneasiness. After all, Mr Browne had been standing beside his boss when the man was shot. Yesterday he was just an assistant, today he was Acting City Engineer, with the power that the position brought in a city filled with burned out buildings, all waiting to be reconstructed.

'Are these the plans for the rebuilding of the city hall?' he asked abruptly.

Thomas Browne dragged his eyes away from the drawing and frowned. 'Perhaps,' he said with an indifferent shrug. 'Can I help you, sergeant?'

'Inspector,' said Patrick abruptly. He had spent many long midnight hours, endeavouring to keep his eyes open, striving to keep his brain from bursting with the knowledge that he was cramming into it, anxiously, intensely studying for that promotion and he was not willing to forgo an iota of the respect due from a man who had probably idled a few years at university after receiving an expensive boarding school education. He looked around, found a chair for himself and nodded to Joe, indicating a small table and chair in the background.

'The constable will take notes of this interview,' he said curtly and watched with annoyance how a look of amusement came into the man's eyes.

'How can I help you, inspector,' said Thomas Browne and even the tone of his voice held a mockery. Patrick felt his face grow warm, but he took a grip on his rising temper and deliberately waited for a moment, sitting very straight and gazing around the walls of the room where framed drawings covered almost every inch of space. There was one of what must be the new city hall, but it looked quite different to the one which Browne was folding up. He decided not to ask about it. The man was so arrogant that he would just think that Patrick was trying to curry favour with him. Make them respect you, the superintendent of the barracks had said on his first day of work and Patrick had always kept that in mind. Polite, distant and firm, that was the image that he tried to convey whether he was interviewing a dock worker or a man who had half a million in the bank. He would not try to lead gently into the matter, but question the man directly.

'Mr Browne, you were present in the English Market yesterday morning when your superior was shot dead?'

'That's right,' said Thomas Browne, still with that look of amusement. 'I believe that I gave my name, address and occupation to the good constable there and told him that I had no idea what happened or who shot Mr Doyle. And, just for the record, inspector, I did not regard him as my superior.'

'But he employed you, that's right, isn't it?'

'No, inspector, the city council employs me. I was Mr Doyle's assistant and now I am Acting City Engineer.' There was a note of triumph in the last words and Patrick felt a slight thrill of excitement. The man was beginning to expose frustrated ambition and jealousy and perhaps he could be needled into saying more.

'So you felt that you were a better engineer than Mr Doyle, or as good as, and you resent it when I call him your superior?' He made his voice as bland as possible. Years of dealing with drunken dock workers had trained this manner. *Never give them an opening to accuse you of bias*; he always kept that in his mind.

Browne resented his comment, though.

'What the hell do you mean? What are you insinuating?'

'I merely asked a question, sir.' From the corner of his eye, Patrick noticed Joe lift his head.

'Well, it came across as damn offensive.' He took a cigar from the drawer of the desk, clipped the end from it and lit it.

Patrick sat silently, and allowed him to have a few long moments to inhale some soothing smoke before he said, 'You'll understand that we have to ask all sorts of questions, sir. I'm sure that you are anxious to have this matter cleared up.'

'But wasn't it that young fellow, the chap with the gun in his hand, Sam O'Mahony, that was his name, wasn't it? I understood that he was sent by the Republicans to assassinate Mr Doyle. Saw something in today's paper about it.' The voice was a bit quieter and the manner not so aggressive.

'We have to consider all aspects, sir,' said Patrick. 'And, of course, the first matter that we have to consider is the victim. People tend to be very kind about a man who has just died, but we would prefer to know the truth – was he a liar, a cheat, a bully, violent, dishonest, anything like that? All these things can form a motive for murder. You would be surprised at the things that we uncover and how sometimes the reason for a killing is hidden in a man's past. Perhaps, sir, you could enlighten us about Mr James Doyle. You would know him well, having worked alongside him for many years, I understand. Could anyone have had a motive for killing him?' Patrick waited for a full half minute and then added quietly, 'In your opinion, sir.'

There was an even longer pause after the question was asked. With satisfaction Patrick saw a flicker of interest in the dark eyes that met his from behind the veil of cigar smoke. Were they his own cigars, he wondered, or some of the possessions of the dead man, like the expensive leather blotter, the gold Waterman pen, the elaborate box of pencils, labelled Günther Wagner, and the marble, carved paperweight.

'Well, I suppose that he was not too popular, the late James

Doyle, just between ourselves, inspector.' Thomas Browne's voice was almost sleepy, but his eyes were watching the police inspector, watching to see whether he was going to swallow the bait, thought Patrick, remembering how he and his friends used to tie bits of dead rats to lengths of string and dangle the tasty morsel in front of the eels that came up through the street drains on days when the river flooded the streets. There had been great excitement in it and a tasty meal afterwards when the eel was boiled in the kettle over the fire. Now he felt some of that old thrill as he added another morsel of bait.

'Of course it may have been a political assassination, but the Republicans could have used someone with a grudge to do the dirty work,' Patrick said, leaning towards the desk and lowering his voice to a confidential undertone.

Thomas Browne gave a short laugh. 'Well, if you're looking for someone with a grudge, inspector, there would be a queue to choose from. The city is full of men with a grudge against the late James Doyle.'

'Such as?' Joe had his pencil poised over his shorthand notebook.

'To start with there are all of those people whose shops, homes, offices were destroyed that night when Cork burned.'

'But Mr Doyle had nothing to do with that, or did he?'

It seemed to Patrick that the acting city engineer hesitated a little over that, but then he waved his cigar. 'Well, let's just say that he wasn't hurrying himself to rebuild the small men's places. Too busy negotiating the big contract.' Thomas Browne puffed at his cigar for the moment and then said maliciously, 'Not that I believed any of the rumours about bribes, of course.'

'But you heard them?'

'This is a city full of gossip, inspector. You'd want to be stone deaf not to hear some of it.'

'Did you contradict the rumours?' Patrick looked steadily across the desk, suddenly feeling rather sorry for the dead man. It must be a strange thing to work closely with someone who was full of hate for you.

Thomas Browne shrugged. 'Not my place. When I make any public statements I like to think that they are true statements.'

'Meaning that you believed the rumours; or, perhaps, that you knew that the rumours were true.' When he didn't answer, Patrick said sharply, 'I have to press you, Mr Browne. This is not a social chat. A man is lying dead in the mortuary at the police barracks and I intend to find out who killed him. I'll ask you again, did Mr Doyle, to your certain knowledge, take bribes?'

Browne allowed a moment's silence, then put down his cigar onto an elaborate ashtray moulded in the form of a sleeping dragon.

'Let's just say that I could not be sure that he had not,' he said eventually.

'From builders?'

'Of course. But the design for the public buildings like the library and, of course, the city hall, had to be his. And, of course, he had great plans to rebuild the English Market and make it a show place. He had his eye on a big job in Dublin, or in London. Never liked Cork. He used to get asthma every time that there was a fog. The place didn't suit him at all, he used to say.'

'So builders who couldn't or wouldn't pay a bribe didn't get the job?'

A shrug answered this and Patrick repressed his anger. This man was infuriating, but he could be a dangerous enemy. He belonged to one of the merchant princes' families, the twenty or so families who had built up the trade in Cork city and whose sons and grandsons had gone to expensive schools and then into the professions, he had that air of affluence, of privilege. He could make a lot of trouble for a humbly born policeman. He looked around the office.

'It would be a great help to us, sir,' he said evenly, 'if you could give us a list of builders available in the city, and, also, if you would be so good, a list of builders employed by this office.'

For a moment he thought that the man would refuse. He had a sarcastic, rather mocking gleam in his eye. Patrick faced him steadily, and did not allow his eyes to drop. In the background he was aware that Joe's busy pencil had ceased and that his assistant sat motionless, his eyes, no doubt, on both protagonists.

In the end it was Thomas Browne who gave way. 'Well, if it's any use to you,' he said with an exaggerated sigh, and he rose, went to a filing cabinet, leafed through the folders and then came out with a list.

'Some of them we used; others we did not,' he said with an exaggeratedly nonchalant manner.

'That's very useful, sir,' said Patrick, surveying the list, but not touching the sheet of typewritten names and addresses. 'I wonder whether you would be kind enough to put a tick opposite to those builders whom you know were employed by this office during the last couple of years.'

For a moment he thought that the man would throw the list in his face, but with a half-suppressed oath, Thomas Browne took the sheet back from him. He picked up the pen from the tray – had a certain amount of difficulty with it, noticed Patrick, seemed unaccustomed to the slant of the nib – and then put ticks opposite to names. When he handed it over, there were gaps against over half of the names.

Patrick looked at it, hoping that his face did not betray him. There would be a lot of work in checking out this dozen or so of building firms that had not been used by the city engineer. And then would come the work of checking through those that had been used. This might, actually, he thought, prove more fruitful. There might be one firm, one man, there who had hoped, because of past experience, to get a prize commission for one of those new splendid build-ings. The Munster Arcade, Cash's and Grant's had all been rebuilt, but there were many, many others which still remained as blackened skeletons.

And, of course, the prize building of all, the city hall – whose design was going to be chosen for that, and which fortunate builder would receive the commission to erect an edifice that would be the focus of admiring eyes from Britain and from the continent of Europe, and perhaps even from America? Once more his eyes went to the drawing on the wall and then to the chest where Thomas Browne had shut up the drawing which he had been working on when they arrived. He had a sudden desire to look at that again. It had been, he thought, quite different to the rather pedestrian sketch on the wall, where the new city hall looked very much like the building that had been around for a few hundred years. He looked at the defensive and rather mocking face of Thomas Browne and thought that he could not justify that request. He would have a word with the Reverend Mother, he thought. She had a great knowledge of the old Cork families. She would know all about Thomas Browne and would have some wise advice for him.

When it came to a matter that involved the merchant princes of Cork city, it was only sensible that a boy from the slums like himself should proceed with great care. He gave a quick glance across at Joe and saw that his assistant had laid down his pencil and so he rose to his feet.

'Thank you very much, sir,' he said quietly. 'You've been immensely helpful to us.'

# EIGHT

St Thomas Aquinas:
*Ordina, Deus meus, statum meum, ut faciam, tribue ut*
*sciam; et da exsequi sicut oportet et expedit animae meae.*
(Regulate, oh God, my life; and grant that I may fulfil it as
is fitting and profitable to my soul)

Lucy was the Reverend Mother's first cousin and a great
friend. Though their lifestyles were so different, they
shared a common background. They were quite near in
age, but Lucy was so well preserved, so well dressed and so
manicured, so much a product of skin cream and expert hair-
dressing, that she looked almost twenty years younger than
her real age. She was the wife of a prosperous solicitor, Rupert
Murphy, the senior member of a well-respected law firm on
the South Mall. Rupert was immensely proud of his pretty
and clever wife and rumour told that he consulted her about
most matters and that he owed quite a lot of success to her
sharp wits as well as her skill as a hostess.

'I hear you were in the front line when James Doyle was
assassinated,' she said now, taking off her hat and studying
her hair in the small mirror that hung over a chest of drawers.
It had been dyed a subtle shade of ash blonde, warm enough
to be flattering, but so cleverly done that it looked quite natural,
neither blonde nor grey, just an elusive hue between both
colours. 'You nuns do get about,' she added, carefully outlining
her lips in soft pink and running a finger over her neat
eyebrows.

'Come and sit by the fire, Lucy.' The Reverend Mother eyed
her with affection. Lucy was her nearest relation, almost a
sister to her, and though very different in almost every way,
they had a relationship where much was understood by a nod
and a quick glance.

'Or don't you think it was an assassination?' Lucy gave her

a keen look before she smoothed her fashionably short skirt and eyed her silk stockings with satisfaction.

'I'm sure that you, out in the world, know more than I,' said the Reverend Mother modestly.

'Rubbish, you always find out about what's going on; and don't think I don't know why I got a royal summons, today. You're looking for information, so you might as well come straight out with it, Dottie.'

'I was thinking about the Newenhams – our cousins. Which one was the father of the present man, Robert?'

'Robert? He's Timothy's son. You remember Timothy, surely. He was gun-mad. And hunting-mad, too. Of course everyone hunted, but he took such a delight in it. Used to go out with the keeper stopping up earths and laying traps for badgers, bashing the unfortunate animal over the head, cutting off the foxes' tails after the dogs had killed them – we never liked him much, did we? Robert is his. Must be in his late thirties. Not the eldest son; that was John. Yes, John was the heir. Robert was at the end of the tail, he went into the army.'

'So he told me.'

'Wouldn't have much money, Timothy pulled some strings to get him that job as town planner. But that would be all that there was to leave him. Even John's not very well off, these days, I seem to remember hearing. Of course the value of land has dropped like a stone after all this wretched fighting. It's bad enough in England; but over here it's a disaster. I was talking to William Boyle the other day and he was saying that you might as well give the acres away these days.'

'So you hob-nob with earls these days, Lucy; you must introduce him to me.' said the Reverend Mother thinking that William Boyle, the Earl of Cork, should contribute to a Cork charity like her new enterprise.

Lucy smiled demurely. 'So what do you want to know about Robert Newenham? He was there, wasn't he, standing there when James Doyle was shot. Rupert had all the news when he came home yesterday. Don't tell me that the young man who shot him was one of your former pupils and you want to prove that he had nothing to do with it, even though half of

Cork saw him with the gun in his hand. You want to muddy the waters, that's it, isn't it?'

'Sam O'Mahony is not one of my pupils and no one really knows who actually did shoot James Doyle. *Post hoc* is not necessarily *propter hoc*, you know.'

'If you are going to talk Latin, I shall put on my hat and go,' said Lucy firmly. 'I suppose what you are trying to say is that it is not completely proved as yet.'

'I don't think that Sam did fire that shot. I think that he is telling the truth when he said that he picked up the gun when he felt it strike his foot. I think that the real murderer hastily dropped or threw the gun from him.'

'And then ran away?'

'Or perhaps, more cleverly still, did not run away but stayed with the crowd and gasped with horror at the deed.'

'It's possible,' said Lucy thoughtfully. 'And you think that it might be our dear cousin or second cousin, Robert, taking after his father, of course. How dear Timothy did love to kill things!'

'It may not have been a random killing; somehow he struck me as a careful, cautious individual. He has a very expensive car, a Rolls Royce,' added the Reverend Mother.

'Hmm,' said Lucy thoughtfully. 'That's interesting. He wouldn't be that well paid, you know. There isn't too much money around, these days. Not one of them, including the city engineer, is well-paid. A bad idea, according to Rupert. You can guess why, can't you?'

The Reverend Mother nodded thoughtfully. 'Leaves them open to bribery, I suppose,' she said placidly.

'Nuns are such realists,' murmured Lucy, sipping her tea elegantly. 'The late lamented James Doyle was widely known as having a preference for builders who met him in a pub, handed him small oblong packets wrapped in plain brown paper and carefully tied with string. Or, better still, just left the packets on the table without a word. Rupert has a story about how James Doyle, pint of Murphy's in one hand, without even glancing at the man, picked up his raincoat with the other hand and placed it neatly over one of these packets and it stayed there, safely hidden, until they had finished their drinks.'

'And Robert Newenham?'

'Never heard anything much about him,' said Lucy regret-
fully. 'He was supposed to be just a "yes man" – did what
James Doyle wanted, signed anything put in front of him. He
wouldn't have the power in the same way, of course. Interesting
that he has such an expensive car, though, isn't it? Where do
you suppose that he got the money? They didn't get much
when they were demobbed, you know.'

'He was in the Dorsetshires Regiment, did you know that?'

Lucy nodded briskly and then with a look at her cousin's
face added, 'And?'

'And so was Captain Charles Schulze, the man in charge
of the regiment of auxiliaries who burned down the buildings
in the city on that night two years ago, or so the postman told
Sister Bernadette, but no doubt Rupert will know if that is
true.' The postman, she thought, probably had it right. He and
the lamplighter usually knew what was going on. Their
currency was gossip and they traded on it in the pubs and on
the doorsteps.

Lucy frowned thoughtfully. 'Interesting,' she said. 'You
know there was a lot of talk about the fact that there was a
list in the pocket of this Captain Schulze on that night. When
someone shouted to him, "Stop your men; the owner of this
shop is a Protestant!" apparently he took a piece of paper out
of his pocket, looked at it and then put it away again and said,
"I can't help it; that number is here on my list." Interesting,
isn't it? And who better to feed details about the owners of
buildings and business premises than a town planner? And the
same thing happened up in Dillons Cross. How could an
Englishman know exactly which houses to burn and which
ones to spare?'

'And you think that Robert Newenham would be paid for
information like that?'

'Of course! Spying and passing information was the best
business in town a couple of years ago, Rupert says. The city
would have been bankrupt, according to him, if the British
weren't pouring in money in an effort to hold onto the country.
But of course, that wouldn't be true any longer now that we've
got our independence. Robert would have bought that car a

couple of years ago, I'd say. He doesn't live anywhere smart, just one of those villas up in Summerhill.'

'That's correct,' said the Reverend Mother. 'The car was bought in January 1921, so a knowledgeable person told me.' Her mind went to six-year-old Paddy Maloney. He was a bright boy. Yes, she thought, she could well describe him as knowledgeable. 'And that,' she added, 'would have been one month after the burning down of Cork.' She thought for a moment and then added, 'If it's true that it was discovered that he gave to Captain Schulze names and addresses of places to burn down in December 1920, then he would be a target for assassination by the Republicans.'

'But it was James Doyle who was assassinated,' pointed out Lucy. 'And he wouldn't have the same sort of knowledge available to him as Robert Newenham. In any case, why do it two years after it was all over and done with?'

The Reverend Mother thought about that. It was true that the burning of Cork had happened more than two years ago. Nevertheless, she, more than Lucy, perhaps, knew that the aftermath of that terrible night had gone on resounding through the lives of ordinary people in the city. People, often quite humble people, like Patsy Mullane, the librarian who now swept the sawdust from the passageways in the English Market; people like Patsy who had lost a richly fulfilling job as a consequence of the burning of the Carnegie Library, and who was still waiting patiently for the rebuilding. And there were others who had lost a house, lost a room that they called home, lost a shop, like Michael Skiddy. And her own gardener who had lost his bicycle shop. Perhaps for these people it was not over and done with, but was a festering sore that needed a bloodletting to clear its effects.

'What about,' she began slowly, her thoughts ranging over the possibilities, 'what about if it was Robert Newenham who gave that list to Captain Schulze, his fellow officer, his friend, perhaps, from their days in the same regiment during the war. He could have done that; been paid for it and so bought his expensive car; thought no one would ever know. And then somehow, James Doyle heard a rumour, got some proof, after all, he must have been in and out of the town planner's office fairly often.'

'Blackmail,' purred Lucy.

'It is possible, isn't it? A list like that would probably have had a rough draft first of all; it would need a bit of checking, wouldn't it? And then when he was sure of his facts he would probably have made a fair copy. In fact the original list may well have been on Cork City Council paper and that would have immediately led back to Robert Newenham if it fell into the hands of the Republicans, so he would have definitely copied it out onto a blank sheet of paper.'

'And you think that that draft fell into the hands of James Doyle?'

'It's possible, isn't it? By all accounts, it was chaotic that night. Something like a sheet of paper, a list, could have been dropped. James Doyle as city engineer would have been in and out of those half-burned-down buildings. There would be measurements to be made, floor space, height of building in comparison to its neighbours, the back yards and the lanes behind to be surveyed. He could have picked up a piece of paper on the Monday morning, or even on that Sunday. I understand that the place was crowded on that Sunday after the morning. All the children were full of tales when they came into school on the Monday morning. It was obvious that there would have to be a great new building project. After all Patrick Street is the focus of shopping in Cork, these days, isn't it?'

Lucy nodded. She wore the air of a woman who knew all that was to be known about the fashionable world and their shopping habits. 'Yes, of course. No one that I know would dream of shopping in North Main Street or South Main Street. And I'll tell you something else. Robert Newenham sent us a card for an invitation to a party to celebrate the reopening of the Munster Arcade and I remember saying to Rupert, "What fancy handwriting!". It was like something that our grandmother might have written. I think he probably had an old-fashioned governess – the Newenhams were rich when we were young, were they not? They probably imported some governess from England, the boys went to school in England; I remember that. It was no wonder that when he left school he joined an English regiment and fought against the Germans. And some of these fellows, according to Rupert, found it hard to settle into the real world when they had left the army.'

The Reverend Mother bowed her head and tucked her hands into her flowing sleeves. These young men who went off to the war in 1914, she thought, young men such as her relative Robert Newenham, and such as Captain Charles Schulze, they were not wholly mature, just overgrown school boys, dropped into a lifestyle as an army officer, where they were encouraged to be as violent as young boys will be if not checked. And then suddenly in 1918, the war was over and they were thrown, rudderless, into a totally different world. But Sam O'Mahony, if innocent, should not hang for the deed of another. She forced her brain to return to the practical matter before her.

'So,' she said briskly, 'if James Doyle came across that piece of paper . . . It might have been scorched, half-burned even, but if the handwriting was as distinctive as you remember it to be, Lucy, then he might have said to himself, "This looks familiar", and he might have wondered why, for the sake of argument, there was a tick or a cross placed opposite to each shop or business place number in the centre of the city.'

'And then guessed,' said Lucy triumphantly. 'I'm sure that you are right. James Doyle was not a pleasant man, but he wasn't stupid.'

'No, he wouldn't be.' Anyone in this city who rose up from a poor background, who rose from being the son of a jobbing tailor, working in a cellar which was workshop and home for himself and his family, anyone who managed to struggle out from that sort of poverty and gain a top position like city engineer would have been clever.

And perhaps ruthless.

'So, of course, if he found the list in Robert Newenham's handwriting, he could have denounced him to the authorities, to the newspapers or he could have kept quiet and blackmailed him,' she finished.

'And, of course, Robert would have to pay and to go on paying. He would have lost his job if this got out, but more seriously, he would have been assassinated by the Republicans. His life would not have been worth this.' And Lucy snapped

a finger against a thumb and the blood-red nail varnish
flashed in the firelight.

'And he wouldn't be rich, you think,' mused the Reverend
Mother.

'Lives very poorly,' confirmed Lucy. 'He has rather dropped
out of society. After all, he could hardly ask anyone to that
poky little house of his in Summerhill, so people have stopped
asking him to their parties. The last time that I met him was
at that affair in the Munster Arcade and, of course, that was
all paid for by the city council funds.' She gave a demure
smile and added, 'Of course, my dearest Rupert would say
that there is not a scrap of real evidence against the men.
Solicitors are always so pernickety. Myself I go by the pricking
of my thumbs, don't you?'

'I'd like to talk to him, to get some idea of what sort of
person he is. Is he capable of murder? You know him. What
do you think?'

'Anyone is capable of murder if the motive is strong enough,'
said Lucy robustly. 'I'm sure that when I was seventeen years
old, if I'd had a pistol in my hand and a means of escape I
would have murdered . . .' She broke off, her mouth tight and
her cousin did not ask her what she meant. The picture of that
man, the sneering words, the threats that he had uttered were
in both their minds, although it had all happened more than
fifty years ago. Lucy had ended up with a happy life, but the
conduct of a man who had been her guardian when she was
in her teens would never be forgiven by her.

But was it true that anyone could murder, she wondered?
She didn't think that Sam O'Mahony had murdered in order
to revenge himself for the loss of a job, but his mother, she
felt sure, would, if the opportunity presented itself, murder in
order to safeguard her son's life. Perhaps it was true that many
people were capable of murder, given a strong emotion: fear
for your safety, for your life, violent hate, motherly love,
intense greed, emotional patriotism; yes, there were many
situations she could envisage that would tempt many people
into taking human life.

'I have an idea,' said Lucy thoughtfully. 'Why don't you
get Robert Newenham here, go on about all your charitable

works, make him think that you are going to ask for a dona-
tion and then when he starts to wriggle out of that, you can
ask him to hold a party to raise funds for you. He's the sort
of man who likes to ingratiate himself with the important
people in the city. The rebuilding of Roches Stores has finished
now – they've made a splendid job of it. The city council will
pay for the food and the drinks. I'll tell you what, find out
when he can come and then let me know and I'll just happen
to be there. I'll take all the catering out of his hands, perhaps
your girls can do some of it – we'll make sure that the convent
is paid for it. I'll pretend to confer with him – he'll be flattered,' said Lucy complacently, sure of her position as a leading
light in Cork society. 'And I'll make sure that he gets the right
sort of guest list. It will be fun. And you will have an opportunity to cross-question him; otherwise you'd probably never
see him again. And you can find out all that was going on in
this rebuilding of Cork. Rupert says that it's a hothouse of
corruption, the whole business.'

'Excuse me, Reverend Mother, excuse me, Mrs Murphy.'
Sister Bernadette glided into the room after a preliminarily
respectful knock on the door and stood there looking hesitant
and worried. 'Captain Robert Newenham is here. I told him
that you were with a visitor but he was very pressing about
speaking to you now. He said that he meant to phone you
yesterday afternoon, but he was detained by business to do
with the death of the city engineer. Shall I tell him that you
will phone him later on, Reverend Mother?'

'No, I'll speak to him now. Bring him in here, please, sister.'
Her eyes met Lucy's, but neither smiled, nor moved until Sister
Bernadette had taken herself off, closing the door with an
emphatic click as an indication of her disapproval of the inter-
ruption of Mrs Rupert Murphy's visit.

'God whispered a word in his ear,' said Lucy mischievously.

'More likely that he wants me to put in a good word for
him with the bishop. It probably suddenly occurred to him
that I would have influence in that direction.' A death always
meant a reshuffling, one saw it in church affairs and no doubt
it was the same in the county council and other such businesses. While Robert Newenham was kept in a state of

apprehension by James Doyle, he would have been reluctant
to call attention to himself, or to attempt to seek a better salary,
but now he would be in line for promotion. The Reverend
Mother arranged her face into a welcoming smile as the heavy
tread in the corridor signalled his arrival.

'Reverend Mother!' he exclaimed heartily. 'I've just come
to see how you are after that terrible event at the market.'

It was a poor excuse and she guessed that he had come to
see whether she had information.

'You know Captain Newenham, of course, don't you,
Mrs Murphy? Captain Newenham, Mrs Murphy,' she finished
stiffly and indicated an upright chair near to the door.

'But of course, of course. We're second cousins, aren't we?'
He walked over towards the fire. Lucy gave him her hand and
smiled up at him. She had decided to play the friendly affable
role in comparison to her cousin's stiffness. Lucy and I would
make a good pair in a music hall, thought the Reverend Mother
as she gazed at him coldly and listened with an inward chuckle
to Lucy's flow of reminiscences of Captain Newenham's father,
now transformed into a spirited and adventurous youth, and
her glowing recollection of the party that he had held to
celebrate the reopening of the Munster Arcade.

'Such fun. So informal. Any chance of another party? A
little bird told me that Roches Stores is now ready to be
reopened. So clever of you to think of holding a party before
all the dreary clothes and pots and pans and cheap furniture is
brought in to spoil the lovely architecture,' she said gazing up
at him roguishly.

'Do sit down, Captain Newenham,' said the Reverend
Mother coldly, while her cousin beamed at the visitor and
patted a chair beside her invitingly.

'Sit here beside me and tell me all about those wonderful
fittings that you have ordered. My husband tells me that you
sent to London for many of them. The marble tiles, he was
telling, you got them from the place that supplied Harrods in
London. Wonderful, isn't it, Reverend Mother?' Lucy didn't wait
for an answer, just swept on. 'I can't wait to see them. You're
so like your poor father. He was a man of great taste. Oh, do
tell me that you are going to allow some guests to see the place

before it's spoiled. Everything is of the best, Reverend Mother, so I've been told. Mahogany and teak and bronze fittings, so I hear.' Lucy went on chanting the perfections of the newly built department store and Robert Newenham glanced from one to the other while the Reverend Mother allowed her mind to wander over the probable cost of all that luxury and of how many homes for the poor could have been built with half the sum expended.

'And you are going to have a party, aren't you, Captain Newenham? Now, don't tell that you won't.' Lucy shook a finger at him. 'I so love a party.' She sighed wistfully and then said, in a voice that she strove to make sound tentative, 'You wouldn't like any help with the guest list, would you? I don't want to put myself forward, but a woman's touch, you know.'

'That would be so extremely kind of you,' he said gallantly, although there was an uneasy look in his eye.

'I know what,' said Lucy clasping her hands together in an ecstasy of admiration of her own cleverness, 'just before you came in, the Reverend Mother and I were discussing a fund-raising initiative which she wanted me to organize for her school. What would you say, Reverend Mother, to have an affair held at Roches Stores? I'm sure that the bishop would come, wouldn't he? Dr Cohalan is such a great supporter of the work done here among the poor. And I wonder whether the Earl of Cork would come? It's so easy to get people when it is for charity, isn't it? And then I can tell him all about your war record. He'll have a great fellow feeling as he fought in the Great War also. In fact, a year or so ago, he was telling me that he was having a chat with Captain Schulze from the Dorsetshires whom he'd met in France.'

It was lightly and airily done. Lucy took bites of her cake in between sentences and leaned over to touch the teapot while she delivered the last sentence. The Reverend Mother, standing slightly in the background was able to observe Captain Newenham's face very carefully. For a moment it seemed as though he were about to deny the acquaintance. His mouth opened quickly, but then he shut it and after a minute bowed his head in a gesture that could have meant anything. There had, she was sure, been a momentary flicker of apprehension in his eyes.

He took his leave a few minutes later, promising to put the proposition to the council and to be in touch with Mrs Murphy about the guest list. The Reverend Mother obligingly provided him with paper and pencil so that he could write down the Montenotte number and she stood close enough to see that his hand slightly shook as he wrote the word and the numerals. A well-groomed man, she thought. Not a hair astray, moustache neatly clipped, boots polished, snowy white handkerchief protruding from his pocket. But as she stood beside him to touch the bell for Sister Bernadette, she was aware of the strong smell of sweat that came from him.

And Lucy was right. Captain Newenham had very ornate handwriting. The first stroke of the letter M curved around to form almost a circle, then rose to twin peaks, before descending to form another swirl. It was beautifully done.

'He's scared,' said Lucy triumphantly, as the sound of the footsteps died away. 'He's scared and it was the mention of Captain Schulze that did it. He has a guilty conscience about him. I'm sure of that, but then, as Rupert says, "opinions don't count in the law". We'll have to get evidence that they knew each other. Leave it to me. I'm going to have fun with this.'

# NINE

W.B. Yeats:
Being young you have not known,
The fool's triumph, nor yet,
Love lost as soon as won,
Nor the best labourer dead
And all the sheaves to bind.
What need have you to dread
The monstrous crying of wind.

Eileen had waited for darkness to fall before she walked up the steep incline of Barrack Street. The fog was thicker than ever. It filled the narrow space between the small, red-brick houses on either side with a miasma of stinking vapour that tasted of sulphur and made her eyes water. It deadened the sound of the bells and obscured buildings – almost as though the progress of centuries had been wiped away and Cork had reverted to being a marsh again. There was something rather eerie about it, almost a sense of floating along in a ghost-like vapour and Eileen purposely made the steel-tipped heels of her boots ring out against the brick pavement. A shivering girl under a gas lamp, misled by the boots, the breeches, the short hair and the jauntily placed cap, called out an invitation to her, but Eileen ignored it. They had to make a living these poor girls, she supposed, but if ever Ireland became a republic the party, and she, would campaign to put an end to prostitution. There would be jobs for all that wanted them, women as well as men, meat in the pot and milk for their children. The glow of satisfaction at the thought warmed her and she ignored the freezing fog and walked briskly up the familiar pavement.

The front door to her mother's cabin was locked – a sign of the troubled times during the last few years. During her childhood, the door had always been on the latch. Eileen tapped softly and waited, keeping well into the shadow of the doorway and alert for any watching eyes.

'Who's there?' Her mother was at the other side of the door instantly. Things were very unsettled; there would have been a time when everyone on Barrack Street would have trusted a neighbour, but the bitter civil war had split communities, streets and even families and now little trust was left.

'It's just me, Eileen,' she whispered at the keyhole and heard the lock turn. In a moment she was through the door and had shut it behind her. The kitchen was warm, she was glad to see. Maureen had a daily job cleaning out Tommy's Bar and Eileen herself brought money home from time to time. It was one of the rules of the Republican Volunteers that support was to be given to a mother if, like in most households, the father had died or disappeared, and Eileen always kept back a portion of the takings from a raid in order to make sure that her mother had plenty to eat and fuel to warm the one-roomed cabin. She slipped a ten-shilling note into the vase on the shelf over the fire and sat down on the settle-bed.

'Kettle's singing,' she said with satisfaction. 'I'd love a cup of tea, Mam.' Now that the moment had come for explanations, she found herself feeling reluctant to start. The ritual of swinging the kettle over the hottest portion of the fire so that the high-pitched note turned to a deeper bubbling sound, the scalding of the tin pot, the careful measurement of the tea leaves, the two mugs unhooked from the dresser, the soda bread extracted from the tin that kept it safe from any rat and, if times were good, spread with a small piece of butter from another tin. The cabin was full of old biscuit tins – their defence against rodents. Her mother carefully saved them when cleaning out the public house.

'I suppose that if you'd become a teacher, you'd have had a house up in St Luke's Cross and a servant to make your tea, Mam,' she said affectionately. It had been one of the tales of her youth, how her mother nearly became a teacher, had stayed on at school after the rest of her classmates had left, had been about to study for an examination, but then had decided to have a little girl of her own instead. As a small child Eileen had been immensely flattered that her mother had chosen her instead of the glittering career as a teacher, but by the time that she was nine or ten years old had guessed the truth. Who was her father, she had often wondered, but had never dared to ask. She knew that she had been luckier than most of her friends. Her mother had the single child, not the nine or ten of other families, had loved that child, supported her, told her stories, taught her to read before she went to school and from that very first day had encouraged her in her studies, had sat with her every evening sharing a pleasure in the stories in her reading book, explaining history, finding new ways to work out sums, teaching her poems and songs.

'Whenever Ireland becomes a republic, I might try to get to university, Mam,' she said now as she sipped the first, too hot, taste of the tea. No soda bread, tonight, she thought and hoped that all was well with her mother, feeling glad that she had brought the ten-shilling note. 'I have to do my best for the country first,' she said apologetically, but knowing that her mother understood. They had shared a dream and the crumbling lime plaster of the walls still held yellowed pictures of the martyred heroes. 'But after that . . .' she finished.

'Please God,' said her mother heroically.

'You've still got Pearse's declaration up on the wall,' said Eileen. 'I told the Reverend Mother about the walls of this room and all the history that is stuck there.'

Her mother clicked her tongue. 'You had no business saying something like that,' she said reprovingly. 'I've always told you to keep your tongue in your mouth and let your brain work before you speak, but you were always a chatterbox, always knew best.' The words were tart but Eileen knew they hid an immense pride.

'I have to try; I have to do my best for Ireland,' she said earnestly, not answering the last statement but the unspoken reproaches that she knew must go through her mother's mind sometimes. If only her daughter had stayed on in school, perhaps she might have won the Honan Scholarship, might have had three years paid for at Cork University, and might now be studying for the further qualification to be a teacher.

'What you have to do, you have to do,' said her mother stoically. 'I sometimes feel bad that I've led you astray. All that poetry and all those stories. Of course, you were as bright as a button and you sucked it all up like a young calf, but I should have had more sense. Poetry can have a great effect on you when you're young.'

'Stop worrying,' said Eileen. 'Nothing in life is safe. You told me that yourself.'

'True for you; look at all the people getting shot on Patrick Street, and even in the English Market, so I've heard. I don't know, it's a hard life.'

Her mother was looking old. And yet she was only in her early thirties. Her back was bent from continually carrying heavy buckets of water and her hands were swollen, red and sore-looking from the harsh bars of Sunlight soap that she used to scrub the stone flags of the public house where she worked. She hadn't much of a life, Eileen thought sadly.

'If we get our republic and I qualify for a good job, you'll never scrub another floor again,' she said passionately.

'Floors have to be scrubbed. Someone has to do it. I don't mind; I'm used to it. I worry about you, though. Still, you're looking blooming on it. Well, I suppose you're just as safe out there in west Cork as you would be here in the city.' Her mother was pursuing her own thoughts. Eileen had never told her that their unit was not in west Cork, but very much nearer, down in Ballinhassig, only seven miles south of the city. The less she knew about her daughter's whereabouts and activities, the better it was for her. 'Was that young man who's supposed to have shot the city engineer, was he one of your crowd? He was, wasn't he? I can see it in your face.'

'No, he wasn't. Sam was completely against everything that we did. He's been set up for this.'

'But you know him, don't you?' Her mother looked at her sharply. 'Sweet Jesus! Don't tell me! He's a boyfriend of yours, is he?'

'He's a reporter on the *Cork Examiner*,' said Eileen. The urge to confide in her mother was becoming irresistible. She could feel the beginnings of a smile tremble at the corners of her mouth and she bit her lips to suppress it.

Maureen heaved a sigh. 'Trust you,' she said affectionately. 'You had all the boys in Barrack Street running after you, and you'd never give any one of them the time of day, and now you have to go and fall in with this fellow. He's a son of Mrs O'Mahony in the English Market, isn't he?'

'That's right,' said Eileen. She leaned down to poke at the mound of half-burned turfs and watched them collapse into a pile of softly-glowing white ash.

'And how did you meet him?'

Eileen was silent for a moment. Outside of her own unit, no one was supposed to know that she wrote a column for the *Cork Examiner* under the byline of 'A Patriot'. She posted it to the newspaper offices and her payment came back to a P.O. box in the General Post Office in Patrick Street. Still, the Reverend Mother had guessed – by the style of writing, apparently and she had told Dr Scher, so perhaps it would do no harm to let her mother into the secret.

'You see one of my jobs for the unit is to, well, I've never told you because I didn't want you to get into trouble because of me, but I'm the one who writes that column in the *Cork Examiner*—'

'You needn't tell me,' interrupted her mother. 'The one by "A Patriot", that's you, isn't it?'

'How did you know?'

'I know how you write, haven't I read enough of your essays when you were in school and you brought a *Cork Examiner* once or twice with you when you came here and I'd find it open at that page. You can't keep any secrets from your mother, you know. I used to tell you that, didn't I?'

'Well, that was how I met Sam. I wrote something for the *Cork Examiner* about the struggle to establish a republic and in the next edition he, Sam O'Mahony, had a column making a mock of all my arguments – he really tore it to shreds, and a lot of what he said was just stupid. I sent him a warning, but he did the same thing the following week and so I waited for him one evening in the laneway. I pretended to take his arm, getting quite close to him and then I put my hand back into my pocket and dug my pistol into his ribs. I told him to say nothing and he just looked at me, with my short hair and my breeches and my cap and my boots and he said out loud without a scrap of bother in him, "You're just a girl, aren't you?".'

A reluctant smile came over her mother's weather-beaten face. 'And what did you say to that, something smart, if I know you?'

'I just poked my pistol a bit more into his ribs and said, sarcastic-like, "Even a girl couldn't miss at this range".' She giggled and then quickly sobered. 'We walked side by side down Patrick Street and we were arguing like mad, stopping every few yards and facing each other. I had all the good arguments, but he kept on dragging other things up and then he stopped at Pavilion Cinema and pulled away from me, just as though he was sure that I wouldn't shoot him.'

'And what happened next?' Her mother, despite her tired, time-worn face, was still the same romantic, enthusiastic mother of Eileen's youth. They two of them devoured the books that she brought home from school, discussed them into the small hours of the night, argued over the meaning of a line of poetry, over Mr Darcy in *Pride and Prejudice* – her mother liked him and Eileen, always the rebel, didn't. She thought that Lizzie could do much better for herself. They had been friends, not just mother and daughter, and for some time now, Eileen had longed to tell her about Sam O'Mahony. She gave a slight giggle at the memory of that first evening when she and Sam had gone into the warm, cigarette-smoke-scented darkness of the cinema.

'He just marched off, bold as brass, and bought two tickets for the stalls, real expensive seats, and then he came back and he took my arm this time and we went upstairs together and he found two seats in the back row – and you don't need to sigh, like that, either, because he didn't get up to any funny stuff.' Not then, anyway, she amended within her mind before going on with the story and telling her mother how they had gone on arguing furiously in whispers but when the main film had come on, *Nanook of the North* they had fallen silent, had been mesmerized by the extraordinary scenes of desolation amid the ice and the snow.

'It's funny, but when it had finished, Sam said, "Imagine living in a place like that, even worse than Cork City!" and we both had a laugh and then, somehow, we seemed like friends and he held my hand as we came out of the cinema,

just like as if he was my boyfriend. He asked me to come and
have a cup of coffee with him, but I had to go because I was
meeting Eamonn down Lavitt's Quay and just as I was going
to slip away, Sam said, "Same time, same place, same day
next week." And, then he just walked off, not giving me time
to reply. And I shouted after him, "You'll be lucky!" but, you
know, Mam, you know how it is . . .'

'You turned up.' Maureen was trying to sound cynical, but
Eileen knew better. Her mother loved a romance.

'Yes, I did,' she admitted. 'I told myself that I hadn't
finished with him. I was going to make him eat his words,
so I turned up outside the cinema and we went in and we
saw *Vanity Fair* and he hadn't read the book, and I had. Do
you remember how you and me, we used to argue about
Becky Sharp? Well, he was like you, he didn't like her and
so we went for a walk down the Mardyke and in the end he
agreed with me that she was much more interesting than
Amelia.' They had kissed that night, she remembered, though
she didn't intend to tell her mother that. His lips had been
warm and his hair had smelled of frost and they had clung
together. Her mother didn't need to know the details of these
late-night strolls in the darkness, of the kisses and caresses
well away from the gas lamps of Western Road. Sam was
different, she told herself, he would not be like that father
whom she had never seen, the man who had made her mother
pregnant and then cleared off on the midnight ferry to
Liverpool. She and Sam were friends. She kept the association secret from everyone except Aoife. Tom Hurley would
have been furious, she knew.

'And now he's killed a man and will hang for it. We've no
luck, you and me.' Her mother sighed heavily.

'He didn't. I'm sure that he didn't. He's so against violence.
We've argued and argued about it. Sam is a pacifist. He says
that nothing justifies killing. And he wasn't a member of the
Republican Party, if that's what you are thinking.'

'No, I don't suppose he was; you'd know, wouldn't you?'

Eileen was silent. Even to Sam she had never broken her
oath to keep secret that unit to which she belonged and the
names of her fellow conspirators. It was, she acknowledged

for a moment, just about possible that secretly he was a member
of another unit. But then she shook her head.

'No, I'm certain that he was a pacifist. Why should he spend
so long arguing with me about violence?'

'They were all talking about it at the pub at lunchtime. I
heard them while I was scrubbing the stairs. They were saying
that everyone saw the gun in his hand, even the Reverend
Mother from St Mary's of the Isle saw him. They were saying,
too, that James Doyle got him sacked from his job at the *Cork
Examiner*. That might be enough to drive a man to murder.
Did he talk to you about that?'

'Of course,' said Eileen shortly. Sam had poured out his
bitterness and yes, he had said wild things but that was only
talk. There was little use in arguing, though. She knew that.
What was needed now was decisive action.

'I want to go to see him, to visit him in gaol, Mam. And I
want you to go with me. We'll pretend to be his auntie and
his cousin. I'll borrow that old shawl of yours.' It would be
fatal for any connection to be made between Sam and the
Republicans, but her mother's respectable presence would
ensure that no questions were asked about the daughter. It was
lucky that the men guarding the political prisoners were always
recruited from another part of the county. No one at the gaol
would know the story of Eileen's involvement with the
Republicans. In any case, she planned to dress so that she
would merge into the mass of the ordinary poor of the city.

One of the first things that Eileen had done when Tom
Hurley had given her back six pence a week from the fee from
the *Cork Examiner* column had been to save up for a new
black shawl for her mother. The old plaid one that had belonged
originally to her grandmother had been thriftily stored in
mothballs below the mattress in the space beneath the settle
bed. It was a huge shawl and would envelop face and figure.
Eileen stood up, lifting the seat and pulling out the old flock
mattress. Under it were also stored some spare clothes, and
another shawl. Eileen was glad to see a worn woollen dress.
It would be too big for her but that didn't matter. The shawl
and the dipping hemline – both would look poor and unob-
trusive. It would definitely not be a place for her smart breeches,

jacket and jaunty cap. She picked out some more things. There were a couple of pairs of bloomers which she had reluctantly sewed when she was at school, another old dress and a still more decrepit shawl.

'When's visiting time?' Her mother sounded resigned.

'It's from three to four o'clock of the afternoon. You'll come then, will you?'

Her mother's only answer was a comforting hug, but Eileen had glimpsed the expression of pity and the tearful eyes before the arms went around her. Maureen probably believed that her daughter's heart was to be broken. She would have heard the matter discussed in the public house and the opinion would probably have been that there was no hope for Sam. He would definitely be hanged.

'He didn't do it, you know!'

'I know,' said her mother comfortingly. 'But don't build up your hopes. He has no one to speak for him. His poor mother! My heart goes out to her. Her only son. They were saying at lunch time that she looked twenty years older, standing behind the stall. Jack was saying that his wife had to ask her twice for a few scraps for the cat. She seemed in a daze. Does she know about you?'

'I don't know,' said Eileen. 'I don't think so. I don't want to meet her, Mam.' She hoped that Sam's mother would not be there when they came. Visitors were only allowed ten minutes. One of the lads of the unit had told her that. Ten minutes would be enough for what she wanted to find out.

Her mother looked keenly at her troubled face and said, 'I could pop into the English Market, to her stall tomorrow morning, tell her how sorry I am, she won't know me, but she'll have everybody saying things like that to her. I'll just find out when she's going to see him. Though I could tell you that for free, now; she's like every mother. She'll be waiting for the jail to open. She'll be in there for the first ten minutes of visiting time. I'd lay any money on it. But I'll find out for you, if you like.'

Eileen nodded, turning away from her mother's keen eyes and tossing another sod of turf onto the fire. She had a plan, had worked it out with the others in her unit. She had encountered great difficulties in the beginning. No one wanted to hazard their lives and Republican property in rescuing a man who had publically criticised their movement. But eventually they had given in. A mixture of standing by a friend and an intense dislike of Tom Hurley's bullying, she thought, though Aoife had asserted that Eamonn was sweet on Eileen. She had not wanted to believe this, as her loyalty had to be given to Sam and she had been very business-like in the planning of the rescue attempt. Eamonn had given her a list of things to observe when she visited the gaol and Liam had promised to lend her his pocket watch so that she could time every movement exactly. Aoife was the one that had suggested taking her mother with her.

'She won't know anything about it,' Aoife had said, 'so she'll be acting natural and you can copy her. Don't forget to keep the shawl well over your head and face and tell your mother to do the same. They might be taking notes about visitors and I wouldn't even put it past them to do little sketches. With a shawl over your head, there won't be much to see. You can pretend to be drying your eyes on it while you pass the guards.'

'You've got something in your head; I know you when you are up to some mischief.' Her mother's voice broke into her thoughts and Eileen immediately banished all the plans from her mind.

'I won't do a thing tomorrow. I promise. I just want to see Sam. While I have a chance,' she added and felt the tears run down her face. There was, she knew, a very small chance that the plan would succeed. It had to be kept a dark secret from Tom Hurley, which added to the excitement, as none of them liked him, but it left only a small number of very inexperienced conspirators to bring the affair to a successful conclusion. She had, she thought now, no right to endanger the lives of her friends in order to rescue a man who had no sympathy for their armed struggle to establish a republic. She felt the sobs rising in her throat, did her best to subdue them, but the familiar kitchen and her mother's presence was robbing her of her courage. For a moment she wished that she were ten years old again and if that were impossible, she wished that she had never met Sam. Everything would be so much easier if she were in love with Eamonn, or Liam, or Paddy.

'You can never choose the one for you.' Her mother's arms were around her as she came and sat on the settle beside her daughter. 'Life is like that; we just have to make the best of things. You don't think that he did it. Talk to him tomorrow. See if he remembers anything. If he didn't do it, then someone else did. Keep your mind on that and see if you can find out who it was. That's the way to help your young man. Goodness only knows, you have brains enough and to spare. The Reverend Mother herself said that to me. "Your daughter is a very clever young lady, Mrs MacSweeney." That's what she said when you told her that you were leaving school. Even came around here to talk to me. I told her that you had a will of iron and that I couldn't do anything with you. It was true then, and it's true now, God help me. I think I brought you up too independent.'

'The Reverend Mother,' said Eileen thoughtfully. This was the second time that her mother had mentioned her former teacher. The Reverend Mother had been a witness to the murder. Perhaps she would have some ideas. Perhaps her mother was right. Perhaps she should be trying to find out what really happened on that Thursday morning when James Doyle was shot and killed in the English Market.

# TEN

St Thomas Aquinas:
*Quomodo enim homo positus in sole caecus, praesens est
illi sol, sed ipse soli absens est.*
(In the same way as when a blind man is standing in the
sun, the sun is present to him, but he himself is absent from
the sun)

Sunday afternoon was always a peaceful time in the
convent of St Mary's of the Isle. The hours between two
and four were times when the families and friends of
the sisters came to visit them, having tea in one of the parlours
and strolling around the gardens. The Reverend Mother usually
found it was her best time to make her long-term plans for
the school and the community. She could normally count on
an uninterrupted few hours, but on the Sunday following the
death of James Doyle she had a visitor.

'I thought that I would pop in and see you.' Dr Scher's
bushy head of iron grey hair appeared behind the flustered
young lay sister who was the only one on duty that afternoon.
'I can see that you have nothing to do and need a friendly
chat,' he continued with a quick look at her littered desk.

'Come and sit by the fire and join me in a cup of tea,'
invited the Reverend Mother. Despite her workload, she knew
that she was glad to see him. Her mind was haunted by Sam
O'Mahony's mother. That tragic face, that heartbroken voice
and the appeal. 'One small lie.' Those words came to her mind
with exhausting frequency. Was her conscience worth a young
life, a neck broken on the end of a rope?

'I suppose you've been asked to do a post-mortem, is that
right?' she enquired as she watched him tip a few more lumps
of coal from the scuttle onto the molten ash and waited patiently
while he fiddled around with tongs and damper settings. A
man who liked his comforts, she thought eyeing him with

affection. What would his decision be if he were asked to lie in order to save a fellow human being, she wondered suddenly? Was it something that he would regard as a ridiculous quibble, or would he feel as she did – that to lie under oath was to endanger the fabric of the society in which they lived?

'Done it,' he said succinctly and for a moment she was so preoccupied with her conscience, she hardly knew what he meant. She said nothing, but waited, listening to the young footsteps in the corridor and then she crossed the room and opened the door. Sister Mary Angela was barely fourteen years old, a former pupil of the school, who was doing her best, by a saintly expression, to convince the Reverend Mother that she had a genuine vocation towards the life of a nun, but after six months, hopefully, she would have had enough of convent life and would find something else. She might, at least, learn to make tea properly, she thought, suppressing a smile at Dr Scher's disappointed face as the pale tan-coloured liquid dripped from a teapot held in a nervous hand. No sandwiches either and only two meagre slices of a plain sponge cake. It was not what Dr Scher was accustomed to receive from the discerning hand of Sister Bernadette. Still, it would do him no harm, she thought, with a glance at the well-rounded stomach beneath the pale grey waistcoat. In any case, there would be no point in upsetting or humiliating the child. She would try to remember to have a word with Sister Bernadette about a little tuition on boiling the water and allowing the tea to stand for a few minutes, before presenting it to a connoisseur like Dr Scher.

'So, you've done the post-mortem,' she said once the door had been closed and footsteps had retreated. 'Anything interesting?'

'Have you ever studied geometry, Reverend Mother?' was his unexpected reply. He chewed on a piece of sponge cake and then put the rest of the slice back on the plate and rinsed the mouthful down with some of the weak tea.

'Geometry?' she queried. 'A very long time ago,' she admitted. 'More than fifty years ago,' she added.

'But you remember about angles, I'm sure,' he returned and then rapidly picked up a teaspoon, reversed it and aimed the handle towards the broad, stiffly starched breastplate that she wore above the black habit. 'Bang,' he said dramatically.

'And I have a bullet through my heart.' The Reverend Mother nodded. 'And,' she continued, 'since we are about the same height and you were holding your pistol straight, I presume that an autopsy would show that the bullet travelled in a straight line through the flesh.'

'Exactly!' Dr Scher clambered onto the chair and stood dramatically pointing his makeshift pistol down at her. 'What about if I fired it now?'

'Well, in that case, I would expect it to carve out an angle of approximately forty-five degrees.'

'Well done,' said Dr Scher admiringly.

The Reverend Mother ignored the patronising inflection. 'What you are trying to tell me is that the bullet was fired by someone taller than the city engineer. Or else, standing at a height.' Her mind went to the market layout. The centre walkway was below the level of the stalls. So someone standing against the wall would have been at a slightly higher level.

'And there are stools behind many of the stalls.'

'But why stand on a stool? It would make you conspicuous. Someone would remember you climbing up. And then you would have to climb down.'

'I suppose so,' admitted Dr Scher. 'And stools are wobbly things. Would never climb on them, myself.'

'Was the gun fired at close quarters?'

'No scorch marks on the coat. Not too close, I'd say. What's in your mind?'

'I was wondering whether someone might have dropped something, or whether he dropped something. That would make him bend down and the bullet would enter his back at an angle.'

Dr Scher borrowed another teaspoon from the second saucer, laid it flat upon the tea tray and pointed the first teaspoon at it.

'Bang,' he said and then grimaced and threw down the two spoons. 'No, the angle is wrong,' he said.

The doorbell pealed and again there were footsteps in the corridor. This time little Sister Mary Angela was blushing scarlet when she opened the door and announced, 'It's Patrick Cashman, Reverend Mother.'

They would have been next-door neighbours when Patrick was a teenager. Nevertheless, the Reverend Mother frowned slightly and said with great emphasis on Patrick's newly acquired title, 'Come in, inspector, come and sit by the fire.'

The young lay sister closed the door, still blushing and then shot in again, this time convulsed with giggles. 'Oh, I do be forgetting,' she said. 'Would you fancy a cup of tay, inspector?'

'No, thank you, sister,' said the Reverend Mother decisively. She, herself, had not touched the second cup and there would be plenty in the pot if he wanted some of the lukewarm, watery liquid. No point in wasting Patrick's time in small talk while they waited for a kettle to boil and another tray to be arranged.

'You've probably heard from Dr Scher about the bullet track,' said Patrick as soon as the door closed and the footsteps died away. He shook his head as the Reverend Mother touched the teapot with an enquiring look and then turned to face Dr Scher.

'I wondered about the gallery upstairs, but the superintendent of the market told me that the door was locked. I went around to see him after I had read his report.'

'That's true,' said the Reverend Mother. 'I remember him handing the bunch of keys to Patsy. He sent her up to light the gas lamps.'

'Where were the keys?' asked Dr Scher.

'In his pocket, apparently,' said Patrick. He looked towards his former headmistress and she nodded a confirmation.

'Yes,' she said. 'I saw him take them out, quite a big bunch, he hauled them up and selected the right key and then handed them to Patsy.'

'So we're back to the crowd around him; I suppose that it must be one of them.' Dr Scher looked exasperated. 'I had forgotten about the gallery, but of course that would have been ideal. A perfect angle.'

'It might have cleared Sam O'Mahony, too,' said the Reverend Mother sadly.

'Perhaps, though, the door to the gallery wasn't locked,'

said Dr Scher hopefully. 'Patsy may not have bothered to mention this. There was so much going on.'

Patrick shook his head. 'No, I checked. I went to see Patsy and she was certain that the door was locked. She said the lock was stiff and she had a bit of a struggle to get it open. We had a little chat about it and it appears that the superintendent of the market is very particular about locking the door when the gallery is not in use. I checked on that, too.'

Patrick, thought the Reverend Mother, always would check. He was that sort of boy. She looked at him with approval.

'And the keys . . .?' There was a question in her voice. In her mind's eye she remembered the size of the bunch as the superintendent had dragged it from his pocket on that Friday morning. Surely the man did not lug them around in his pocket every day.

'I found out about that, too.' There was a faint smile of appreciation on Patrick's lips and she knew that he had read her mind. 'Normally,' he said, looking directly across at her, 'the keys are kept in the weighmaster's office, but this morning he knew that the city engineer would be likely to want to go upstairs, perhaps talk to him in his office, look at the original 1790 plans and so he kept them in his pocket. I checked on the position of the weighmaster's office. It's in the Grand Parade section of the market. There is always someone there, unless the office is locked. The superintendent said he took the keys out of there before the market opened for business on that Friday morning. "Off the hook and straight into my pocket": these were his words.'

'Pity,' grunted Dr Scher. 'I was beginning to fancy myself as a bit of a Sherlock Holmes. I could just hear my evidence in court. "The bullet, m'lord, sliced through the man's flesh and entered the heart at an exact angle of forty-three degrees. Having borrowed a . . ." What's it called, you know, the thingamajig that engineers use to calculate angles?' He appealed to Patrick, but it was the Reverend Mother who answered.

'The word you are seeking is theodolite, Dr Scher,' she said crisply and enjoyed momentarily the respectful look in both men's eyes before adding, 'but the same angle could have been achieved, could it not, if the man had bent down and was just straightening himself?'

'Perhaps,' admitted Dr Scher. 'But wouldn't someone have noticed that? I wasn't there myself, but surely someone would have noticed him bending down.'

'No one mentioned that,' said Patrick. He had, guessed the Reverend Mother, been over and over the evidence gathered during the last couple of days.

'Well, I was present,' she said, 'and I certainly don't remember him bending down, but then I don't suppose there would be any reason for me to remember such a trivial matter – a man retying a shoe lace, picking up a dropped pencil, perhaps even flicking a thread of lint from his trousers.'

'I still think that the assassin was above him, perhaps standing near a stall, or even behind a stall,' said Dr Scher.

'Or the assassin was someone very much taller,' said the Reverend Mother. Her mind went to her cousin. He was an extremely tall man, probably about six foot four inches high, she reckoned. Her eyes went to Dr Scher and he nodded reluctantly.

'The corpse measured five foot four inches,' he said with precision. Once again he picked up the two teaspoons and moved them further and nearer apart, raising one higher than the other. She watched him indulgently. There would have been a sixth of a difference in height between Robert Newenham and James Doyle, the one the product of rich feeding for three or even four generations, the other the son of a struggling tailor from a basement.

'I suppose it might be possible, what do you think, Patrick?' Dr Scher manipulated his spoons under Patrick's eye. But then he threw them both down with disgust.

'Yes, but why would a man raise his hand and point downwards towards his victim? Surely he would aim at the heart. It's not possible. It's insolvable, this crime.'

'Not insolvable, surely. Saint Thomas Aquinas says that insight, or light, is always with us, but we don't always see it; he used the analogy of a blind man standing in sunlight, probably aware of the heat, but yet absent from a real understanding of the sun, of its shape, colour and size,' said the

Reverend Mother mildly and then bit back a smile as Dr Scher
gave a snort of annoyance. It was, she thought privately,
possible that Robert Newenham had raised his gun in order
to shoot over the head of a bystander. This would account for
the angle in which the bullet entered the man's back.

'Interesting,' murmured Patrick. He took out his notebook,
licked the tip of the indelible pencil which all policemen,
working in the wet streets of Cork, invariably carried. 'Just a
note to myself to check on the heights and the positions of
everyone who may have had an interest in the death of the
city engineer,' he explained without raising his eyes from his
page. And then he looked up and straight across.

'Reverend Mother,' he said respectfully, 'what's your
memory of Sam O'Mahony's position?'

The Reverend Mother paused, but only for a second. 'Sam
O'Mahony, when I noticed him, was standing in front of his
mother's drisheen and tripe stall,' she said.

'And when you heard the pistol ring out?'

This time she did not pause. 'I was not aware of Sam
O'Mahony at the moment of the shot,' she said.

And then the die was cast. She could not go back on this
statement. There had, she thought, never been any doubt in
her mind. She could not – would not – lie under oath and that
being so there was no point in prevaricating at this stage. Sam
O'Mahony she sincerely believed was innocent, but he could
not be cleared of this crime by false witness.

And certainly, she thought, picturing his face when he was
aware of the gun in his hands, he had looked bewildered – and
innocent. The word came to her mind and she retained it. If
Sam was innocent, then his name had to be cleared and he
had to be released from prison. She looked across at Dr Scher
still gazing at his two spoons.

'The nearer the two lines, the greater the angle,' she said
crisply and then as they both looked at her in a puzzled fashion,
she crossed over to a small table near to the door and picked up
a child's copy book. It had been sent up to her by Sister Philomena
in the hands of a tearful Tommy O'Reilly who had been guilty
of defacing a book meant for neat sums by drawing a tank with
guns and enormous wheels, on the back page. It had been a

remarkably good drawing for a six-year-old and the Reverend Mother had been torn between backing up Sister Philomena's discipline and admiring the child's skill and compromised by retaining the copy book and decreeing that he had to do his work on pieces of paper for the whole of the following week. Now, without compunction, she tore out the middle page and drew an upright line, five squares high and then a series of lines at regular intervals across the page, joining them to the taller line.

'You can see,' she said with satisfaction, 'the nearer the position, the steeper the angle.'

'And, of course, the man may have held the gun quite high,' said Patrick rapidly. 'I understand from everyone that the place was quite dark and full of shadows. Some of the stallholders had lit candles, but only some of them, is that right, Reverend Mother?'

She thought for a moment. 'As far as I remember, the only well-lit area in the Princes Street Market was Michael Skiddy's soap and candles stall. The goods themselves were lit up, but behind the stall it seemed even blacker than elsewhere. In fact, there was, I think, one gas lamp burning on the rail of the gallery on the other side, just above Mrs O'Mahony's drisheen and tripe stall and it made that side of the market less dark.' She hesitated for a moment and then reminded herself of the necessity to establish the truth. 'I told you, Patrick, about the man there, at Michael Skiddy's stall, the one who caught my attention. He wore a belted raincoat, and a soft hat, pulled well down to hide his face. I noticed him because he did not appear to be shopping. He had no basket, no bag with him. He spoke with Michael Skiddy for a moment or two and then he stepped back.' The Reverend Mother paused, seeing the scene on that dark, foggy morning and then added, 'He stepped back into the shadows behind the stall. That's about all that I can tell you, Patrick.'

He jumped to his feet. 'Thank you, Reverend Mother, and you, Dr Scher. You've both given me plenty to think about. I'll go around to the market and see Michael Skiddy tomorrow morning. And I'll get Joe onto checking heights and positions of everyone who could have had any interest in this murder.'

'You could do as the Emperor Napoleon did,' said the Reverend Mother. 'He, I understand, used to have models

made of his courtiers. And then before each grand event he
had the models dressed in clothing of his choice and he used
to move them around and check how they looked in groups
around him. One of the facts that I picked up in an expensive
education,' she added.

'And I have to make do with teaspoons,' said Dr Scher
sadly, but Patrick was already at the door. The Reverend Mother
touched the bell for little Sister Mary Angela. Let the child
have the excitement of showing out her hero. The neighbourhood around the convent was very proud of Patrick, and though
slightly built, his dark eyes and curly hair made him quite a
good-looking boy. The would-be lay sister might well change
her mind about immuring herself in a convent if she realized
that there was a world out there to explore, and that she would
do well to know what it was all about before renouncing it.

The Reverend Mother shook hands with them both and
allowed Dr Scher to linger for a few minutes while Sister
Mary Angela fetched Patrick's coat and fussed about removing
a smudge of limewash from its navy blue surface.

'Conscientious boy, isn't he?' said Dr Scher in a low voice
and with a nod towards Patrick. 'There's not many a policeman
would look twice for another suspect after the evidence against
young Sam O'Mahony was dished up to him on a plate.'

'Did you know Sam?' enquired the Reverend Mother.

'Seen him around,' said Dr Scher briefly. 'Good lad. Bright,
too. Interviewed me about the body of that man found in the
limekiln. Asked all the right questions. Produced a good report
afterwards, too. Made me sound quite intelligent. Pity he ever
got above himself and criticized the city engineer.' He looked
at her enquiringly, but she did not respond. Dr Scher would,
she suspected have, with any encouragement, lingered longer,
but now she needed to get back to work.

And to sort out her thoughts about the murder of James
Doyle in full view of fifty Cork citizens. Sam O'Mahony, she
thought, had learned to use the power of the pen. She wondered
whether anyone who had experience of that sort of a weapon
did readily turn to the cruder weapon of pistol and bullet. He
had made no effort to escape, relying on words to protest his
innocence and to keep him safe.

# ELEVEN

Alan Ellis
Reporter on *Cork Examiner*:

'The Auxiliaries and Black and Tans, supported by
some regular troops, many wearing scarves over their
faces, were firing shops in Grand Parade and Washington
Street. A jeweller's shop in Washington Street had been
looted, as well as shops along Marlboro' Street. Witnesses
saw soldiers carrying away kitbags full of booty. Murphy
Brothers, the clothing shop, on Washington Street was also
looted and set on fire and there was a danger that the fire
would spread to the Church and Priory of St Augustine,
next door.'

Michael Skiddy's wrecked shop had been situated in
Berry's Lane, behind Washington Street. He had been
unlucky, thought Patrick as he surveyed the charred
timbers and the empty windows of the roofless building. The
shop had been tiny, just a place for the people of the marsh
to buy their candles to illuminate the houses where no one
even thought of bringing gas. And a place to buy their bars
of Sunlight soap to scrub clothes and children. The Black and
Tans would never have dreamt of wasting petrol on such a
humble place. Unfortunately it had backed onto a prosperous
menswear shop on Washington Street and the fire had spread
to its decaying timbers. Patrick spent a few minutes surveying
it. A neat little shop in its time, he thought. A steady trade,
without too much expenditure. The candles, he remembered
them well from his mother's cottage, would have been made
from tallow, and in Cork where there was a continual export
of beef to England, the tallow was a by-product – most
butchers were delighted to get rid of the lumps of fat and
seldom charged more than a couple of pence. In a city where

there was either rain or fog on most of the days in the year, candles were a necessity.

'Are you looking for Michael?' The voice was aggressive and Patrick turned carefully towards the speaker. The guards were not popular in many of these small lanes. There was great support for the Republicans around here and many a man on the run was hidden in one of the small tumbledown cabins, or in the rooms above the meagre shops.

The question was asked by a woman with a shawl drawn over her head. Not old, he thought. One side of the face showed smooth young skin, but the other side was marred with puckered scars. She saw his eyes go towards it and pulled the shawl a little further forward and repeated her question angrily.

Patrick pulled himself together, deliberately turning his gaze from the ravaged face and looking back at the building. 'Does he still live here?' he asked.

He sensed rather than saw the shrug. It was a wet morning and the shawl would be heavy with rain.

'Where else?' she answered and there was a sarcastic, angry tone to her voice. 'Where else? We haven't got a country mansion, you know. Just this one place that was belonging to Michael's father and his father before him. And I suppose this dump of stone and plaster will be the birthright of his son.' She was, Patrick noticed, heavily pregnant under the all-concealing shawl.

'Are you Michael's wife?' he asked.

'What do you want him for?' she said without answering his question.

'Nothing much,' he said. He wondered what Michael Skiddy must feel about the failure of the city engineer to rebuild the houses and shops of the poor, despite the large sums of money paid by the British government in compensation for the burning of Cork by their troops. With a pregnant wife and only a burned-down hovel to shelter her and a newborn baby, his fury might have spilled over into direct action. Or, perhaps, a word in the right place had brought a killer to his stall that morning. 'I just want to ask him a few questions about the shooting at the English Market,' he continued. 'Someone mentioned that he was talking to a man in a raincoat and a soft hat who suddenly disappeared at the moment of the gunshot.' From experience he kept his voice as neutral as possible. *Walk slow and talk soft.* The superintendent had said that to him on his first day at work and although the man was a pompous fool he had nearly fifty years of policing the rebel city behind him and his advice was sometimes worth listening to.

The alarm in her face was perceptible and her hand went to her mouth with an instinctive gesture of terror. With an effort she pulled it away and locked her fingers together.

'Man, what man?' she asked aggressively. 'Michael talked with no man.'

'You weren't there, were you?' he asked, making sure that his voice was unthreatening.

'No, of course I wasn't. Otherwise you would have my name down, wouldn't you?' She snapped out the words, but he could see from how she bit her lip that she realized she had made a mistake. They had discussed the matter, she and her husband. This was obvious.

'The strange thing was,' he went on smoothly, 'that this man disappeared after the shot was fired and before the superintendent closed the two entrances from the Princes Street market. A witness saw him and then he vanished. I'd like to have a word with Michael and get his name.'

'He didn't know him from Adam,' she snapped.

'So he spoke of him to you,' said Patrick gently.

She paused for a moment, searching, he thought, for the words to avert his suspicion.

'Yes,' she said. 'Michael told me that he had just sold a bundle of candles to a man that he had never seen before in his life, *a stranger*, them were his words, and at the very minute that he had taken the money, the lights went out and then he heard the shot. And when he looked again, the man had disappeared. Michael had never seen him before in his life,' she repeated. 'He thought he might have been from the country because of the way he spoke.'

Her own sing-song Cork accent reached a high pitch as she watched him anxiously and he nodded gently. He could guess that Michael Skiddy was already at work in the market and he could find him there. He would not distress this poor pregnant woman any longer.

'I see,' he said. He looked again at the ruined house, at the broken roof, the chimney leaning at an angle, the boarded-up windows. 'You and Michael manage all right in there?' he asked with a nod towards the patched and still scorched front door.

She shrugged, the shawl falling open and revealing the enormous mound of her pregnancy – the unborn baby seemed almost as big as herself.

'We've still got the dipping wheel and the boiler for the wax; we must stay here,' she said fatalistically.

He found a shilling in his pocket and slipped it into her hand. 'Buy the baby something nice with this,' he said with a smile and was relieved when she fastened her fingers around it.

'Thanks,' she said awkwardly. 'Sorry if I sounded a bit rough-like. Me nerves are bad.'

'No wonder,' he said lightly. 'It's an anxious time for you. Let's hope they get this place rebuilt as soon as possible.'

It looked, he thought, as he strode down the lane and re-entered Washington Street, as if it could tumble down at any moment. But, of course, the rents at the English Market had been recently increased to the huge sum of twenty-six shillings in the week, so every penny that Michael Skiddy made, over and above that, would have to go on food. There would be nothing left over to hire lodgings for himself and his wife.

The candle stall was bare of customers when Patrick approached it. Sam O'Mahony's mother averted her eyes as he walked past, but he gave her a courteous 'good morning' and even hesitated for a minute in order to give her time to ask him a question if she wanted to. This, he thought, was the hardest part of the job. He would have preferred to break up a fight between a crowd of drunken dock workers than face the devastated mother of an arrested man who might be hung for a murder that he, perhaps, did not commit. Mrs O'Mahony said nothing, however, just turned her back and rearranged the pale sausage rolls of drisheen on the shelf behind where she stood and so he passed on, conscious that every stallholder and every customer in the place was eyeing him with suspicion as he approached the candle maker's stall.

'Good morning, inspector,' said Michael nervously. He fiddled for a moment with the burning candle in front of him, scraping off a drip of wax from its side with his fingernail, placing it into a tin box where other crisp candle drippings were stored and then carefully reversing it so that the draught from the open door of the Princes Street Market would blow on the higher side of the candle. A strong smell of tallow filled the air for a moment and then the flame straightened and began to burn more steadily.

'Just wanted to have a word with you about that man in the raincoat with his hat pulled down over his face,' said Patrick briskly. He watched Michael's face as he spoke and could have sworn that he looked deeply uneasy.

'Man in a raincoat,' he said tentatively.

'The one you told your wife about; the man whom you had just served at the moment that the shot went off,' said Patrick and could have sworn that a flash of anger crossed Michael Skiddy's face. He didn't blame him. It was a nasty business tricking information out of a heavily pregnant woman, but Patrick had learned to keep one aim in mind while engaged on solving a crime. He had to find out the truth; had to know whether Sam O'Mahony was guilty, or whether he had been falsely accused and imprisoned.

'Lots of people in raincoats on that morning, last Friday. Nasty dirty weather.'

Michael, Patrick thought, was talking for the sake of talking, giving himself time to think. He was prevaricating, of course. The slouch hat pulled down over one side of the face was almost a trademark for the Republicans. The candle maker knew quite well what Patrick was asking but he was giving himself time to think. His dilemma was clear. Either he could lie to the police, or he could find himself in trouble with the Republicans. There were nasty rumours around the city about the fate of informers and many a body was dragged from the river with a bullet wound in the head.

'You're right, of course,' he said in an easy way. 'The only reason why we are interested in this fellow is that, according to one witness, he just vanished before the superintendent had time to order the gate to be shut and the entrance to the Grand Parade side of the market to be blocked off.' He stopped for a moment to allow Patsy Mullane to sweep the sawdust from beneath where he was standing and then carried on. 'I wondered whether you could put a name to the fellow, or whether you knew where he came from.'

'Never saw him before in my life.' Michael's voice was loud and emphatic. Several stallholders looked across at him or turned their head momentarily from their own customers. A sudden hush subdued the normal hum of business and Patrick found every head turned towards him. He cursed himself briefly and then decided to make the best of things. Many of the people shopping here this morning may have been at the market at the same hour on Friday morning. Shoppers tended to be regular in habits and to have a loyalty towards particular stalls.

'I wonder whether anyone who was here on Friday recollects someone disappearing before the superintendent closed off the two entrances?' he asked and heard his voice boom against the gallery floor over his head. The superintendent emerged from his office above and came hurrying down the stairs. 'A man in a belted raincoat and with a slouch hat pulled well down over his face,' he added.

There was a dead silence. No one looked at a neighbour, nor commented. Everyone probably knew or had heard that there had been a member of the Republican army who had rapidly disappeared, probably just after the shot had been fired. Still, the moment might not be wasted. An approach might be made to him in secret later on in the day, or even on the following day. He would make sure he was available, to be a conspicuous presence in the city centre, to instruct the constable on duty in the police barracks to detain with welcoming cups of tea anyone looking to speak to him and to send an urgent messenger after him if he happened to be out.

'I suppose it's hard to remember all of your customers,' he said turning back to Michael Skiddy. No sense in alarming the man. 'Well, it was worth a try, but if you don't know him, then you don't know him. I'll have one of those two pound candles, as I'm here,' he said casually and then, as he handed over the money, he said in a low voice, 'Anything that you tell me will be in confidence. Just pop into the barracks, or send someone to me with a message.'

And then he accepted his change and his brown-paper-wrapped parcel and crossed over to Mrs O'Mahony's stall. Carefully he removed his cap and stood respectfully in front of her.

'You'll be going to see Sam today, Mrs O'Mahony,' he said.

'That's right,' she said curtly. 'I don't suppose that he will be coming home with me, though, as he should do if right were right.'

He bowed his head at that and gave her pronouncement a moment's silence. No point in trying to justify the police action, he thought. He had been in charge, he was the one who had made the decision to arrest Sam, he, in her eyes, was guilty.

'There's a lot in his favour,' he said carefully. 'The very fact that he did not run away, that he waited, that he allowed himself to be held by the two beadles and made no struggle. Tell him to keep his spirits up.' He had said more than he should have done, perhaps, but it was a shame to think that if he had arrested any of the men standing around James Doyle, if he had arrested Robert Newenham, the town planner; Father de Courcy, the bishop's secretary; Thomas Browne, the assistant city engineer; or any of the others, then by now they would have a well-paid and well-informed solicitor acting for them and pointing out all the reasons why his client should no longer remain in custody. One law for the rich, and one for the poor, he thought, as he checked that Mrs O'Mahony knew the visiting hour and that she would be allowed to stay only for ten minutes and that anything she brought to Sam would have to be examined first of all.

'I'll bring him a book,' she said slightly, unbending from the air of frigid mistrust with which she had first regarded him. 'He's a great lad for reading, always was.' She hesitated for a minute and then looked at him very directly. 'Tell me something, inspector, will it go against him that he threw the gun away?'

He did not make the mistake of brushing aside her fear. It was a valid point and he took a thoughtful moment before he answered it.

'It may,' he admitted. 'It's a pity, perhaps, that he did not straight away go over to the superintendent of the market or someone else and say: "I picked up this gun", but it's easy to be wise after the event. The chances are that it might have felt hot, smelled of burning, and that was why he threw it into the fountain.' Once again, he thought that he was exceeding his duty; that a point like that would be something that a lawyer for the defence would bring out in court. Still the words were out and he could not unsay them. 'I'll leave you now; don't want this uniform to put off your customers,' he said with an effort at humour. He thought briefly about purchasing some drisheen, but he loathed the stuff and Mrs O'Mahony might find his purchase to be patronising. Tucking his brown-paper-wrapped candle into his attaché case, he made his way out and into the busy thoroughfare of Princes Street. He had gone a hundred yards when he felt a light touch to his arm. He looked down and saw Patsy Mullane.

She must be in her forties, he thought. There was no doubt that she had been around in the city library when he was quite a young boy. He remembered Sister Philomena bringing the whole class there to choose a book, which would be read when they were back in the school. Patsy Mullane, Miss Mullane, Sister Philomena had addressed her as, looked middle-aged then, but perhaps not too different from her present appearance. An educated woman; he remembered asking her for something about ants and how swiftly she had scanned the shelves before coming up with a volume of *The Children's Encyclopaedia* and quickly finding the right page for him. It was stamped 'Reference Library' but she had consented to him borrowing it on the promise of extreme care being taken of it and he had revelled in it day after day, even forgoing playtime in the yard on occasion in order to finish an article. It was a shame, he thought, that she had been reduced to work such as sweeping up the sawdust in the English Market. Normally a boy or girl, just out of school, took a job like that, before graduating to the position of a messenger who would deliver goods from the stalls, and be presented with a bicycle. Once again he took off his cap and carefully addressed her as 'Miss Mullane'.

'Oh, Patrick,' she said and then covered her mouth with her hand. 'I mean, inspector.'

'We're old friends,' he said gently smiling. 'I remember how good you were to me and how you found books for me when I was studying for my school certificate.'

Her face bore a wistful look. 'Ah, the library,' she said. 'Will we ever see it replaced, do you think?' And then, without waiting for an answer to her question, she said rapidly, 'I've something to tell you . . .'

'About the murder, is that right?'

She hesitated and then said defensively, 'It's not that I meant to listen, or anything – and of course, I wouldn't dream of interfering.' She flushed a mottled purple, her cheeks, he noted with pity were chapped and weather-beaten. The English Market, despite all its refinements, was stone-cold during the winter. What a change for the poor thing from the library where she, he remembered, had a soft chair and a cosy fire to snuggle up to when there were no eager children looking for advice on a library book.

'Anything that you can tell me will be of help, Miss Mullane, and, of course, will be treated in strict confidence,' he said gravely.

'It's just that I heard you asking about the man at Michael Skiddy's stall last Friday and I think that I know who it is.'

'That would be most useful information.'

She cast a frightened glance around and stopped in the shadow of a doorway to a derelict shop. He paused also, bending down to tie a shoelace and heard her voice in his ear as she leaned towards him. 'I think that he's the son of old Mr Hurley who was the caretaker at the library. Do you remember him?'

'Vaguely,' said Patrick, searching his memory. He straightened up. There would be more to come, he knew. Patsy was an intelligent woman. She would not have followed him without a good reason. The caretaker. He cast his mind back to his school days and remembered a figure with a broom who appeared to spend most of his time on the steps of the library. A grumpy old man, he recollected.

'Died six months after the burning down of the library. God rest his soul.' Patsy said piously and Patrick's interest sharpened.

'And the son?' he queried.

'That would be Tom. The eldest fellow died of TB. He was a real, nice man. John, his name was. But Tom,' hissed Patsy in his ear, 'he was very wild. Fought in the 1916 rising and was a commander in the Troubles. Still is, so they say.'

And with that, Patsy shot hurriedly back down Princes Street and he saw her turn into the market entrance.

So, thought Patrick as he made his way amongst the shoppers, I now have a name for the man in the raincoat, and, as he had surmised, it was perhaps a Republican assassination. But why put the gun down at Sam O'Mahony's feet? Why didn't Tom Hurley, if that was who it was, just take the gun with him and only jettison it if there was a pursuit? In the event, there was no pursuit, no one had noticed his disappearance at the time and the entrances had been blocked off too late to detain everyone present when the shot was fired.

In a way, he thought, as he reached the Grand Parade, it almost seemed as though the involvement of Sam O'Mahony could have been deliberate, that someone had wanted the young reporter to be found guilty. He glanced up the roadway at the clock above Woodford & Bourne's. Ten o'clock. He would, he thought, go past the convent of St Mary's of the Isle on the way back to the police barracks. The children would be out for their morning break in the yard by the time that he reached there, and the Reverend Mother was often to be seen strolling around, surveying her flock, present to lend an ear to any tale of distress or to rebuke any misbehaviour or fighting. He would have a quick word with her about this development. She might have some suggestion to make.

'And here comes Inspector Cashman. Let him see how beautifully you make the numbers. Remember that when you make a five, you go straight down, curve around and then put its hat on.' The Reverend Mother, to his pleasure, was superintending some five-year-olds who were drawing out a hopscotch oblong on the rough concrete of the playground. He took her words for an invitation and opened the cast iron gate, closing it carefully behind him and coming over to stand beside her as a chilly-looking little girl completed the last two numerals and looked up at him for praise.

'It's perfect,' he said. 'Much better than I could do it. Can I play, too?'

'You're too big,' she said gravely surveying him and he nodded with relief.

'Let me see you do it,' he said and then went to stand beside the Reverend Mother as the game began, warming the poorly dressed children, and filling the corner with shouts of triumph and encouragement and rhythmic counting of the numbers.

'You look troubled,' she said under the cover of the shrill voices of the hopping children.

'I was wondering whether we have the wrong man under lock and key,' he said.

'By accident or by design?' she said, as always going straight to the heart of the matter.

'I've begun to think by design, not mine, but the real murderer's.'

'Very possible.' She seemed unmoved, just looked steadily ahead, her eyes on the bouncing figures of the five-year-olds.

'You see,' he went on, 'I've always thought that there was a possibility that Sam was innocent and that gun landed on his foot by accident, but now that I have another suspect in mind, I think it might have been a deliberate effort to cast the blame on him. We've had information about the man who disappeared after the shot. The man in a raincoat, with his hat pulled down over his face.'

'Was your suspect standing at a stall on the other side of the market thoroughfare?'

'I think so,' he said.

'By the soap and candle stall.' The Reverend Mother sent a stern glance over at a small boy who was sticking his leg out to trip up one of the girls and he retreated immediately with a bland expression of innocence on his face.

'And we have a name for him,' Patrick said. 'Tom Hurley. He's a commander of a Republican section.'

'A political assassination, then.'

'Possibly, or possibly a private grudge. Apparently his father was caretaker of the library and he died six months after the burning down of the place. Tom Hurley might have wanted revenge on all those who seemed to have profited from that night. But it's not terribly helpful. Tom Hurley's got a crowd of young fellows under his thumb. Much more likely to send one of them to do a public job like that. He would keep himself for the big stuff, the raids on army barracks, the seizure of lorries with ammunition, that sort of thing.'

She looked at him gravely. 'And your informant is reliable?' Her voice made a query out of the statement.

He compressed his lips. 'Oh, I'd say that she told the truth. I'd say that it was Tom Hurley, all right.'

She, thought the Reverend Mother. Probably Patsy Mullane. But why? Most people would be very afraid of naming a Republican activist to the police. She watched Patrick's puzzled face attentively.

'It just doesn't bear the hallmark of a Republican assassination,' he said after a minute. 'I'd have expected it all to be much slicker, not a last-minute escape like that. He risked a lot, if it was Tom Hurley. And then the involvement of Sam O'Mahony. What was the point of dropping the gun on the man's foot? The Republicans need all of the guns that they can get. They're rumoured to be running out of guns and ammunition and the government is taking huge care, these days, when any troops are moved. They go in convoys, and an advance party of armoured cars clear the road ahead of them.'

'You're puzzled because you are beginning to believe that Sam O'Mahony is not guilty but has had suspicion deliberately thrust on him.'

He nodded. 'But if that's right, then I don't think that Tom Hurley is the murderer. I don't think he'd bother. He'd know that we'd find it virtually impossible to bring him to justice. And if he had something against Sam O'Mahony, well, he'd just meet him in a dark street one night and shoot him, or else have him shot. There would be none of this business . . .'

He paused and then continued, eyeing her closely, 'There would be none of this business of casting Sam as the patsy, if you know that American expression, Reverend Mother?'

'I think that you are probably right, Patrick.'

So it was Patsy Mullane who had informed on Tom Hurley, commander of a section of the Republicans. Very brave of her; or did she have a pressing motive? The Reverend Mother considered the matter thoughtfully, while she intervened in a couple of incipient fights, supplied more chalk for hopscotch players, looked sternly at a man who had paused by the playground railings and then, with relief, rang the bell for the children to return to their classrooms.

# TWELVE

W.B. Yeats:
The old brown thorn-trees break in two high over
Cummen Strand
Under a bitter black wind that blows from the left hand;
Our courage breaks like an old tree in a black wind and dies,
But we have hidden in our hearts the flame out of the eyes
Of Cathleen, the daughter of Houlihan.

'That woman at number 23 is a police spy, Eileen. Did you know that?'

Eileen choked over her cup of tea. She had half-chewed the hunk of dry and very stale bread that was all the food available for breakfast, had taken a gulp of tea to soften it and both had got stuck in her gullet. It took a few minutes of vigorous thumping by her mother and coughing from Eileen before her windpipe was clear.

'You should eat properly,' said Maureen severely. 'At your age, too.'

'It's your fault,' retorted Eileen. 'You startled me. How do you know that she's a spy?'

'People say that she is,' said Maureen. 'Her cousin is a peeler, a guard, you know.' She didn't sound too concerned, but Eileen frowned with annoyance. Everyone in the street knew about Maureen's rebel daughter and she didn't want to get her mother into more trouble by being seen to visit her. It might result in a visit from a policeman and an interrogation of her mother. Generally she never visited by daylight.

'I'd better not go out by the front door, then. I'll just get over the wall and into the back lane,' she said. 'If we go out together, she'll know that it is me, shawl or no shawl. I'll go now and I'll meet you at the prison at half past three. If you're right, and his mother visits at three o'clock, then she'll be well gone by half past. They only allow ten minutes for each visit.' She could easily pass the morning on her own. Wearing the old black dress and the shawl she would merge into the background of the poor that flooded the streets of Cork. She choked down the rest of the unappetising bread and then took off her boots, breeches and jacket and stuffed them into a basket. She would go barefoot, she thought, but then changed her mind. The dress that she had selected the night before was too long for wall climbing. She had thought about tearing a strip off it, but in the end she decided to leave it as it was and put on the boots again. The length of the dress would be enough to hide their shining beauty and these days she was quite unused to bare feet and would find it hard to walk through the streets, let alone climb a crumbling wall with exposed, jagged pieces of broken stone. If her plan did not work out, then a quick getaway might be necessary.

'You're up to something,' said her mother suspiciously. 'I can see it.'

'Nothing, not today, anyway,' said Eileen, suppressing the thought of the piece of paper which she planned to pass over to Sam when they shook hands. 'I wouldn't involve you. I just need you today for a bit of a disguise. You'll make me look respectable. You're always telling me that you wished I was respectable, and not go around wearing breeches and boots, so now you'll have your wish. There'll be a pair of us – a respectable mother with a respectable daughter.' Quickly she shoved the basket with the clothes behind the settle. She would have preferred to take them with her, but there would be a search at the door of the prison. She had been warned about that. She would just have to return afterwards to collect them.

'What was all that writing about last night? I could hear your pencil going scratch, scratch until I fell asleep and then there was all that burned paper among the ashes in the fire this morning?' Her mother sounded amused, even proud, but Eileen was conscious of a moment's alarm. It was important that her mother be totally unaware of the plan. She had to appear just concerned for the prisoner, sorry for him, but not hugging a secret to herself. Maureen showed the world her thoughts. Her daughter would not wish to involve her in any secrets. Furtively she stirred the cold ashes in the fireplace with the toe of her boot. Her mother watched indulgently.

'Want some more breakfast?' she asked, but did not protest when her daughter shook her head. Her mother never breakfasted at home. There would always be scraps of uneaten food in the pub when she cleaned up after the night's drinking. In any case, there was little enough food in the house. Eileen wished now that she had taken some more money from the jar on the mantelpiece in the hideout. She was hungry. She was used to a substantial cooked breakfast at this time of the morning. The farmer who sheltered them was generous enough to tell them they could take what eggs they could find from the barn that sheltered his hens at night, and he often dropped off some home-cured bacon for them. They fed well, the soldiers of destiny, she thought. She knew that she had filled out ever since she had joined them and the fact that she looked so well had reconciled her mother to the life that her only daughter was leading.

'Don't worry,' Maureen said. 'I'm not after your secrets. Just wondered what you were writing, that's all. You used always show me your essays.'

'Just trying out an article,' said Eileen shortly. Her effort to compress all of the information Sam would need onto a piece of paper which would fit in the palm of her hand, and could be passed to him as she greeted him, had been more difficult to write than any thousand-word article for the *Cork Examiner*. It was essential that he understood the plan, essential that there should be no fumbling, no hesitation, and no missed chances.

'See you later, then,' she said lightly, as she slipped through the back door, down to the privy at the back of the yard. There was a loose stone here which could be removed to make a stepping stone, high enough for her arms to reach the top of the wall; she remembered that stone from the days of her childhood, when it had always seemed to be more fun to climb over the back wall than to walk out of the front door like a civilized human being, as her mother used to put it.

She would approach the gaol by the back streets, she planned. No waiting around the gates, no awkward encounter with Mrs O'Mahony. She would go up to the top of Barrack Street, around by Gillabbey Street. From there she would walk along College Road, wait for the right moment when no one was in sight, no nursemaid wheeling out one of the babies from these houses of the privileged classes, no delivery boys cycling along the steep incline. She used to envy these bicycles so much, though she thought that the metal strip on the crossbar bearing the name of shop or stall rather spoilt their smartness. No, she would wait for the right moment and then she would slip into the university grounds, make her way to the tree-lined patch near to the river and conceal herself there. If any of the students spotted her, they would just imagine that she was some girl coming in to scrub the floor or make the cups of tea in the university restaurant's kitchen.

She had two pieces of luck. First of all she found an abandoned hunk of cake lying on the wall of the bridge, left there for the birds, doubtless by some student suffering a hangover. Eileen consumed it in two large bites and then when she had penetrated a little further along beside the river she found an old willow tree, which, when she had climbed up it, made a very good place to hide and was perfectly situated to provide a view of the prison.

Cork gaol was a small, one-storey building, constructed, like its neighbour the university, of fine white limestone. There was a high wall all around the buildings and standing clear of them. The entrance was closed on the outside by a pair of heavy wrought-iron gates in one of which was inserted a small wicket door. These outer gates gave access to a yard that had another pair of iron gates which extended the full height of the archway. Between the two sets of gates and to the left was the visitors' waiting room, in which she had been told a warder was always on duty.

Prisoners awaiting trial were allowed visits of ten minutes' duration each between three and four p.m. Not more than six persons were allowed in the waiting room at the same time and they were all searched and had to wait their turn under the eye of the warder. Eileen's plan was based on that. The visiting cell, she knew from what Tom Hurley had told her, was situated near the centre of the prison and was approached from the main gate by a path running inside the wall that led to the prison buildings at which the military sentry was on duty. She could see the path from where she sat on the branch. Three minutes to walk it, she reckoned, and probably at a run the distance could be covered in under a minute. Speed and silence were to be their watchwords. And, of course, meticulous and careful preparation.

Tom Hurley, she thought idly, as she watched for her mother to appear, had proved to be very useful unknown to himself. He had spent six months in Cork gaol after taking part in a parade down St Patrick Street and he remembered the layout of it fairly exactly. He was easy to flatter and she had found that he was very ready to describe the gaol, and even had unbent enough to draw a sketch map of the place and its surroundings. Her plan, she knew, was a good one, if everyone could keep their head and if Sam O'Mahony could be forewarned and be ready for the rescue.

There was a sound of a bell from the university and she hoped that it meant half-past three. She was getting tired of sitting on the branch of the willow tree and every nerve in her body was on edge like an over-strung fiddle. Her mother was coming now, she could see her turn in from Western Road and cross the stone bridge. She was wearing her shawl well pulled up over her head. Swiftly Eileen slid down and pulled up her own shawl, feeling pleased that the strong smell of mothballs had begun to evaporate. She brushed the catkins from her dress and dragged it well down to cover the shining splendour of her knee-high boots and then she rearranged her shawl, folding it into a triangular shape and carefully pinning it under her chin. It felt uncomfortable like that and the pin dug into the soft flesh of her neck, but not being used to a shawl she didn't want it to fall off just as she was passing the note to Sam.

Maureen gave a nervous start when her daughter joined her in Gaol Walk. Her eyes, inside the framing shawl were wide and frightened. It was good that she was so much taller than her daughter, thought Eileen, glancing up with a reassuring smile. Maureen had been brought up in her early years by an aunt who lived on a farm and only returned to her own mother

when she had been seven years old. The early good feeding
had helped her to grow tall and strong, Eileen had often
thought. She linked her arm with her mother's, leaning her
shoulder against the woman's arm and mentally assessing the
height difference. It should work. Luckily Liam was not too
tall and quite slight in build. Confidently she marched up
towards the lofty limestone archway.

'Yes,' said the warder at the gate abruptly.

'If you please, officer, we've come to see my cousin, Sam
O'Mahony,' said Eileen, speaking in a shy soft low voice. She
felt her mother's arm tremble and she pressed it comfortingly
to her side. Now that the play had begun, she herself was not
nervous. Just keyed up and excited. And yes, he took a bunch
of keys from his pocket.

'A pity you didn't come at the same time as his mother,' he
grumbled as he unlocked the wicket gate. 'Can't you families
get yourselves organized? You'll have to wait your turn, now.
There are two other sets of people in front of you.' This wicket
gate, noted Eileen, bowing her head as though chastened by the
reproof, was barely the height of a man. If a vehicle stormed
the prison, then the two outer and the two inner gates would
all have to be broken down first. Big heavy gates, too, made
from wrought iron set into stone archways, no, it would be
impossible to force them open; her plan was a better one. Brains
over brawn, she said to herself.

Demurely Eileen waited, her arm locked into her mother's,
her head hanging, looking, she hoped, the epitome of a bashful
country girl. The warder now relocked the outside gate, and
walked them across to a one-storey building, made of the same
white limestone as the gaol itself. There was another warder
standing at the door to this, smoking a cigarette and looking
bored.

'Visitors for Sam O'Mahony. Aunt and cousin,' said the
first warder briefly.

'Lucky man. Second visit today. Don't know why you didn't
all come together.' He held out his packet of cigarettes to the
first warder and jerked his head at them to go inside. Eileen
exerted a gentle pressure on her mother's arm and went in.
The room was furnished with three wooden benches and was

freezing cold and filled with the miasma of fog. The door was left open, but the two warders were talking loudly about last night in the pub and Eileen seized the opportunity and turned to one of the male visitors.

'We're visiting Sam O'Mahony. Who have you come to see?' she asked.

He turned out to be living in the east Cork town of Midleton and introduced himself as Tom O'Brien. 'Me and Augustus are here to visit our youngest brother, George, someone accused him of robbing his pocket, brought a lorry-load of witnesses,' he said, his voice wavering between family solidarity and unease about the weighty evidence for the crime.

'Sam is in for murder,' said Eileen and sadly dabbed her eyes with the corner of her plaid shawl.

'That's bad,' said a third man sympathetically. 'And I bet he's as innocent as a babe unborn. That's the way with things. Them peelers, *guards*, they call themselves, "guardians of the peace"; well that's a laugh, that is. "Persecutors of the poor", that would be more like it, isn't that right, Maggie,' he said to his wife.

'They say that he stole ten shillings from the butcher's at Fermoy, as if my Colm would do a thing like that!' Maggie ignored Eileen and leaned over towards Maureen's well-built and more motherly form.

'Visitors for Colm O'Sullivan,' shouted the second warder. The first warder, Eileen noted, flung down his cigarette and walked across to meet a couple of women emerging from the inner gate. One warder at the outside gate, a second at the visitor's waiting room, and a third at the inner gate, noted Eileen. She kept her face down and partially covered by the shawl in order to conceal her excitement. She would be able to memorize the positions of the prison warders and now she had the names of two of the other prisoners awaiting trial and so allowed visitors on a daily basis.

'Tom O'Brien, Colm O'Sullivan,' she repeated soundlessly to herself. And the wonderful thing was that one man lived in Midleton and the other in Fermoy, both towns at a considerable distance from the city. It would be most unlikely that the families would be able to visit the prisoners again tomorrow.

Nevertheless, an unconvicted prisoner could receive visitors every day of the week, except for Saturday and Sunday. She stopped listening to the story of Tom's woes and looked keenly around the bare little room, noting the position of the warder behind what looked almost like a shop counter. There was, she noted also, a telephone on top of it and her eyes found the socket in the wall above a steel safe.

The ten minutes allowed for the O'Sullivans' visit to their son were not long in passing. Soon they reappeared, escorted by a warder, were handed over to the warder at the inner gate, then there was a wait while the keys were produced and the gate unlocked. Next three warders came together: the first warder to escort them to the wicket in the other gate, the second beckoned Eileen and her mother from the visiting room, and the third still stood with the keys dangling loosely from his hand. This will be the crucial moment, thought Eileen, as she followed him meekly, peeping at the overlooking windows and keeping alert for the presence of other prison warders.

No other warder appeared though. The man tapped on a door in the middle of the building and then, as soon as it was unlocked, he thrust the two women inside and then left. He had not exchanged a word with the warder of the prison cell and this one, thought Eileen, was a surly-looking fellow, tall and tough-looking. He nodded to them to sit opposite a wooden barrier and to put their hands on the shelf beneath it.

'Spread the fingers,' he ordered. 'Just a handshake is allowed through the barrier. No hugging or kissing. Too easy to pass things like that,' he said sourly, glaring at them. 'Any gifts,' he queried and when they shook heads silently, went straight over to the phone on his desk at the back of the room and just said, 'Prisoner 41.'

So they don't search the visitors, thought Eileen. Just hands are inspected, and not even them at the two outside gates. Another fact to remember. She was slightly trembling, she noticed, and was annoyed with herself. This was a serious affair and she was supposed to belong to an army. She had never yet taken part in a raid; her job was to do the writing: propaganda agent, press secretary, planner, even. Tom Hurley was old-fashioned and he didn't like women entangled with the fighting force.

But now it was serious. Sam's life probably depended on her. She clenched her hands as she heard the heavy footsteps tramping down the corridor. There was a knock at the door opposite to the one where she and her mother had entered. Two doors. She reminded herself to check whether both would be locked during the ten-minute visit time.

And then the inner door was unlocked and Sam was thrust into the room. No chances were taken. The door was immediately relocked and then there was just one warder, the prisoner and the two visitors – two against one, she thought excitedly, though reminding herself that the one was armed and that there was a telephone by his hand.

'Just a handshake, remember,' he said now in a monotonous tone, turning his attention back to the *Cork Examiner* which he had taken from a ledge beneath the top of his desk.

There was an odd look on Sam's face. He seemed defensive, unhappy, embarrassed, even annoyed. For a moment it was almost as if he had not recognized her, shrouded in her faded plaid shawl and then he suddenly flushed a dark red. He avoided Eileen's eyes, looking with an air of bewilderment at Maureen. Eileen nudged her mother firmly and Maureen held out a tentative hand. He seemed not to know what to do for a moment and then reluctantly he shook it. Eileen gave him a moment to recover and then took her own hand from beneath the shawl. She had meant to have given it a quick lick, but in the event she was sweating heavily with a mixture of fear, compassion and excitement. The small piece of paper stuck to it firmly. She forced herself not to glance over her shoulder at the prison warder. She had looked once and twice would show anxiety.

'How are you, Sam?' she said passing her hand beneath the barrier and gripping his firmly.

'Not too bad,' he said and she could not tell from his expression whether he had felt the small, thin piece of paper torn from a cheap jotter. She kept her hand in his.

'Don't despair, Sam,' she said earnestly. 'We're all –' she allowed a small pause to ensue before finishing with the conventional – 'praying for you.' He knew her link with the Republicans and knew that daring raids and rescues had been effected by them. He himself had written a dramatic article about the attack on St Luke's Barracks.

She felt his hand move within hers and the slight scratch of well-trimmed nails and then he had taken his hand away. She took her own hand back and laid both hands, palms upturned on the shelf beneath the barrier. The piece of paper had disappeared.

'We all know that you didn't do it, Sam,' she said earnestly.

'No talking about the case,' said the warder from behind her and that gave her an opportunity to turn and look at him. She got up and moved over and stood before him, her head bowed, the very picture, she hoped, of submission and respectable poverty.

'What can I talk about, sir,' she whispered loudly.

He looked at her with amusement. 'Talk about anything you like, my darling, talk dirty to your young man if you want to. I don't care. I'll just be sitting here reading my newspaper peacefully. Just don't mention the case that has yet to be tried.' And then ostentatiously he yawned and turned over to the death notices in the *Examiner*. She waited for an extra moment, as though overwhelmed with fear or embarrassment and then she moved back and took her seat again beside her mother. Sam, she noticed with satisfaction, had just finished chewing something and now his hands lay in front of him, conspicuously empty. He was a quick reader. He would have had plenty of time to understand and memorize the short message. There was a new expression on his face, now, though she could see how he tried to subdue it.

'We got a lift in this morning with the man who brings fowl to the English Market,' said her mother suddenly. 'You wouldn't believe this, Sam, but he turned out to be a cousin of mine, and a cousin to your grandmother, too, Lord have mercy on her soul. He was talking to me about her. She was buried on the night of the Big Wind, would you credit that?'

Sam was looking slightly startled but he rallied enough to insert the conventional: 'It's a small world' and then sat back and allowed her to fill the uneasy silence with a long and

complicated tale about this mythical relation that Sam shared
with them and of the various things that had happened to her
throughout her life. Eileen watched him and saw him relax
into a grin. There was nothing that he and she could discuss.
Not the murder, not their love for each other, not her belief
in his innocence. She blessed her mother's talent for making
up stories. No one could object to this flow of reminiscences
and anecdotes. Beneath it, her eyes met Sam's and she deliberately looked around, directing his towards the figure of the
warder, immersed in his newspaper and the telephone and
the door to the outside. And then their eyes locked for a long
moment.

'I remember her,' he said aloud, addressing himself to her
mother. 'She drank a few pints of stout a day, a great one for
the stout, she was, wasn't she?'

'Never!' By now her mother had begun to believe in this
mythical grandmother of Sam's and her voice was loud and
emphatic. 'I'll have you know, young man, that your grandmother was a living saint. Wore out her knees, she did, what
with all the praying. And the rosaries that she would be saying
all the night long!'

Eileen began to feel that her mother had gone beyond her
brief. If it were the same warder tomorrow, he would be
astonished that such a talkative woman had suddenly turned
dumb. In any event, he gave an enormous yawn, as though he
was finding the conversation to be very dull.

'One more minute,' he said warningly and she seized the
opportunity.

'We'll come again tomorrow at the same time, Sam,' she
said and then added in as petulant a tone as she could manage,
'And perhaps I'll be allowed to do a bit of the talking myself
then, otherwise, I'm just not coming.'

And her mother, her magnificent mother, born to be on the
stage, said in resigned tones, 'I won't say a word, *alannah*,
cross my heart and hope to die. You can talk to your heart's
content. I won't say a word from start to finish.'

'That will be the day,' said the warder. He gave a wink at
Sam, and then he bent over his desk, lifted the telephone and
said abruptly into it, 'Visitors are leaving.' He put the

instrument down, turned around, dragging the keys from his pocket, and leaned down to open the door.

Eileen, followed by her mother, was right behind him, waiting patiently to be escorted out and through the double set of gates.

# THIRTEEN

St Thomas Aquinas:
*Etsi homines falles, deum fallere non poteris.*
(You may deceive men, however, it is not possible to
deceive God)

'Dr Scher to see you, Reverend Mother,' said Sister Bernadette, adding hastily, 'he said to tell you that it was urgent and that he wouldn't keep you for too long.'

The Reverend Mother paused. She had been on her way to the senior classroom on this Tuesday morning. She was loathe to allow anything to interfere with her precious teaching time, but Dr Scher had never before sent a request like that. His usual practice was to arrive at the end of the school day, or during the weekend, with, always, a joking pretence of just passing the door and being overwhelmed with longing for Sister Bernadette's fruitcake, or else using the excuse of visiting Sister Assumpta who had been gently fading away for the past twenty years and would probably have another year or two in the same state. He was not a man to say that a matter was urgent unless it truly was. Quickly she thrust the pile of copy books into Sister Bernadette's hands.

'Bring Dr Scher into my room, and then find Sister Mary Immaculate and ask her to take my class for the moment. The girls can be doing their corrections and reading my notes. Oh, and, sister,' she called after the retreating figure, 'we won't need any tea or refreshments.'

If Dr Scher said it was urgent, then she wanted no interruptions, no small talk while awaiting the appearance of the tea trolley. She hoped that her face had not betrayed her, but she was apprehensive. There was a name in her mind. Dr Scher knew that Eileen had been a pupil of hers and that she was fond of the girl. Had she been arrested for some illegal activity? Her heart gave a painful lurch. The new Free State had proved itself even more savage than the occupying English troops in crushing all opposition. There had been several Republicans shot or hanged inside the grounds of Cork Gaol and their bodies thrown into an unmarked grave.

She seated herself at the desk and awaited him, quietly tucking her hands into the large sleeves of her habit and placing her feet side by side beneath the desk. Her face, she knew, would show nothing.

Dr Scher's face, though, was filled with distress. He often, she had thought in the past, had the comfortable, chubby look of one of those teddy bears displayed in the windows of the expensive shops in St Patrick Street at Christmas time, but now he wore a wilted, depressed look, and there were black shadows under his brown eyes. He came in silently and dropped into a chair beside the fire without saying a word.

'What's the matter?' she asked as soon as the door had closed behind a puzzled Sister Bernadette.

'There was a shoot-up at the Coal Quay Market last night,' he said, not looking at her. 'A ship had delivered corn and the prices were sky high. The Republicans wanted a free distribution of a hundred-weight sack for each family. Just the one-off distribution and after that the corn could be sold at any prices they liked. Well, of course, that could not be allowed. A bit too Utopian, wasn't it? The army was sent down from Collins Barracks and it all turned into a pitched battle. The usual thing. Luckily no deaths, but lots of gunshot wounds and one lorry crashed into a wall when the driver was shot in the arm and the fellows in it were all badly injured, really smashed up, not like good, clean gunshot wounds. Anyway,' he said and he bore, she thought, the aspect of a man reluctantly coming to the point, 'anyway,' he repeated, 'the hospital was working at full strength so when the guards were called out to a woman who had taken poison, Patrick sent someone for me. He's a sensible lad; knew that taking her to hospital would probably end with a long wait and then a dead body; they would have had no time to deal with her with men bleeding to death under their hands.'

The Reverend Mother cautiously let out a breath. The

woman, it appeared, was not dead. But would Dr Scher call the seventeen-year-old Eileen a woman?

'Who was the woman?'

He did not reply to this question, but bent down and opened his attaché case. 'This was on the table in her room. It's addressed to you.'

He handed over a brown-paper-wrapped small parcel addressed in strong bold capital letters to: 'THE REVEREND MOTHER, ST MARY'S OF THE ISLE'.

Not Eileen, she thought, as she struggled with the knots in the string. She knew her handwriting, a close imitation of her own italic hand. The parcel felt limp and flexible and once the brown paper was off she could see that it was a parcel of three school copy books, just like the ones that she had sent across to Sister Mary Immaculate. These, however, were twice the usual bulk and not filled with written work, but every page had a cut-out article from the *Cork Examiner* pasted upon it. The Reverend Mother turned over the pages. The first article was dated almost three years ago and the last in the book at the bottom of the pile was dated several months ago and dealt with the corruption among those charged with the rebuilding of the burned-down city and ended with a list of questions aimed at the city engineer's office. Well-written and no doubt the young author of the articles was clever enough to know that you cannot libel an office, only an individual. Nevertheless, Sam O'Mahony had lost his job at the *Cork Examiner*. She put down the third copy book carefully on her desk and looked up at Dr Scher who was now striding restlessly around the room.

'Mrs O'Mahony?' There was a question in her voice, though she had already guessed the answer, and he just nodded in reply.

'What happened?' she asked.

'The woman in the room below the O'Mahony's place heard the sound of terrible banging, as though someone was calling for her, she thought. She went up the stairs as quickly as she could go but by the time she raised the latch the sounds had stopped and Mrs O'Mahony was lying unconscious on the floor. She didn't know what to do, but she ran down into the street and by a piece of luck, Patrick was there, patrolling Kryls Quay with his men. The disturbance at the Coal Quay Market was over and done with, but he was just making sure that all was quiet before he left the place. It was lucky that the woman found him. He sent one of his men to the hospital for an ambulance and sent young Joe down to the South Terrace to get me.

'And?'

'Well, violent shaking and then unconsciousness sounded like rat poison to me, so I grabbed some tannic acid and some chloroform and jumped into my car and was there in a few minutes. She was too far gone to be sure of saving her, but I did my best until the ambulance came. They pumped out her stomach when they got her there.'

'Did they find out what was wrong with her?'

'What I had expected. She had swallowed rat poison. A lot of the deaths in this city, by accident or by design, are due to rat poison. The place is full of it.'

'Was it an accident?'

Dr Scher shook his head sadly. 'She left a note . . .' He hesitated for a moment and then said, 'It was beside the parcel that she had addressed to you. She had meant to slip it inside, I think.'

'What did it say?' The Reverend Mother had begun to stretch out her hand and then withdrew it. No doubt the note was now in possession of the police.

'It said: "I can't go on" . . .' Dr Scher said the four words slowly and his brown eyes were moist. 'Poor woman,' he added. 'There was an ink blot on the page as though she had dropped the pen then, probably had begun to feel ill. She would have been shaking violently. That's what happens. A sort of rigor sets in. I don't think there is much hope for her, to be honest. Her jaw had begun to lock. I gave her as much chloroform as I could before I left the hospital and now it's a matter of waiting. Poor thing. A terrible way to kill herself.'

'Suicide?' The Reverend Mother heard her voice shake. Mrs O'Mahony had threatened it in her hearing. What was it that she had said? *I can't see myself wanting to live if Sam is taken from me – so you will have my death, also, on your head.*

'I wouldn't have thought that she would do such a thing,' she said after a long breath to control her voice. 'Not while there was still hope, not while Sam was still alive and needed her.'

'The dark hours of the night . . .' said Dr Scher. 'She had had her supper, but she hadn't eaten all of it. There was half a drisheen left in a frying pan and it looked as though she had an egg with it and she had eaten half a slice of soda bread. And there was an empty cup with tea leaves in it.'

The last supper, thought the Reverend Mother. In the Bible the Last Supper had been followed by despair. Mrs O'Mahony had no one to watch with her during her agony. She bowed her head and said nothing. She heard, rather than saw, Dr Scher move towards the doorway. His words came back to her.

'I'll drop in again later on. I'm off to the hospital now. I haven't much hope, though. That rat poison is terrible stuff. That poor boy in prison. What a terrible, terrible thing. Someone will have to break very bad news to him, I fear.'

And with that he went away abruptly, not waiting for her to ring the bell so that Sister Bernadette could conduct him to the doorway with her usual ceremony. When he left the room, the Reverend Mother tried to rise to her feet, but she felt her legs trembling. She seemed to hear the words of Mrs O'Mahony scurrying around in her head. *What's a small lie compared to a human life. We tell lies all the time; and it's not a lie; Sam was standing just in front of my stall and I saw the pencil in one hand and the notebook in the other. I saw him a second before I heard the gun.*

And then more words, self-accusing words: *vain-glorious; puritanical; hypocritical; false, unkind, uncharitable.*

She put both hands on to her desk and managed to lever herself up. Sister Mary Immaculate and all of her senior class for English Studies would have seen Dr Scher go down the pathway towards the gate and they would be expecting her. She forced herself to walk in as upright a fashion as she could manage and to ignore the trembling of her legs as she entered the classroom, thanked Sister Mary Immaculate and then turned to the girls.

'Before we start, I would like you to say three Hail Marys for a special intention,' she said.

And as the young voices chanted the words at the usual breakneck speed, her mind, gravely and solemnly enunciated the sentence from the Bible: 'Though I speak with the tongues of men and of angels, and have not charity, I am become as sounding brass, or a tinkling cymbal.'

Dr Scher's battered Humber car was in the roadway when the children were going home from school that afternoon. The Reverend Mother was at the gate lending an ear to the mother of a fourteen-year-old girl who had taken to slipping out of the family's one-roomed accommodation late in the evening and walking around the quays with her school friends.

'I've talked and talked until I am blue in the face, but not a blind bit of notice will she take of me. So I said to myself, I'll just pop along and have a word with the Reverend Mother and she'll be able to sort her out.' The woman looked at her trustfully.

'I'll have a word with them all,' said the Reverend Mother. Her tone, she realized with compunction, was a little absent-minded. She was busy studying Dr Scher's face. Was the news good or bad? It was difficult to tell. Death, for a doctor, especially for one who conducted autopsies for the police, was probably a weekly occurrence, at least, she thought. And suicide, as well as murder, happened often in this city of abject poverty living side-by-side with great wealth. With an effort she turned back to the woman.

'You're quite right, Mrs O'Callaghan,' she said briskly. 'I'll have a word with Annie and the other girls about the dangers of going down the quays at night. And remember, you're the mother and she is the child. It's for you to say what she should or should not do. Don't allow any argument.' Privately she felt sorry for the lively girls who did not want to spend their evenings cooped up in one damp room with a depressed parent and lots of small brothers and sisters. If only some philanthropist would set up a place where these girls and boys could go of an evening. Her cousin Lucy's grandchildren were mad on jazz, according to Lucy. No doubt, the girls of her school would like an opportunity to listen to music, also. The difference was that instead of listening to records in their own or in friends' houses, going to concert halls and cinemas, these children had to hang around the public houses. How much, she wondered, as she took leave of Mrs O'Callaghan, would a Victrola phonograph cost? And which rich businessman could she persuade to donate one to the school?

And then she forgot about Annie O'Callaghan and her friends. Dr Scher had got out of his car, moodily slamming the slightly warped door with a noise which caused heads to turn. As he came towards her, she read the news in his downcast face. She asked no question, however, when he approached her.

'Come in and join me in a cup of tea, doctor,' she said quietly. 'I usually have one just after school finishes.' She gave a quick glance around. Child abuse and child prostitution was a major problem in this part of the city and she tried to make sure that every child in her school was collected by a parent or went home with neighbours, or in a large enough group of the older girls so that a predator could not target a solitary unhappy youngster and win confidence with presents of sweets or some tawdry ribbons.

Not even Sister Bernadette's fruitcake raised a smile from Dr Scher, though he roused himself to thank her. A difficult occupation for such a soft-hearted man, thought the Reverend Mother as she waited until Sister Bernadette's slippers ceased to sound from the corridor. Then she looked at him and said, 'Is Mrs O'Mahony dead?'

'That's right,' he said. 'May her God have mercy on her soul! I don't suppose that he will, though, will he? Don't you holy Catholics believe that someone who commits suicide will go straight to hell? Don't you decree that a suicide should be denied the right of a proper funeral and burial?'

The Reverend Mother made no answer. Let him relieve his feelings by the usual rant against organized religion and hypocrisy. She leaned over and poured out a cup of Sister Bernadette's tea. It was dark orange in colour and the fragrant smell filled the room. She added a couple of spoons of sugar and a small dash of milk. 'Drink this,' she commanded.

He drank thirstily and when he had drained the cup, she refilled it. Halfway through the second cup he seemed to relax, though he did not touch the tempting slice of rich fruitcake.

'I did everything I could do,' he said, speaking, she thought, as much to himself as to her. 'There's no real cure, though, if you can't get to them immediately.' He stayed for a long moment staring across the room. She understood his frustration. Time after time again she had found herself thinking: *If only; if only I had more money, more knowledge, more patience, more understanding.* It was the road to madness, she had decided and tried always to banish such thoughts and to get on with the next pressing task. Her nature, though, she thought, was less mercurial than Dr Scher's.

'I can't stay for long,' he said after a minute. 'The coroner has ordered an autopsy. There'll be a proper inquest afterwards, I suppose, though I don't know why they bother. Doesn't do the dead person any good. Still, I suppose that it keeps the lawyers rich.'

'I think that it is important for society that death is marked by its rituals,' said the Reverend Mother. 'After all the family of the deceased person would want to know all of the facts.' And then with a feeling of dread, she asked tentatively, 'Does Sam know of the death of his mother?'

Dr Scher shook his head. 'No,' he said briefly. 'Patrick said that he will go around to the gaol this evening. I offered to do it for him, but he said that it was something that he had to face. He knows that Sam will blame him, but you know Patrick. The very fact that it will be difficult and unpleasant would make him do it. He's a fine young fellow.'

'He is, indeed,' agreed the Reverend Mother. And Sam O'Mahony was a fine young fellow, also, her mind told her. She had browsed through some of his articles during her few spare minutes in the morning, and she had been impressed by their vigour and their style, and also, surprisingly, their humanity. A bit opinionated, but an intelligent and a courageous young man. And his mother was a courageous, hard-working, almost undaunted woman. But her Achilles heel was her son.

'Well, I must be going,' said Dr Scher. He drained his second cup of tea and then rose to his feet. 'I have to do the autopsy now. I'll pop in a bit later and let you know the result. Though I could tell you now that she died of a dose of strychnine. Still, the judge and lawyers have to have their day in court and so do I. Only difference is that I don't get a fee for attending.'

This grumble appeared to cheer him up. He stuffed some cake into his mouth and she could hear him call out cheerfully to Sister Bernadette as he went down the corridor towards the entrance door.

The Reverend Mother did not rise, nor did she follow him out of the room. She sat quietly in her chair and stared towards the window. The fog was descending again as the air cooled and she was conscious of a feeling of depression and of a desire to leave this city of almost perpetual greyness. Rome, she thought. A city full of warmth and sunshine. The bishop had wanted her to go there. Had she been stupid to refuse? She thought about it for a moment, thought about Rome and then she shook her head vigorously. Never look back, never repine, she told herself firmly.

Her mind slid back to the idea of a Victrola phonograph. She had seen one of them in Lucy's house. It looked almost like a small cupboard with a flap that came out and there was a turntable inside where the record, like a large, black dinner plate, made, she understood, from shellac and ground slate, was inserted. The phonograph could easily be placed in the senior classroom and there could, perhaps, be an afterschool club for the older girls where they could listen to records, and perhaps dance to the music. She would buy a few recordings of sacred hymns and music to keep people like Sister Mary Immaculate happy and the jazz records could be slipped into the cupboard beneath.

Energised by the thought, she rose to her feet and crossed over to the window, closing the curtains decisively to shut out the vision of fog and smoke.

'I can't go on wasting my energies in futile regrets,' she muttered as she took from the drawer of her desk a list of the merchants in Cork. Beside each company name, in her fine italic handwriting, she had written the dates when each was approached and the amount they had donated to her various charitable enterprises. At the bottom of the list she wrote the name Robert Newenham. She paused for a moment and then resolutely turned her mind back to the matter in hand. The money raised could be used for the religious and musical education of the girls at her school. Lucy could organize the catering, the lighting. Her cousin Lucy could grandmaster the event and she would provide the focus for the evening's fundraising. Then she pulled a fresh piece of paper to her and began to write down a list of benefits which would accrue to the school by the possession of such a machine and then began to add as many names of pieces of sacred music that she could think of. *Panis Angelicus* she wrote and then a few more titles.

There was, she thought, as her fluent pen began to move down the page, nothing that she could do about Mrs O'Mahony, but perhaps she could do something for the son whom she had loved so intensely. She would do her best to clear him of the charge which, instinctively, she felt was a false one.

The first thing was to have a penetrating look at the men who had stood around James Doyle when he fell to the ground on that fatal Friday – men who would have something to gain by his death, unlike Sam O'Mahony who had nothing other than a futile revenge. She pulled out her watch from its pocket, pressed the button to open its lid and checked the time. Yes, this would be a good time to ring Lucy to discuss their plans. A music room would be a good focus for the fundraising and would undoubtedly gain the support of the bishop. The bishop's secretary, Father de Courcy, was, she had heard, a keen violinist. He would be a useful man to have on her side.

And, of course, she thought, as she moved at a stately pace down the corridor towards the telephone, Father de Courcy was standing just behind James Doyle, in the dim murky interior of the English Market, just two minutes before the city engineer was shot in the back. She herself had seen him there and had noticed how his eyes had wandered away from the speaker and were roving over the market itself.

'I had such a good idea last night,' said Lucy. 'I was just about to telephone you, so I'm glad that you rang. I heard that there is to be a town planning meeting this afternoon. It's to discuss the plans for the new city hall. Everyone will be there.'

Everyone who was at the English Market with James Doyle on last Friday morning, interpreted the Reverend Mother. Lucy, like she, was always aware of the possibility of listening ears – either in the house or at the telephone exchange.

'That sounds an excellent idea. And Mr Newenham?'

'He's delighted to be of help.' Lucy's voice bore the undercurrent of a laugh.

'And the time?'

'Half-past four of the afternoon.'

'I'll be there,' said the Reverend Mother crisply and then she disconnected.

Once back in her own room, she began to make another list, a list which she knew she would shred and then burn before she left the room. Her mind was one that did its best work with a pen in her hand. She wrote the names of all those officials who had clustered around the city engineer as he expounded his philosophy for the rebuilding of Cork so that the city would appear in the forefront of western Europe. And then opposite to each name she wrote her thoughts. When she finished, she sat back and studied her list for a moment. There were, she thought, more question marks than solid facts. Nevertheless, she had made a start and she hoped that tomorrow would fill in the gaps. She added a few lines and then laid it down. A new thought had suddenly come to her.

Her own words of earlier on had sounded in her mind, like those from a far-off echo from across a valley.

*I can't go on*

She had finished her sentence with the words: 'wasting my energies in futile regrets', but others may have made a different sentence with the same beginning. Many thoughts, many sentiments could have started with those four words. Mrs O'Mahony had the vigorous practised hand of someone used to writing – she had been a sharp, intelligent woman, had built up a highly successful business against strong competition. She had wanted a good education for her son and the chances were that she had received a good education herself, thought the Reverend Mother. Not, she thought, a woman to give up and to despair before all avenues were explored. And even then, she thought, Mrs O'Mahony would have stayed beside her son to the very last moment, not abandoned him at the moment of his greatest need.

She would have to see Patrick as soon as possible, she thought. She wanted to look at that note left by the dead woman, probably addressed to herself.

Or she could just ask him a simple question, if that was not possible.

Had there been a full stop after the word 'on'?

# FOURTEEN

W.B. Yeats
The Political Prisoner:
She that but little patience knew,
From childhood on, had now so much
A grey gull lost its fear and flew
Down to her cell and there alit,
And there endured her fingers' touch
And from her fingers ate its bit.

Eileen found herself trembling with excitement. Yesterday had been the dress rehearsal but today was the real performance. If it came off, then Sam would be free by the evening. She found herself looking around at the house and the farmyard at Ballinhassig, trying to see it with his eyes. She had picked out her companions for this adventure and all, she thought with a moment's compunction, were doing it for her sake, for the sake of the deep friendship which had grown up between them, holed up together and continuously in fear of arrest and even execution. They were a good crowd, she thought affectionately. There would be Eamonn, clear-minded and quick to react, Danny who had the best motorbike and was the cleverest rider, Fred, though a bit of a show-off, immensely strong and muscular, a man who always got the better of his opponent in any fight. And then there was Liam who was a meticulous planner and timekeeper, and who could be relied upon to keep calm. She arranged that he would be the one to be her companion on the visit to Sam. Everyone was ready now except for Liam who was making a big fuss about dressing up as Eileen's mother. The seam of the old dress split as he dragged it on reluctantly. He had insisted on retaining his own trousers and as Aoife pulled it down the old material gave way.

'Oh, put a stitch in it,' he said impatiently. 'God, it stinks of mothballs.' He had already sworn that the old plaid shawl had to be hung out in the wind for a few hours before he would be able to wear it and at the moment it flapped from the branch of an ash tree near to the gate. Eamonn was on watch further down the lane, keeping a close eye out to make sure that Tom Hurley would not pay a surprise visit and interrupt their plans.

'You can't wear your trousers. They show,' said Eileen firmly. She was not going to allow any silly scruples to spoil her plan at this stage.

'I have to; where can I keep my pistol, if I don't have a proper pocket. That pocket in the dress is too small. The gun will show up if anyone looks at me carefully. And it could fall out.'

'You can do what I'm doing. You can wear one of the pairs of bloomers that I made when I was in school,' said Eileen. 'Sister Mary Immaculate made us all make them to the same pattern – the same size as her own – so they are huge. My mother kept them in the space under the settle bed. Wait, I'll get you my second pair.' Before he could object she ran back into the house, giggling to herself at what Sister Mary Immaculate would say if she knew that a pair of bloomers, stitched under her eagle eye, would be worn by a young man. And that both he, and Eileen herself, would be using them to conceal firearms.

'Here you are,' she said when she returned. Each girl had been forced to make two. Eileen had managed to secure one piece of navy-blue flannel before having to fall back on the nauseating shade of pink which Sister Mary Immaculate had favoured. She handed the navy blue pair to Liam and shook it insistently in front of him before he reluctantly accepted it. 'Go on, put them on,' she said impatiently. 'They've got really strong elastic in the waist and on the ends of the legs. They'll come down to your knees. You can stick the pistol in there and then you'll just need to hitch up the skirt a little to grab the pistol. Make him put them on, Fred. Go on, Liam, stop making such a fuss. Go behind the bale of straw if you're all that modest. Aoife, go out and see if Eamonn has any news. Just whistle loudly if there's any sign of Tom Hurley. Liam and I'll hide behind the bales of straw in the barn until he goes away; he never stays for long.' Eileen went over the arrangements in her mind. Eamonn had borrowed a clerical collar from a sympathetic priest and Eamonn, Danny and Fred were going in their normal clothes.

Almost everything, however, depended on herself and Liam. She had chosen him because he was the nearest in height and build to her mother, as well as being someone who appeared to be without nerves. Together they would, hopefully, look just like the same pair who had come into the prison on Monday afternoon. She smiled to herself to think of her mother's fluent evocation of distant relatives and had prepared her own words for today's visit. 'Make it boring,' her mother had advised. 'If it's long-winded enough, your man will get lost in his *Cork Examiner*.' The thought of her mother reminded her of something.

'My mother went into the English Market to see Mrs O'Mahony,' she told them. 'It seems that Mrs O'Mahony planned on going into see Sam first thing each afternoon. She had an agreement with the woman in the stall next to her that she would look after the drisheen and tripe for an hour. Mam had quite a chat with her. She said that everyone was being so nice to the poor woman, bringing her little presents for herself and to bring to Sam in the gaol.'

'Doesn't matter anyway, even if we do meet her,' said Liam, eyeing himself with a grimace in the little hand mirror that Aoife held up in front of him. 'I don't suppose that she knows every one of Sam's friends. She certainly doesn't know any of us. And not even my own mother would know me in this rig-out, I'm glad to say.'

'No sign of Tom Hurley,' said Eamonn returning from his vigil. 'Let's go. It doesn't matter if we're early. We need to leave the two ladies off at a bit of a distance, anyway. Got your pistol, Lily darling,' he said to Liam as he walked up and down the yard, moving in an awkward, stiff-legged fashion. 'Just hope that the prison warder doesn't take a fancy to you and give you a squeeze.'

'Or take a notion to get inside his bloomers,' said Fred.

'Oh, shut up,' said Liam bitterly.

No one, thought Eileen, as she climbed up behind Eamonn, would ever imagine that they were going on an expedition where they could all end up shot, or else imprisoned. She found herself giggling as Eamonn in his clerical collar began to intone '*Miserere mei, Deus*' at the top of his voice. Liam joined in the psalm in a high falsetto voice, singing counterpoint to Eamonn's baritone and Danny performed his party piece which was an imitation of an organ, done through his nose.

They went at a leisurely pace, but even so it was well before three o'clock by the university clock when Eileen and Liam were dropped off on College Road. The plan was for them to go through along a back pathway and to hide in the lower grounds of the university until quarter past three and then they would turn up at the gaol gate. The others would park the motorbikes in the space beside the engineering buildings and then walk along the Western Road and into the gaol at twenty-five minutes past three. They would give the names of the other two prisoners whose relatives Eileen had met in the visiting room the previous day: Colm O'Sullivan and Tom O'Brien. Danny and Fred would make a big affair of giving way to Eamonn, as would be expected by any decent men when faced with a priest's collar. With some luck, the waiting room might be empty, but it didn't really matter. No one was likely to get in their way once the stunning of the prison warders had begun. It would be instantly recognized as a Republican raid and Cork people knew that it was wiser not to get involved in these matters.

'You again,' said the warder on the gate when Eileen and Liam presented themselves. 'You're falling in love with me, darling, aren't you?' he addressed himself to Eileen and then looked slightly taken aback as she fumbled in her pocket and took out her mother's rosary beads, looking shyly down at them and passing the worn string between her fingers. Once the other four arrived in the waiting room, Liam produced a similar set and they prayed soundlessly and just nodded a greeting when the others came in. Eamonn immediately clasped his hands in prayer and the other three followed suit. Eileen was only sorry that she had not been able to round up some more sets of rosary beads but they were not a religious crowd. Very few Republicans now even went to mass. The bishop of Cork had excommunicated all who had taken part in raids.

Still, the rosary was a very useful prayer, thought Eileen. She remembered how much she had resented the time spent on her knees when she was in school, trying to disguise from Sister Mary Immaculate the fact that she had a book open on the floor under her desk. Without a book to read the whole process had seemed interminable: fifty times *Hail Mary . . .* five times *Our Father . . .* five times *Glory Be . . .* and then followed by the *Apostles' Creed.*

'Visitors for Sam O'Mahony,' said the warder into the phone. Outside in the yard a man and woman were returning from the main block. She noticed that the hand with which Liam put away the rosary trembled slightly and she felt sorry for him. He had not her advantage of knowing exactly how everything should work out. He would have to trust to a girl who had never been on a raid before and that, she guessed, was very difficult for him.

And then she forgot about Liam and concentrated on the part that she was going to play. 'Now remember that you promised to let me do the talking,' she said in a penetrating whisper into the ear of her supposed mother. 'Yesterday, you talked and talked and I couldn't get a word in edgewise.'

Liam, she was glad to notice, recovered enough to give an exaggerated sigh. She hoped that he wouldn't get so confident that he would attempt to talk in that awful falsetto that he had been using on the ride into town, but she daren't whisper a warning. She had gone over and over the procedure last evening, rehearsing again and again. Now, she told herself, was the time to relax and to play her own part as well as she could.

Everything happened as yesterday. The two were put on chairs in front of the barrier. Eileen stretched out her hands and laid them, palms upside, on the counter and Liam copied her. There was a moment's unease when she noticed the hairiness of his fingers but by the time the warder came near, only the palms were visible. The warder gave a cursory glance and

then went back to his telephone. Eileen saw Liam's eyes go
to the telephone wire and she frowned at him. The more he
kept his head down and his face hidden inside the hooded arch
of the shawl, the safer they would be.

And then Sam came in. He had a worried look on his face
and his greeting to her was almost absent-minded. She wondered
what was bothering him.

'Well, even if yer ma didn't turn up today, at least your
auntie and your cousin are here,' said the warder. He had an
unpleasant jeering note in his voice, but to Eileen's relief she
heard the rustle of the newspaper and guessed that he was
probably going back to his study of the racing pages.

'Your mam couldn't come today, Sam, and she's that sorry,'
she said earnestly. 'She told me to tell you to expect her
tomorrow without fail. The thing is she got a big new order
for some drisheen for the hospital. A doctor there has discovered that it is the best possible thing to give patients that are
recovering from an operation. She's been up all night getting
the sausages ready.'

Did Mrs O'Mahony prepare the drisheen herself, or did she
just buy it in and resell it? Eileen realized that she hadn't a
clue. Sam had never really spoken much about his mother, apart
from saying how hard she worked to send him to school and
how depressed he felt that now she was having to work even
harder in order to maintain a man of his age who had not been
able to get a new job. Eileen had always discouraged those
conversations because, sooner or later, they would end with
Sam declaring despairingly that he would have to go to England.

Liam, she noticed, had uttered a loud sigh of what was
intended to be boredom. He fished out his pocket watch from
his pocket, pressed the spring to open the lid and stared fixedly
at its face. The toe of his boot nudged the side of her foot.
Only another few minutes to go, she noticed as she glanced
swiftly down at the timepiece.

'And, you'd never believe it, Sam, but your mam is thinking
of advertising in the *Evening Echo* for a messenger boy. Of
course it would be an awful expense. She would have to buy
him a bicycle. But then, you see, she knows a man who would
get her one cheap.'

'She'd be better off not to bother,' said Sam in a voice that he tried to make sulky. 'She'll have to pay for one of those metal nameplates as well. And then there'll be the cost of painting the name on it. And if the messenger boy gets into trouble, then she'll be blamed.'

'But you could paint the name on for her, couldn't you, Sam?' pleaded Eileen in as soft and coaxing a voice as she could manage.

'Time's up,' said the warder. He picked up the phone and said into it, 'Visitors coming out.' Eileen felt her legs tremble as she stood up. By now, she thought, the boys in the waiting room should have stunned the warder, taken his keys and ripped out the telephone wire.

Beside her Liam had sprung to his feet with an alacrity that she feared might betray them to the warder. But when she turned around, the man had already pulled the keys out from his pocket and was, his back turned to them, bending down to open the door. Liam picked up the stool that he had been sitting on and whacked it down on the man's skull. He fell with a crash that Eileen feared might be heard throughout the prison. In a second, Sam had leaped over the barrier and joined them. Liam put his hand in the warder's pocket and drew out a pistol.

'Leave that,' said Sam. 'I want no violence.'

'Shut up,' hissed Liam. 'Mind your own business. We're only doing this as a favour to Eileen. Either you come along with us and keep your mouth closed, or else trot back to your prison cell like a good little dog.'

'Sam!' Eileen looked at him imploringly. He was stubborn and inflexible she knew, but there was no time for argument. Already Liam had opened the door, looking left and right cautiously. He handed the keys to her and then boldly marched across to the waiting room.

'Take this,' she said and before Sam could object, she had taken off the huge enveloping shawl, opened it out and put it over his head, fastening it with the safety pin under his chin. It came down to below his knees and would hide the prison uniform from a casual glance. Quickly she locked the door of the visiting cell behind them. Now they were just two female figures, one with a shawl and the other bareheaded. Eileen thrust her arm into his and forced him to walk slowly across the yard. Anyone casually glancing out of a window would see nothing unusual. In any case, not many windows looked out on the space between them and the inner gate. All the cells and corridors radiated out from the visiting cell in the centre.

As soon as they emerged from the door, for a moment she thought that all had gone according to plan. Eamonn's clerical collar gleamed white in the mist and Fred's tall figure had gone ahead of him. There was a slumped-over figure lying on the ground and Eamonn was tying a gag over his mouth. Hands and feet had already been tied together with the man's own belt. But why was Eamonn delaying over such matters?

Now she began to worry. Why had Fred gone ahead of Eamonn? She had planned that Eamonn was to be the one to go first towards the outside gate. This was the dangerous part. The warder at that gate would expect his friend at the inner gate to be the first through it. She had relied on the near certainty that he would be deferential towards a priest and hesitate to challenge him. Fred, she thought with exasperation, could never resist being in the limelight.

Steadily Eileen marched on, keeping a grip on Sam's arm. Just one more gate to pass through. She could see the gate. It was very near. The warder had come out from the small wooden shed where he sheltered and she saw, even through the mist, the gleam of a pistol in his hand. Something had alerted him. He would have expected a telephone call and then the figure of his colleague. He shouted out a warning and Fred started to run towards him. The man lifted his pistol, took aim and then fired. A shot rang out. Fred fell to the ground.

For a moment, everything seemed to stop, almost as though a cinema reel had been frozen. Fred was on the ground groaning; Eamonn was bending over him; the warder was pointing his gun from one to the other. And then, with the gun still steadily held in an outstretched hand, he began to back towards his shed. Through the open door the telephone was clearly visible.

And its wires had not yet been cut.

Eileen dropped Sam's arm. Quickly she groped for her pistol, securely stored inside the bulging leg of the bloomers. There was a tearing sound. The stitches were giving way. Impatiently Eileen tore her skirt from her waist. The threadbare, half-rotten material ripped away in an instant, leaving Eileen dressed only in Sister Mary Immaculate's bright pink bloomers.

And a pair of well-polished, knee-high boots.

The man stopped. The sight mesmerized him for one dangerous second. By then Eileen had pulled the pistol from inside the stout elastic of the knickers. Every fibre of energy within her exploded as she raced towards him. The pistol was still in his hand, held outstretched; she saw it waver and she did not hesitate or slacken her pace. Sam's life was hanging from a thread. If she failed now, he would die on the rope. Only the one warder was between them and freedom. She tried to fire, but somehow her finger refused to press the trigger. The first death, she knew from the hushed talk of the boys in the unit, was the watershed, after that, things got easier. She just could not pull the trigger and be sure of her target. Fortunately the man seemed to be mesmerized by the bright pink bloomers. Her eyes were fixed on his right arm and she aimed her body as though it were an arrow. In a moment she was on him, holding him for that vital second before Eamonn came up and brought the butt of a pistol down on top of the man's head.

He dropped like a stone. Eileen gave one glance and at that instant the telephone began to ring. She instantly ripped out the wire, but it was probably too late. Probably the shot at Fred had been heard. In a moment all of the warders from inside the gaol would come pouring out, guns exploding. There was not a moment to be lost. She grabbed the bunch of keys from the unconscious man's pocket and with steady hands unlocked the front gate. Eamonn and Danny had picked up Fred. He was groaning, so that was good; he was alive. Sam, to her exasperation, just stood very still and looked stunned and bewildered. The rain had begun to fall heavily and his glasses were misted over with it, giving him an odd, defenceless look. He still wore the shawl over his head, pinned under his chin and she hoped that he would keep it on until they could hide him somewhere safe.

'Come on, come on, let's get out, get out of here quickly,' she hissed. Regardless of her strange appearance in pink bloomers and black shawl, she grabbed his hand and pulled hard. Then he started to run fast, dropping her hand in order to gather his shawl around him and hold it pinioned to his sides. She followed him. Now they were at the locked outside gate, and Eamonn and Danny, carrying Fred, were just behind them. There was no sign of Liam, but he had probably kept his head and stopped to gag and tie up the stunned warder.

All they needed to do was to get into the university, recover the motorbikes and the boys could take Sam back to Ballinhassig, as was planned, while Eileen herself stayed the night with her mother. She stood beside him and reached out to take his hand. Liam joined them, no longer wearing dress and shawl, but the respectable overcoat of the prison warder, which came down almost to ankle length on him, neatly covering the embarrassing bloomers. He had a set of keys in his hand. It took a few long minutes before he managed to find the small key that unlocked the wicket gate. Eileen waited, shivering with cold and excitement.

And then the key was in the lock and there was a click. Liam pushed the wicket gate open. At the last minute Eileen realized that they should have taken another prison warder overcoat for Sam; the shawl looked odd with a pair of trousers beneath it, but it was too late to think of that. She pushed him through the narrow opening, Liam followed her and then Eamonn and then Danny clutching Fred's good arm in a firm, supporting grip. The other arm was tied firmly to Fred's chest with Liam's discarded shawl.

But then things started to go wrong. There was a roar of a powerful engine, a strong smell of diesel and an army lorry turned in from Western Road and raced up Gaol Walk, pulling up outside the gates to the gaol.

The five looked at each other with dismay. An army lorry from Collins Barracks was outside the gate, no doubt with some Republican prisoners within it who were to be held in the gaol. The impatient driver was sounding the horn and then alternating its raucous squawks with the rhythmic pulse of the siren. From behind them came the sound of shouts and of tremendous crashing blows against the door that she had locked to the visitors' cell.

'Unlock the gate,' shouted Eamonn, and Danny obeyed him without a moment's hesitation. Why unlock the gate? Won't the soldiers arrest us? Eileen's mind screamed the questions, but a second later, she realized that Eamonn had made the right decision. The big diesel engine powered up with a roar and a blast of evil-smelling smoke and it shot through the open gates without a moment's hesitation. Somehow, with the mist and murk on the windscreen, the driver had seen nothing amiss. Two seconds later they were all through the gates and out onto Gaol Walk.

'The bikes are down here,' said Eamonn, his voice low and controlled. He set a steady pace, not running, but walking fast.

'Give that shawl to the girl before she gets pneumonia,' he said curtly to Sam and without a word Sam handed it over. The fog was getting worse. Sam in his dark clothes would be more inconspicuous than she with her torn dress. She was glad of the warmth of the shawl, but sorry that Eamonn had ordered Sam to do it. And he had handed it over without even looking at her. What was wrong with him? Wasn't he grateful to be rescued?

'Quick!' said Eamonn. There was a shout from behind them and the noise of running feet. The engine of the lorry roared into action again. There was a sound of raised voices and of yelled commands.

'Run!' shouted Eamonn and Eileen blessed the fact that she no longer had the awkward skirt tangling around her knees. Liam, she noticed, had stuffed his skirt into the enormous bloomers and was overtaking Eamonn. Eamonn had torn off the clerical collar as if it might impede his breathing. Quickly she overtook him and ran to catch up with Eamonn. His was the slowest bike and she was the lightest weight. She would go with him. She could not risk being traced back to her mother's house and putting Maureen into danger. She would go with the rest of them back to their hiding place in Ballinhassig.

Without wasting a second, Danny leaped on his bike and Liam used his shawl to bind the wounded Fred to Danny's back. Then he was on his own bike and Sam had climbed up behind him. They shot out into the Western Road, going away from the city.

And then they heard the sound of the lorry reversing at high speed.

The soldiers from Collins Barracks had seen the stunned and bound figure of the guard and now they were after the gaol breakers.

# FIFTEEN

St Thomas Aquinas:
*. . . maledictus enim homo qui confidit in homine;*
(. . . cursed be the man that trusts in man;)

Lucy had rung after lunch to remind the Reverend Mother that the meeting was to take place in Captain Newenham's office which was situated in the Custom House. The Reverend Mother arrived by taxi and stood for a moment outside the building. Not even the fog could mar its beauty. Built at the spot where the north channel and the south channel of the River Lee diverged, it was a two-storied, three-bayed building, made from dressed limestone, and set over subterranean vaults. The recessed arcades had perfectly rounded arches and these were matched by the semi-circular tops of the three tall segmented windows on the next storey. The Reverend Mother gazed for a moment up at the Cork coat of arms on the pediment above the windows. *Statio Bene Fida Carinis*, it said beneath a carved picture of two castles sheltering a sailing boat.

A safe harbour for ships, she thought as she passed through the door opened for her with a flourish by a splendidly suited individual; a good harbour, but, perhaps not a good living place for a large number who inhabited crumbling houses built on top of the old marsh, not *bene* for those with bad lungs who breathed in the poisonous air of fog, smoke and gas fumes for most of the winter.

'Mr Newenham is expecting you, Reverend Mother,' said the official and politely preceded her up the carpeted stairway and then through the magnificently ornate boardroom. 'They are all in the Committee Room,' he said. He turned the handle of a door at the end of the boardroom and stepping in, announced, 'Reverend Mother Aquinas,' and then stepped back to allow her to enter.

'What a beautiful room,' she said politely as Robert Newenham advanced to meet her. The walls were panelled in wood to door height, with a pale cream and gold wallpaper above it and then delicately patterned ceilings. Here and there hung some impressive maritime pictures.

They do well for themselves, she thought as she shook hands with the committee that Lucy had organized. Yes, Thomas Browne, lately assistant to the assassinated James Doyle and now acting city engineer – he was there. And so was the bishop's secretary, Father de Courcy, a man of immense power, she had often heard it said. Little went on in the city of Cork without his knowledge. Apart from herself, Lucy was the only woman present and that, she thought with amusement, would suit her cousin. She had managed to have assembled, as far as the Reverend Mother could see, most of those who had been in James Doyle's retinue when he came to give a key speech at the market about the wisdom of building a grand new market to replace the old. Knowing Lucy, she would have arrived just at the minute when the meeting was due to end, got herself taken upstairs to Captain Newenham and then flattered and tricked everyone else into remaining for a short presentation of Reverend Mother Aquinas's latest charitable project.

'It's so good of you to come, Reverend Mother.' Lucy came forward to plant a light kiss on her cousin's cheek and then added, 'We're all admiring Mr Browne's proposal for the rebuilding of city hall.' The cluster of expensively-suited gentlemen moved obediently aside and the Reverend Mother saw that an easel had been set up, just where the light of the window would fall upon it. It was a marvellously-executed drawing, its decisive pen strokes delicately coloured in pastel shades.

For a moment, the Reverend Mother thought that it was a picture of Venice. The sky was a shade of sapphire blue, seldom seen in Cork. The river sparkled in the background and in front of it was a wonderfully baroque building, just as she had often admired in paintings of that city. Then she looked a little more closely at the background where the spire of St Fin Barre's Cathedral rose against that eastern sky and where the cabins of Barrack Street, artistically depicted as picturesque rather than sordid, trailed uphill, muted and slightly smudged, as insubstantial as clouds in the sky.

'Why, it must be drawn from the Grand Parade,' she exclaimed.

'That's right.' Lucy was beside her. 'You see, Mr Browne thought that the Grand Parade would be an ideal approach to the city hall, instead of having it stuck on Albert Quay, out of the town like the old place.'

'What I propose, Reverend Mother, is that a portion of the Lee would be arched over.' Thomas Browne was brimming over with excitement and confidence. 'And then,' he continued, 'there could be a fine square built in front of the building, and the Grand Parade itself could be planted with trees on either side. It would be truly a parade then, and the fountain would form a wonderful centrepiece.'

On the window seat beside the easel, half rolled up, was another drawing. The Reverend Mother could see that it, also, was a proposal for the rebuilding of the city hall. The name JAMES DOYLE was printed on the back of the sheet. It was slightly squashed in the middle as though carelessly thrown aside. It would, she thought, looking sideways at it, have made use of the original site at Albert Quay and would doubtless have been far cheaper than this grandiose plan for the new city hall.

'It seems a wonderfully ambitious scheme,' she said turning her eyes back to the glittering prospect on the easel. If money was found to do this, then Thomas Browne's name would become famous throughout Ireland and Britain, and even throughout Europe, perhaps. It would, of course, mean that the scheme to rehouse the people living in houses on the marsh would have to be abandoned. And, doubtless, the rebuilding of the library would have to be postponed till some later date. But it was, she had to admit, a stroke of genius to envisage turning the present ramshackle aspect of the Grand Parade, which was, as Mr Browne rightly remarked, presently used as a parking and dumping place, into something to rival the Champs-Élysées in Paris.

'Marvellous,' she said again. Had he, she thought as he

politely pulled out a chair for her, ever mentioned this plan to the now dead city engineer? No doubt he had. A drawing like that could not have been executed in a few short days without months of previous planning. And if he had proposed that idea, had he been rejected?

Or had he, she suddenly thought as she turned an attentive face towards Lucy who had taken it upon herself to chair this meeting, had he decided that the plan was too good, too original, to be handed over to his superior? Perhaps, during the dark winter evenings he had brooded on this sunlit image and had thought, *If only I were city engineer . . .*

'So when the Reverend Mother talked to me about extending the education of those poor girls, I wondered if there was any way that I could help her, and I had a chat with Captain Newenham.' She flashed a smile at her distant cousin and he looked immensely flattered. 'We put our heads together and thought the forthcoming reopening of Roches Stores could be a venue to raise funds, and, now,' said Lucy with the air of someone who has just had a brainwave, 'I have suddenly thought of a most brilliant idea. Why don't we display that wonderful, inspirational picture to the people of Cork and get their opinions on the future of the city?' She beamed all around and there was a murmur of excitement. Everyone, including Robert Newenham, of course, wanted to be closely associated with this exciting project. Her own little project would provide a cover for these gentlemen to aggrandize their own ambitions. Thomas Browne gazed ahead, with a certain detachment, but there was a curve to his well-cut mouth and a sparkle in those dark eyes. He had the look of a man for whom a dream was about to come true.

'I'll just ask the Reverend Mother to explain her ideas to us; I know she will do it so much better than I,' said Lucy modestly and then listened enraptured, occasionally sighing in ecstasy when names like Caruso and the Irish tenor John McCormack were mentioned.

'And this will all be for the sake of extending the education of these girls, is that right, Reverend Mother?' The overweight committee member who asked the question was deferential, but others around the table looked at him in shocked surprise.

'I'm sure that the Reverend Mother will make very good use of the money,' said Lucy gently but reproachfully.

'Yes, yes, I know that. It was just that I didn't . . . we don't want . . . want to encourage . . .' Conscious of the eyes of all those around the table fixed on him, he ground to a halt. 'Yes, I'm sure that the Reverend Mother will make very good use of the money,' he agreed deferentially.

'Thank you,' said the Reverend Mother gravely. And never, she thought, would she divulge that her main aim with this project was to provide evenings of fun in order to keep young girls off the streets and the quays of night-time Cork; a city, she had heard once, which had more prostitution than most others in Europe.

Her eyes ranged over the prosperous, well-fed faces around the committee table. Thomas Browne's still glowed. The praise of his plans for the new city hall had gone to his head like a flask of good wine. Robert Newenham, the town planner, Captain Robert Newenham, the former distinguished member of the Dorsetshire Regiment, friend, perhaps of the notorious Captain Schulze, author of Cork city's destruction. And then there were the Barrys, Crawfords, Murphys, Clancys, Maguires, Lanes; they were all there, all eager to show themselves ready to be philanthropic towards the poor of the city. She would, she thought cynically, be happy to exploit them all with the aim of achieving her dreams. She sat there, trying to look humble, tucking her arms inside her sleeves, and allowing her cousin Lucy, wife of the foremost solicitor in Cork city and an accomplished do-gooder, to conduct the meeting along well-ordered lines.

Lucy really was handling matters well. Father de Courcy had constituted himself to be her secretary and was already furnished with a blotter, pen, ink pot and a sheaf of paper. He sat beside her left hand and from time to time turned to her respectfully. The Reverend Mother considered his flushed eager face thoughtfully from under the shadow of her wimple. A lady's man, she reckoned, and wondered what he would be like with other women, young women, women who were fifty years younger than Lucy. There had been an air of easy assurance in the way in which he had pulled out Lucy's chair, in the way that he bent over her, smiled at her. Some of those young priests were not suited for the life of celibacy. Looking at his high colour, his well-styled hair and his carefully brushed clothes, she wondered if he had slipped. Had been seen with a girl from the quays? Did he have a so-called housekeeper who was a wife in all but name to him? Did he have a little girl secreted in a country cottage whom he visited a couple of times a week? Was he that kind of man? Considering his fleshy under lip and the high complexion and the ardent light in his blue eyes, yes, she thought, yes, I do think that he is the sort of man who is very fond of women. And that would have been a very dangerous weakness in the bishop's secretary.

And, of course, James Doyle, the deceased city engineer, may have been a man who knew about things like that, a man who made it his business to find out something discreditable about people who had power to influence decisions about the city. There was no doubt that young Father de Courcy was quite a power behind the bishop's throne.

'The bishop,' he was saying now with great confidence, 'will be absolutely delighted to support a scheme like this. In fact, I can go so far, I believe, as to promise that his Lordship will be pleased to be present on the evening of the grand reopening of Roches Stores.'

There was a little buzz of interest at this. It would be a vitally important point to be able to put, on the invitations, that all would take place by the kind patronage of the Bishop of Cork, Dr Daniel Cohalan.

'This will ensure the success of the evening,' said Captain Newenham, and Thomas Browne's eyes wandered back once again to the splendid picture of the new city hall, which like a phoenix would arise from the ashes of the burning of Cork.

'If only Captain Schulze could see how such good is about to arise from such evil,' said the Reverend Mother aloud, and then looked around at the surprised faces. 'Have I got the name wrong?' she enquired. 'I thought it was a Captain Schulze who was in command when those Auxiliary troops behaved so disgracefully and set our city on fire?' She could, she thought, go as far as that. The bishop mightn't like it much but after all the British government had reluctantly accepted responsibility and had paid compensation.

She did not bother to even look towards the bishop's secretary. Her eyes, under their hooded lids were fixed on Robert Newenham. There was no doubt, she noted, that he was aware of her gaze and that he was uncomfortable at her sudden mention of the man.

'What about a small concert?' said Lucy, cleverly changing the subject. 'Nothing too long, just a short affair. Now, who could we persuade to lend their talent?'

Suggestions poured in and Father de Courcy scribbled enthusiastically. The Reverend Mother modestly contributed her suggestion about naming the event 'The Phoenix Evening', a suggestion which Lucy considered to be brilliant and which everyone else agreed to be a good idea. A businessman with his own printing works offered to print out cards of invitation and then Lucy summed up efficiently and the committee began to disperse.

'Want a lift home or have you other fish to fry?' said Lucy quietly in her ear as the Reverend Mother took another long look at the sketch of the splendid new building set against an azure sky, with the river and the hillside as a background and a magnificent square in front of it. One man's dream, she thought. Her thoughts strayed to Walter Raleigh, a man whose lifetime was spent in a dream of finding gold. He had set out from Cork on his last voyage to the West Indies, had been the cause of hundreds of deaths and had then died on the scaffold on his return to London. *Such men are dangerous*, quoted the Reverend Mother to herself. Would Thomas Browne have considered that the death of one rather unpleasant and venal man was a small price to pay for the fulfilment of his dream? With a slight sigh she turned back to her cousin.

'Oh, it's no problem, Mrs Murphy,' she said aloud. 'Please do not worry about me. I can easily get a taxi, or perhaps . . .?' Her eyes went to the tall figure standing rather awkwardly to one side of the genial crowd. His forehead was slightly knit, and his eyes were fixed on her as if puzzling over something. He was wondering, she thought, whether the mention of Captain Schulze was accidental, or whether the Reverend Mother,

reputed to be the repository of many secrets, had heard some
rumour about a connection between the two men. He came
forward very willingly, though, almost too willingly.

'Certainly, I shall be delighted to take the Reverend Mother
home,' he said.

'I just must call in at my dressmaker,' said Lucy, improvising
rapidly. 'And the shop will be closed unless I hurry, so if
you're sure that it will be no trouble, Captain Newenham . . .'

'There is no problem,' he said politely. 'I shall be only too
pleased. Perhaps you would care to take a look around the
building before you go, Reverend Mother. It's a splendid place.
I was so lucky to get an office here after the city hall burned
down.'

It was, she thought, possibly an invitation to divulge any
information that she might possess about the events on that
night of December 11th three years ago. If it were, the Reverend
Mother did not take it up. Let him wonder, she thought as she
exclaimed with pleasure at the prospect of seeing the rest of
Custom House.

The boardroom was even more magnificent than the
committee room, with pale cream and gold walls and a ceiling
of the palest blue, beautifully patterned with ornamental stucco.
The Reverend Mother admired it, but allowed herself to be
led to the river side of the Custom House, passing through
rows of clerks checking bills and glimpsing outside one
window the long line of dock workers waiting patiently for
the next ship to arrive in the hope of getting an unloading job.

'Fine-looking fellows, aren't they? You'd think that they
would find something better to do with their time rather than
lounge around here all day long,' he said as they passed on
up the stairs.

'Yes, they are big strong men,' she said mildly. It was no
part of her plan to argue with him. She wanted to lull him
into a sense of false security, convince him that her remark
at the meeting had been purely that of an old lady sighing
over the past.

'They have to pass a test before they are allowed to join
the queue. They have to lift a heavy weight of about sixty
stone before they are taken on.'

'I suppose that the burning down of the city caused a great drop in trade,' she remarked, noting that there were many empty desks among the clerks' positions in this room. 'What's above this room?' she asked, not waiting for a reply to her previous comment.

'That's some more storage space for when the vaults are full. They don't use it much these days.' His tone was absent-minded. She looked sideways at him through the transparent weave of her veil. It appeared to her that he was looking very intently at her. She sensed that he was trying to make up his mind about her. Did she know anything? Her reputation in the city was of one who knew many secrets. She looked him full in the face, knowing that her own expression would be enigmatic as always.

'That burning down of Cork was such a terrible thing,' she sighed. 'And of course what makes it even worse was that apparently, it was not just a matter of some drunken soldiers getting of control. No, I understand it was not that at all,' she went on, though he had said nothing to contradict her. 'Had you heard anything about that, Captain Newenham?'

'No,' he said abruptly. She saw his eyes go to the clerks. One man had just dipped a pen into the inkwell in front of him. The pen remained in the ink for a long moment while its owner turned around to look at another worker, standing at a desk behind him.

'The late city engineer, Mr Doyle, was most worried about that report of planned arson, for some reason,' she added, looking at him intently. 'I understand that he had some information about some list or other. Someone was telling me that there was a rumour that Captain Schulze referred to a list when there was an appeal to spare one shop.'

And now her bolt was shot. She was conscious of a slight tingling of apprehension, but then she remembered Mrs O'Mahony and forced herself to look casually out of one of the windows and then back again at him. His high-coloured face was a shade redder, she fancied, and the eyes were fixed intently upon her.

'Almost as though he had inside knowledge – so the rumour went, according to Dr Scher.' And now, surely he must react, she thought and braced herself, glad of the presence of the clerks. She would not, she thought prudently, accept his offer of a lift home in his Rolls Royce car. When they went downstairs again, she would insist on calling a taxi. It would be easy enough to pretend that she had said that in order to put her cousin's mind at rest. He was unlikely to argue too much. She watched him with interest and waited to see what he would say next.

Captain Newenham opened his mouth and then shut it again. He stood very still for a moment. The scratching of pens from behind them ceased. He cast a look around at the clerks and instantly pens began to move again.

'I wonder would you like to see upstairs. There is a magnificent view up the river towards Blackrock.' His tone was polite, but he did not look at her and averted his gaze when she turned her head.

Without waiting for an answer he ushered her towards a flight of steps, leading the way and switching on some lights as he went up the stairs.

Not much of a day for admiring the view, thought the Reverend Mother, as she followed him. There was a chime from the clock on the outside of the building and she reckoned that it must be about half-past five. The fog was thickening fast as the evening drew near and the smoke from the various buildings around the quays had condensed it to an almost impenetrable consistency. Nevertheless she followed him. She could not draw back now. She had to try to establish as much of the truth as she could.

There was no one in the top storey of the building, just a scurry of rats as they came up. And then something seemed to swing down in front of the Reverend Mother's eyes, still not used to the murky light. For a moment her heart stopped as what looked like a rope moved almost in front of her face, but a plaintive meow sounded in her ears and a large and very furry black cat, with enormous and luminous green eyes, dropped down at her feet.

'The men feed it,' said Captain Newenham, turning back. 'It's getting fat and lazy. Easier to eat crusts than to do its job and catch the rats.' He aimed the toe of his boot at the cat and instantly it hissed vehemently.

Didn't like him, thought the Reverend Mother. She remembered Lucy's words about Robert's father and his liking to
kill things. She made no remark, though. The cat was a match
for the town planner and with a contemptuous flick of its
tail, bounded up onto a high shelf and strolled along slightly
above their heads. The man took no notice. He seemed to
be concentrating on keeping so closely ahead of her that she
could not see where she was going.

'There you are,' he said after a few moments. 'Look at that
for a view.'

And then everything seemed to happen all at once. Robert
Newenham stepped back, almost brushing her cloak as he did
so. She had a confused impression of an open archway ahead
and then he shouted, 'Take care, Reverend Mother!' at the top
of his voice. The cat yowled and then jumped. The Reverend
Mother pulled back instinctively, realising that a large black
rat had run from beneath the floorboards. In an instant, the
cat had leaped upon it, catching the neck in its jaws.

And it was only then that the Reverend Mother realized that
between her and the open archway was a gaping hatch with
a winch for pulling up goods from ships below. She stepped
back further and without a word made her way to the top of
the steps. There were a couple of alarmed clerks at the foot
of the stairs, staring upwards.

'I'm perfectly all right,' she assured them. 'Just rather
stupidly went a bit too near the hatch. I think I gave Captain
Newenham a fright.' She did not look back, but holding on
to the rail she made her way back down the stairs towards
them. If she had fallen, the clerks would have borne witness
to the fact that Robert had shouted to her to take care, but
none, in the dim light, would have been able to see that she
had been pushed. She was uncertain whether any harm had
been meant to her. On the one hand, it would be feasible
that Robert Newenham was so used to the hatch that he might
not realize it could be a danger to a visitor. Nevertheless, it
was also possible that he had seen it as a way of getting rid
of a threat. As a soldier he would have been used to acting
swiftly on the impulse of a moment. She dismissed the
thought from her mind. Now she had to get safely away.

Later she would ponder on what was possibly an attempt to murder her.

'Perhaps,' she said calmly, 'one of you might be good enough to phone for a taxi for me.' She directed her request at a pimply-faced young man with a pen behind his ear and he nodded cheerfully and went clattering down the next flight of stairs. She turned then towards the captain and held out her hand.

'Goodbye, Captain Newenham, and thank you very much for showing me around this magnificent building. Don't worry about taking me home. I've just remembered that you live at the opposite side of town, at St Luke's Cross, isn't it? And I certainly don't want to take you out of your way.'

She had recovered her equilibrium more quickly than he did. His hand, in hers, trembled slightly and there was a clammy feel to its skin. Murder, she thought charitably, must be a stressful business, especially if you are new to it.

But the thought occurred to her as she sat in the back of the taxi that Robert Newenham had probably killed dozens, if not hundreds, during the Great War.

And, perhaps one more man after the war was well over.

# SIXTEEN

Alan Ellis
Reporter on *Cork Examiner*:

'There had been sporadic gunfire all evening and my ears
had grown so accustomed to it that I did not really notice
it. I then became aware of the thud of nearby explosions.
I knew by then what a bomb sounded like. There were
numerous groups of Auxiliaries, men recruited to make
up numbers in the depleted Royal Irish Constabulary.'

There was not much traffic on that Tuesday afternoon as
they sped away from the jail. From behind them came
the ear-splitting sound of the siren from the army lorry.
Eileen clung to Eamonn, her two arms wrapped tightly around
his waist, her head against the space between his shoulder
blades. And despite the dangers, despite her fear that Sam might
be caught, she was conscious of a thrill of excitement. She
loved to go fast and seeing the way Eamonn's bike wove its
way in and out of the early-evening traffic, she felt optimistically that they had a good chance of getting away from the
heavy lorry. It might, she thought, have been easier to evade
the large vehicle if he had decided to go the back routes through
Glasheen and Togher, but Eamonn was not a native of Cork
city and it was probably best for him to go the straightforward
route that was familiar to him. She turned her head and looked
over her shoulder. Danny, with Fred tied to him, was just behind
them and a little further back were Liam and Sam.

By the time that they reached Victoria Cross, the lorry had
almost caught up with Liam and Sam and she bit her lip in
agony of worry. Perhaps Sam should have gone with Eamonn.
His was the best bike.

Luckily there was not too much traffic at the crossroads and
they dashed across. The warning siren from the army lorry

had its effect and cars were pulling in to the side of the road. A man with a horse and cart were just ahead of them and the horse took fright and started to rear up in a dangerous fashion. Eamonn slipped neatly past, overtaking on the left-hand side. He was weaving erratically in and out of traffic now and she did not dare to look back again, but just clung tightly to him, body and head pressed against his back, doing her best not to impede him in any way. She briefly noticed the telephone exchange as they roared up the hill. Would the soldiers think of stopping there and phoning ahead to a Garda barracks? It would be a good idea but the thrill of the chase had overtaken the soldiers and the lorry's siren continued its raucous sounds.

Stupid, thought Eileen contemptuously. Didn't they realize that the diesel-belching monster could never overtake their lithe, swift bikes? What fun they would have tonight, she thought, imagining the telling of the tale to the others in the house and the applause and the laughter and the jokes and toasts. Perhaps one of the boys might slip down to the nearby public house for a few beers. The siren, she thought, contemptuously, was probably worse than useless. The incessant, deafening noise was confusing people, causing horses to panic and cars to swerve. Pedestrians began to cross the road and then, like frightened hens, turned back again. Horns blew, horses neighed and dogs barked hysterically.

We'll easily get away, thought Eileen as she snuggled into Eamonn's back. On the whole, whatever their political loyalties, the people of Cork were opposed to seeing citizens pursued by armed forces on their streets and roads. There were, she thought, several cars which could have got out of the way more quickly and one or two who had deliberately turned around in the middle of the road after the bikes had sped past.

And then came a piece of the most appalling bad luck. As they roared up the hill and passed through Dennehy's Cross, above the sound of the siren and the blowing of car horns, came a deep, sombre note. The church bell was ringing. Eileen sensed how Eamonn slowed down. She straightened up and peeped over his shoulder.

Coming out of the entrance to Christ the King church was a hearse and behind it, dressed in solemn black, came the mourners, two by two, a weeping woman supported by a teenage boy, behind her two priests and then a procession of men, women and some children.

And behind them, moving at walking speed, was a procession of cars and horses and carts.

Eileen was a city girl and she knew what these city funerals were like. Every single one of the neighbours, every friend, everyone who knew the deceased, everyone who knew any of the mourners, everyone who lived in the immediate neighbourhood of the church; all of these would be attending. It might take at least fifteen minutes for the procession to come out from the church.

And after that there would be the long slow walk up the hill towards the cemetery.

Eamonn did not hesitate. Immediately he swung to the left, bumping his machine onto the pavement. A minute later she saw, from over her shoulder, that Danny and the wounded Fred had joined him and then there was another roar in her ear and she hoped that Liam, carrying Sam, had also got onto the pavement. She could not be sure, however, because there was a scream from a woman at a gate and a yell of, 'Get off that pavement, you young hooligans!'

Eamonn lurched back onto the road. Looking back Eileen could see that the hearse, with its coffin and its wreaths, was now about a hundred yards behind them. The road ahead had only the usual traffic. There was no sign of the lorry. She breathed a sigh of relief. Perhaps the funeral was a lucky break for them. There was no way in which that big heavy lorry could travel on the pavement. She managed to take a look backwards. A second, and then a third motorbike had emerged onto the road and now they were all on a clear road racing up towards Wilton. They swung onto the Bishopstown Road without a problem. This was well outside the town and the traffic was light at this hour in the evening. If only the funeral could hold up the lorry. There was a great respect for funerals in the city. Perhaps the Free State troops would decide that they should stay behind. Eileen began to wish that she still believed in prayer. It would, she thought, be a great blessing to be able to breathe a Hail Mary and have confidence that

the request would be listened to. But it was no good. Another
glance over her shoulder made her heart sink. The funeral
party, despite their deep mourning, had moved to the side of
the road and had allowed the insistent klaxon of the siren to
override their grief.

The lorry load of soldiers was still on their tail, and no
doubt they were still resolute about capturing these six people
who had rushed out of the gaol and had made their getaway
on motorbikes. Whether they knew or not that a man called
Sam O'Mahony, accused of murder, had fled the gaol, she did
not know, but she could imagine their triumph when they
discovered that one of the six was dressed in a prison uniform.
She cast an agonized glance over her shoulder. She so intensely
wished that she had her own motorcycle and that she could
ride it. If only she had Sam behind her, she felt that she
would be capable of any feat in order to escape recapture and
possible death sentence.

The three motorbikes were now quite near to each other
as they roared along the almost deserted road of Bishopstown.
But the lorry was not that far behind and in the absence of
other traffic it was making good progress. They reached
Hawkes Road and then swung on to Waterfall Road. Now
they were out into the empty roads of the countryside and it
would be a matter of who could go the fastest and whether
the motorbikes could outstrip the lorry sufficiently in order
to risk betraying their place of refuge by turning off to
Ballinhassig.

A nice long stretch, but it benefitted the lorry even more
than the motorbikes. Their advantage had come and gone
amongst city traffic where they could weave in and out, but
here where there was no other vehicle to be seen, their chances
of escape began to diminish. There was an ominous, clonking
sound from the engine of Eamonn's bike, almost as though it
were protesting at the rough usage that it had been subjected
to. Eileen did not dare to look back. Eamonn's bike was
lovingly maintained by its owner; she was not sure that Liam
paid that much attention to his.

They were now heading steadily down the Waterfall Road,
going underneath the viaduct where the railway between the

city and Bandon ran above the road. Another few miles and they would be able to turn off to Ballinhassig.

But while the lorry was on their trail, they dared not betray their hiding place to the enemy. Eileen wished that there was a possibility of talking, of a discussion of what might be the best thing to do, but that was impossible with the high-pitched whine from the three motorbikes and in the distance the roar of the diesel engine, punctuated by the beat of the siren.

But the lorry sound was beginning to fade. For a moment Eileen thought that it was her imagination; that it was just wishful thinking, but after a minute of careful listening, she began to feel her courage returning. There was no doubt that the sound had diminished. Perhaps, after all, they would be able to turn off on to the Ballinhassig Road. In any case, Eamonn was clever and quick-thinking. She had little doubt that he had some plan in his mind as they sped along at a speed that whipped her bobbed hair straight back from her head and made her cheeks burn with the wind. It was good to be out of the city, she thought. Not a trace of fog, just clean fresh air blowing in from the Atlantic. She glanced over her shoulder. She could see the other two bikes quite near to them. Danny, with the wounded Fred behind him, had moved out into the middle of the road. Eamonn glanced in his mirror and then pulled in a little, allowing Danny to overtake. For a moment Eileen worried. Why was Danny overtaking? Had Fred's wound started to bleed, again? But she had a glance at him as they passed and his head was up and he seemed alert.

Then a new sound came to her ears and she realized why Danny had overtaken them. He, alone, must have heard it. It was not the lorry. This sound was coming from ahead of them, ahead and to the right. A clattering sound and then the sudden beep-beep of an alarm.

They rounded a corner and Eileen heard herself cry out in dismay. She had forgotten all about the level crossing. Lights were flashing. Danny's motorbike accelerated. An official came out from the small cottage on the side of the road. He was carrying a lantern, a warning light which cast a red beam on the road. Danny shot past him, and the man shouted something after him, but it was too late. Danny's bike had bumped across the railway line and had gone speeding down the road before the other two bikes came up.

It was too late for them. The gates had shut with a clang. The man gave a sour nod at them as they pulled up with a squeal of brakes and then went back into his cottage. A clear plume of blue-grey smoke rose up from the chimney and Eileen could picture him sitting in front of a cosy fire, perhaps eating his supper, and waiting for the parting shriek of the train before he came out again to reopen the gates.

'Quick!' she said urgently in Eamonn's ear. 'Let's get off the road.' She swung a leg over the pillion seat and was on the ground, looking all around for the best place to hide.

He understood her point straight away. Once the lorry came up, they would be like sitting ducks, stuck in front of a barrier with ten rifles aimed at them. In a second he too had slipped off the bike and was pushing his machine towards a gap in the roadside hedge. Eileen delayed only long enough to signal frantically to Liam and then she was behind the bike, helping to push it over some very uneven ground and into the field. A herd of cows had broken through here, she thought and blessed them, though the ground beneath their feet was boggy and uneven. A sharp smell of water mint came to her nostrils and then they were through and on the other side. A minute later Sam and Liam had joined them and all four looked around them in dismay.

It was a terrible field. Some careless farmer had overwintered his cows in it and the land had turned into a sea of mud, pitted with humps and hollows. There would be no prospect of even pushing the bikes through it and it would be impossible to ride across it.

'Let's scatter,' said Eamonn. 'That will confuse the issue. No point in keeping together. We'll meet up at the house after dark.'

'I'm taking Sam to the hiding place,' said Eileen defiantly. He was a city boy and he had no knowledge of this place. During the year when she had been a Republican Volunteer, hiding out in the safe house, Eileen had developed a good knowledge of the surrounding countryside. Now she was sure that she could see, in the distance, Goggin's Hill. She was looking at it from an unfamiliar angle, but screwing up her eyes she could just see the viaduct where the train entered the tunnel.

'See you tonight,' she said firmly and seized Sam's hand and began to set a quick pace up the side of the field, keeping close to the hedge. Eamonn and Liam were heaping the remains of a mouldy bale of hay over the two bikes. When they had hidden them completely they would probably scatter; one man by himself in this farming community was much less noticeable than a pair, but she had to take care of Sam. She was beginning to shiver; Sister Mary Immaculate's bloomers, though made from the best flannel, were not as warm and windproof as the tweed breeches and the threadbare, ancient shawl was nothing but a nuisance. Still she dared not discard it; the bright pink of those wretched bloomers would show up in this countryside of browns and greens. *What can't be cured must be endured*; where had she heard that? And then she remembered the Reverend Mother had set the top class an essay with this title, followed by the word 'discuss'. She had been very pleased when Eileen had argued vehemently against this spiritless acceptance of the status quo, though she had forced her to defend her thesis against the rest of the girls, and the Reverend Mother herself. It was, remembered Eileen, after that the idea of going to university with a Honan scholarship had been introduced.

'Run!' she whispered to Sam as she pushed her way through one of the badly maintained hedges. Now they were in a straight line to Goggin's Hill. She could see the church tower in the village of Ballinhassig and Waterfall Ridge was clearly visible.

When they reached the field where Aoife and she had picked the cowslips only a few days ago she heard a new sound, over and above the monotonous sound of the siren in the lorry. She had giggled a little at the insistent raucous note. What did those stupid soldiers think that the man at the crossing could do? Everyone knew that it was impossible to stop a train at a moment's notice. The lorry would have to wait its turn before going through. But now quite suddenly the siren was switched off. The noise was gone and only the singing of a thrush on a bare, leafless ash tree could be heard.

Had they been seen?

The sudden cessation of noise was almost more shocking than the previous wailing, uneven note that had been in their ears for what seemed like hours. Eileen dragged Sam towards the ditch.

She was straining her ears for a sound and when it came she knew that her worst fears had been realized. Triumphant shouts! The bikes had been discovered. Could she possibly get Sam into the underground tunnel before the soldiers captured them? It crossed her mind briefly that she could go to prison for the crime of helping a prisoner to escape. She eyed the ash tree. For one who had spent her childhood swarming up slippery, dripping wet gas lamp posts, *waxing a gazza,* as they said in Barrack Street, this did not present much of a challenge.

If only she were not wearing those pink bloomers and the threadbare shawl that fluttered in every breeze. No good asking Sam, she thought reluctantly. His eyesight, even with his glasses, was very poor and he did not seem too competent in getting up the sloping field and tended to trip over clods of earth and random stones.

Swiftly she dropped the shawl and put a stone on it so that it would not blow away. She had thought of a use for it. And then, heroically, she stepped into the ditch and smeared the bloomers with some rich brown liquid mud. The magnificent elastic stood up to the extra weight but they began to feel cold and clammy and she could feel the wet penetrate her own drawers. Still she couldn't bother about that and at least her feet, inside her woollen socks and her knee-high boots were cosily warm.

'Wait here. Keep down,' she whispered to Sam and then cautiously began to scale the ash tree. There were some ten soldiers in full uniform climbing the hill about five hundred yards away from them. They were, she thought with relief as she climbed back down again, following the trail left by Eamonn and Liam and had not seen herself and Sam.

Carefully, Eileen arranged her shawl over a low, squat black-thorn bush and then seized Sam's hand. He seemed to be mesmerized by the sight of the soldiers on the hill.

'Quick,' she said. 'Quick, while they are searching on the other side of the hill.' He muttered something, but she ignored him, ducking through a gate and setting off in a different direction, moving in a semi-circular fashion around the side of the hillside. If they saw the shawl they would go straight up, she reckoned. They would not expect them to have gone back down the hill and then in a different direction. It was taking a risk, but she had to get them off the trail of Eamonn and Liam. She and Sam would have the perfect hiding place once they reached the field with the tunnel hatch.

And luck was with them. By the time that they had reached the far side of the field, it had begun to rain, a steady, heavy drizzle which would reduce visibility to a matter of yards. Quickly she found a cow-sized gap in the hedge and edged her way through the sprouting brambles. She was chilled through, but a feeling of triumph was beginning to rise within her. If they could get safely to the top of the field in the dense shelter of this untidy hedge, then they could turn back again and go into the shaft that led down to the tunnel. She could feel beneath her feet the vibration of the train. That must be the one that had closed the road to them.

'Wish that I had never taken part in this tomfoolery,' muttered Sam from behind her. She turned around sharply and saw him stop to clear the rain from his glasses. She thought of saying something, of retorting that they all had risked their lives for him, that two valuable motorbikes would now probably be lost and possibly their safe house be discovered. Tom Hurley would be rightly furious if he found out how they had put everything at risk for someone who was not even a member of their organisation. It was not the moment for a row, though. The job had to be finished, the mission accomplished. Without another glance at him she went on moving fast, but keeping her head down to below hedge level. She hoped that he had the sense to do likewise.

In the distance she heard a shot. And then another and another. Were the soldiers firing at a moving target, or just firing out of frustration? There was talk that the army was quite untrained, quite undisciplined. There had been an article in the *Cork Examiner* and in the *Irish Times* saying that once the civil war was over their numbers would be cut.

All of the crowd at Ballinhassig had cheered wildly at that announcement. The army were a nuisance to them, too trigger-happy, said Eamonn disapprovingly. The police were more predictable and could be relied upon to keep the law.

A few more shots – no, she doubted that they had managed to capture Eamonn and Liam. These shots sounded random. 'Give yerselves up,' shouted a voice in a strong Kerry accent, but there was no reply and a moment later a few shots again. They hadn't seen her shawl, she thought. They were still occupied over at the far side of the hill. They must have sighted Eamonn and Liam going up the hill. Thank God, she thought as she turned around to make sure that Sam was following her, thank God that Fred was not with them, a chase across a hillside in the rain would be no place for a man with a bullet in his arm. Danny, she thought with admiration, had been quick thinking and decisive when he had overtaken them on the road and had courageously sped through the closing barrier. She glanced back at Sam, who had once more stopped to wipe his glasses. A man for peacetime, perhaps, but he appeared poor-spirited, now, in comparison with Eamonn and the others.

'Come on,' she said shortly. 'We can't hang around. We might as well get you safe.'

He didn't respond and she gave him an annoyed glance. Did he realize how much she had sacrificed for him? And how she had induced four idealistic nationalistic young men to hazard their lives, which they had sworn to devote to the ideal of a free Ireland, to risking all to liberate a young man who did not sympathize with their views, who was against all they stood for. And who had little sympathy with their conviction that only an armed struggle would obtain a republic where there would be justice for all, rich and poor. She swallowed hard. The enterprise had been planned and dictated by her; her friends had agreed to it out of affection for her and she had to bring it to a successful conclusion.

'Come on, Sam,' she said gently. 'It's not too far now. Do you see that blackthorn bush over there? We must get across there without being seen.'

Important, she thought, not just for Sam's safety, but for the future of her unit at Ballinhassig.

'Bend down,' she said urgently. 'Make sure that you stay down. Don't betray us, will you?'

She saw him look slightly taken aback, but she said no more, just set an example by getting down upon her hands and knees and beginning a slow and careful crawl across the field. For a few yards, she was imbued with energy, but then the wet, prickly rushes and thistles abraded the skin on her knees and the palms of her hands and the muscles in her thighs ached fiercely. From time to time she glanced back at him. He was lagging dangerously behind her, but she dared not call out to him. They might be within sight and hearing of the soldiers and she was determined not to be instrumental in betraying their hiding place.

By the time she reached the blackthorn bush, every muscle was trembling. However there was no sound from the soldiers, not even a shot, now. Perhaps they had gone back to their lorry, had given up the chase. If there really is a God then He should look after Eamonn and Liam, of course. But Eamonn was a very good boy. He had a fierce and burning love for his country and great plans for its future. He had obtained first honours at the end of his first year at university, had come top of the whole class but had thrown away the prospect of a happy and successful and prosperous life, in order to sacrifice himself to the goal of Ireland's freedom as a republic. Liam, too. None of them was from as poor a background as she. All of them had made far more sacrifices than she had done.

'Keep down,' she hissed back at Sam. He had stopped and tried to straighten up. It was unlikely that he would be seen with his dark prison uniform, now thoroughly soaked through, and his black hair. Nevertheless, she was not willing to run any risks. They had all sworn to keep this tunnel shaft a secret and only to use it in the case of a dire emergency.

There was still no sound when they reached the blackthorn bush. Eileen longed to stand up for a moment and to stretch, but she dared not do it. She wriggled across the wet grass, keeping her head down, until she was lying full length beside the open mouth of the shaft. A smell of smoke came up to her nostrils, but there was now only a distant rumble to be heard. The train was speeding on its way to Ballinhassig Station and from there would go on to Bandon. There would not be another one for a whole hour. They had timed these trains, she and Aoife, lying up there, tucked snuggly into a tarpaulin with Eamonn's watch and a piece of paper and a volume of Yeats' poetry to pass the time.

The ladder had been well fixed to the wall and was easy to climb down. The bloomers were still clammily wet and it was a relief to be able to move as quickly as she wanted to go. Eileen was down it in a flash and then waited impatiently as Sam fumbled his way down, occasionally missing a step and once dangling for a moment by his arms. Eileen's heart skipped a beat. If he fell, he would break a leg, or even his neck. Had he never swarmed up and down gas posts when he was young, she thought impatiently. His mother, she supposed, kept him indoors and away from rough boys of the neighbourhood. He would have been mocked. Going to a posh school, wearing a smart blazer and, of course, the glasses would not have helped.

'Is this place safe?' he asked when he got down. She could hear him, but not see him. The tunnel was quite dark to her just now, but she knew that after a few minutes her eyes would adjust and the faint circle of light that came from the top of the shaft would help to illuminate their surroundings. She made no reply. It was, she thought, a stupid question. What's safety, she thought. She didn't think that she had ever felt safe. Perhaps when she was a baby. But once she had reached the age of five or six, she could remember worrying with her mother whether they had enough money, in the vase on the mantelpiece, to pay the rent man at the end of the week and the anguish when a rat had stolen half a loaf of bread that had been left to her care. She had been terrified of rats and been unable to compel herself to defend the bread. And, of course, she could remember the terror of coming from school and finding street battles going on, men with machine guns blocking her way home.

'How long will we have to stay here?' There was a petulant note in his voice and once again she did not reply. There was a lump of disappointment, heavy as lead, within her. Fred had been injured. Eamonn and Liam may have been caught, their safe house may have been imperilled and worst of all, Sam, for whom she had done everything, seemed to be angry, almost as though he wished that she had left him in peace within his prison.

And then a shot rang out, and then another and another. They were coming nearer, the sound was magnified by the tunnel. And then a voice shouted out, 'We can see you. Come out with yer hands above yer heads.' Sam made a restless movement, but she touched his arm and stayed very still, her back against the wall. The men were bluffing. They had not seen the tunnel with its protective screen of blackthorn.

They were firing into the bush, though she guessed they would not see the entrance hole to the shaft as the thorny branches that she and Aoife had so carefully monitored covered it completely unless you were beside it. Nevertheless, a bullet struck the side of the stone-lined shaft and fell at their feet, rolling over and striking the iron rails of the line below the narrow safety platform. More bullets overhead. Eileen made up her mind. Sooner or later the soldiers would tire of this and then they would do one of two things. Either they would go off to search another field, or else they would investigate the bush to see whether there might be a dead body there, which would undoubtedly mean they would discover the shaft and its ladder. She and Sam would be sitting ducks once that happened. She glanced around. Her night vision had come to her. The tunnel was now palely grey. It was, she remembered, reputed to be nine hundred feet long and the shaft was about halfway along it.

'Come on, let's get out of here,' she whispered in Sam's ear.

# SEVENTEEN

St Thomas Aquinas:
*. . . maius est contemplata allis tradere quam solum
contemplare*
(. . . it is better to convey your thoughts to someone,
rather than merely to contemplate)

'Have you heard the news, Reverend Mother?' Sister
Bernadette was bubbling over with excitement as she
brought in the monthly butcher and baker bills for
her superior to enter the amounts in her accounts book and to
write cheques. The last Tuesday evening in the month was
known throughout the convent as the time when the Reverend
Mother paid bills, added up the running costs of the convent
and of the school. Tuesday evening was when she was shut
up in her room and was not to be disturbed unless for some
serious reason. Sister Bernadette, however, stood her ground,
despite a frosty look from the Reverend Mother.

'The postman told me all about it when he brought the
letters this afternoon whilst you were out,' said Sister Bernadette
undeterred. 'It seems that Sam O'Mahony was a member of
the Republicans, after all. They sprung him from the gaol.
That's what the postman said,' she finished, hastily disclaiming
responsibility for the slang expression which might incur the
displeasure of the Reverend Mother. 'And,' she continued, 'his
own mother committed suicide. Or so the butcher told him.
She took rat poison, so they say.'

'Thank you, Sister Bernadette.' She waited until the lay
sister had gone off, leaving untidy sheaves of bills lying on
her desk and then she sat back.

And so that suicide was unnecessary. The woman's son had
now been released from prison. Did Mrs O'Mahony know that
Sam was a member of the Republican Party? If she did know,
then it would have been strange that she despaired so quickly.

The Republicans had a reputation for daring releases. There had been a few already from the gaol and many from the police station. But did she know? Had Sam kept this a secret from her? He may have done, but after all, they were very close, mother and son. According to Dr Scher they shared one small, two-roomed attic, the mother sleeping in the kitchen/living room and Sam in a small closet-like bedroom. If he were a member, it would seem almost impossible that a bright, intelligent woman like Mrs O'Mahony would not know such a thing about her son.

But was he?

Disregarding the pile of bills on her desk, the Reverend Mother opened a drawer and took from it the three copy books that Mrs O'Mahony had wrapped up for her not long before her terrible death. She had never met Sam O'Mahony but she had before her the fruits of his brain. He conveyed his thoughts clearly and well, she thought. The articles started with the conventional writing up of funerals, though even with these there was a flavour of his personality, and then moving on rapidly to more individual expressions of beliefs and opinions. The Reverend Mother's eye lingered over an article about the murder of an RIC man, a policeman working for the English instituted Royal Irish Constabulary, but a Cork man born and bred. Sam had written movingly about the man's last morning, about his walk down St Patrick Street, about the last recorded conversation with a friend when he had chatted about collecting his bicycle, about his visit to the English Market to buy some drisheen for his supper that night. About his trip out to catch fish from the River Lee. It was well done, thought the Reverend Mother. She remembered Shylock's passionate outcry in Shakespeare's *Merchant of Venice*. 'Hath not a Jew eyes . . . if you prick us, do we not bleed?' Sam, a well-educated young man, had used the same plea for this murdered RIC officer. A man, he seemed to say in his article, a man like others; a man who was part of humanity. Why had he to lose his life for the sake of a doctrinaire philosophy? She mused over the article for a moment. Was it likely that a man who wrote this, and wrote it with passionate sincerity, would be a member of the Republican Party? She thought it unlikely.

Abandoning her accounts she went swiftly down the corridor and dialled a number.

Dr Scher's housekeeper was sure that he would want to speak with the Reverend Mother. No, he was not seeing a patient. He was, confided the housekeeper, just having a cup of tea and sitting beside his stove, reading the *Cork Examiner*. She was back two minutes later with the message that Dr Scher had been meaning to visit Sister Assumpta and could be at the convent in ten minutes, if that would suit her.

The Reverend Mother went back into her room and with sudden decision, gathered all the bills into a neat pile, slipped a rubber band around them and tidied them, and her accounts book, into a drawer. Then she went back to reading those pasted-in articles, a tribute to a mother's love, but also a window into the son's mind. She read through them all with her usual speed, from time to time marking ones of special interest. She had just finished when she heard Sister Bernadette in the corridor, responding gaily to Dr Scher's mellow baritone. And then a lower, deeper voice said something and the Reverend Mother raised her head. Patrick, also, had come.

'Patrick has a message for you,' were Dr Scher's first words once Sister Bernadette had left the room leaving the two visitors behind. 'He wanted to bring it himself.'

'There was no full stop after the word "on" in the message, that's right, isn't it?' said the Reverend Mother. Her mind was full of sombre thoughts, but she could not resist a slight smile at the disappointed expression on Dr Scher's face.

'Has anyone ever told you, Reverend Mother, that this habit of yours of always knowing everything is extremely annoying? Patrick, of course, is too polite to say so, but I'm sure that he is very disappointed after coming all the way over here at my request and then not even being allowed to deliver his message. And he an inspector in charge of this case.' Dr Scher patted Patrick's shoulder with heavy-handed sympathy.

'I'll bear that in mind,' she said and then said gravely, 'it is, as I am sure that you both appreciate, an extremely important point. "I cannot go on", followed by a full stop might indeed be interpreted as a suicide note, but "I cannot go on" without a full stop could be followed by any number of phrases.' She gazed thoughtfully at him. Dr Scher was looking a little puzzled, but Patrick's eyes were alert and speculative.

'In this case,' she went on, 'I venture to think that these words could have been followed by something like "reading these articles over and over again". Yes, I think that would fit quite well with the fact that she had already packed up the three copy books with the articles pasted into them.'

'Strange, isn't it, that she sent these to you? Why do you think that she did that?'

The Reverend Mother paused. Not even to Dr Scher, and certainly not to Patrick, would she disclose the proposition that the dead woman had made to her. That was between her and God now, she thought.

'Perhaps,' she said, 'she assumed that I would be interested.'

'More likely she thought that one of the articles contained a key to a possible murderer, to someone other than her son. What do you think, Patrick? She was a smart woman, so they say. She may have felt that you would be a good person to advise her, may have been interested in your opinion, in whether you, also, had picked out the article that had taken her attention. If she didn't commit suicide, then she would be trying desperately to do something to help her son.' Dr Scher's eyes were bright with this new insight.

'It's possible,' admitted Patrick. 'Which is the book with the latest articles in it?'

The Reverend Mother picked up the top copy book on the little pile. 'This one begins in last May, and, of course ends in October when Sam was sacked from the *Cork Examiner*.'

'Well, this will be the one,' Dr Scher said with conviction. 'What do you think, Patrick? It should show us what way her mind was working.' He turned to the last page and looked up at the Reverend Mother. 'I suppose you've read the article that got Sam fired from the *Cork Examiner*, any clues in that?'

The Reverend Mother shook her head sadly.

'I wonder what made him write it?' said Dr Scher. 'I remember reading it and thinking that the *Examiner* could not keep him on after that. He named the man as well as the office. It was the height of stupidity. Of course he was, between ourselves, saying no more than they were saying in every hotel bar and public house in the town, but you'd think he would have been more careful, wouldn't you, Reverend Mother?'

'Very unwise,' she said, 'but of course he was very young. And he had probably begun to be more and more arrogant. If you look back, in the earlier articles he was more inclined to attack the Republicans, and I must say that he spoke out courageously and boldly against violence, but in the later months, before he lost his job, he had changed the focus of his articles. He had begun by attacking the shoddy work of some anonymous builders, had then moved on to veiled hints about corruption in high places, had even written an article attacking the town planning office, all carefully couched in a series of questions which he declared had been put to him by some "man in the street" about the town planning office—'

'Let me read that one,' interrupted Dr Scher. He leafed through the book and then thrust it impatiently at her. She found the article instantly and handed it to him, surreptitiously straightening a bent-over corner as she did so.

'Hmm,' he said, fumbling for his glasses and then focussing on the print. 'You know, of course, that Robert Newenham, the town planner, was standing just beside James Doyle when he was shot? That's right, isn't it, Patrick?' he said after a moment.

'So I noticed,' said the Reverend Mother placidly. 'As were also many others,' she added.

'This is clever; did you notice how he implies that there was some sort of old boy relationship between Robert Newenham and the late James Doyle. Do you think that they went to school together?'

'Hardly,' said the Reverend Mother, suppressing a smile. Dr Scher, she thought, was still quite naïve about the class structure in Cork city. He and Patrick were looking at her hopefully, but she shook her head. 'Mr Doyle, I understand, went to the local Model School in Anglesea Street, and Mr Newenham, someone told me, went to school in England.'

'But the city engineer would have had to get the permission from the town planner,' said Patrick. 'This article implies that the engineer had the planner in his pocket. Do you think that he bribed him?'

'I have heard that the post of city engineer is not very highly paid,' said the Reverend Mother. 'In fact,' she said, picking her words carefully, 'I understand that there are various rumours that James Doyle was a man who took bribes rather than gave them.' She had a moment's compunction about passing on Lucy's gossip, but reflected that her patron saint, Thomas Aquinas, had advised that it was better to pass on a contemplated truth, rather than merely to contemplate. After her experience yesterday, she was almost certain that there was a strong reason why Robert Newenham had meekly done James Doyle's bidding, and had fallen in with all his corrupt plans for allowing wealthy builders to become even wealthier during the rebuilding of Cork. His violent reaction to the mention of Captain Schulze seemed to point to something more akin to blackmail. She wrestled with her conscience only for a second. Even if Sam had been rescued from the gaol by the Republicans, his re-arrest, followed by a trial, still hung over his head. She owed it to him, and to Patrick, to help as much as possible to uncover the facts around this assassination or murder of James Doyle.

'It has come to my ears,' she said carefully, 'that there was an association between Captain Schulze, commander of the Black and Tans here in Cork, and Captain Newenham. Both served in the Dorsetshire Regiment during the last war.'

Both men stared at her with interest. Patrick was the first to find his voice.

'I heard it said that the Black and Tans were supposed to have had a list . . .'

The Reverend Mother smiled with pride at her former pupil. She said nothing, however. Lucy fed her information, but trusted her implicitly to keep her sources to herself.

'And if there were a list,' said Dr Scher triumphantly, 'well, then, who better to write it than the town planner who would know every shop, every business place—'

'And every man's religion,' put in Patrick. 'They say that they just burned the business and homes of Catholics and left those owned by Protestants untouched. But that is over two years ago, though, isn't it?' he ended with a note of doubt in his mind.

'Memories are still very strong,' said the Reverend Mother. 'There is a lot of bitterness about what happened.'

'And the lack of progress since,' said Patrick, nodding his head.

'It was an interesting collection of people there at the English Market last Friday.' The Reverend Mother reflected for a moment while they looked at her. 'You see,' she went on, 'there would be no legal objection to the town planner giving a list of businesses in the city to a man who, at the time, was in command of what was reckoned to be a police force. In the privacy of this room, we may speculate about that possibility, but no legal action would be taken against him for providing such a list. But, of course, in the eyes of the Republicans, and indeed, perhaps in the eyes of many who had suffered so badly on that terrible night, this would seem a heinous crime.'

'So if Captain Newenham felt threatened by James Doyle, perhaps James Doyle even whispered a threat that he would have a word with the man in the raincoat and the slouch hat, unless the hush money was increased, then Captain Newenham might decide to get rid of him while there was a crowd all around him.'

'And spotting Sam O'Mahony standing there, he thought that the police hunt for a killer could be neatly diverted to this man who would be expected to hate James Doyle, the person who had caused him to lose his job.'

'And, of course, Captain Newenham would dislike Sam because of that article on the *Examiner*.' The Reverend Mother completed the case and then thought about it. There were three questions, she thought. Was Robert Newenham capable of murder? Could he have thought and acted so quickly? And thirdly, would a threat of disclosure to the Republicans be enough to warrant murder?

The answer to all three questions, she thought, was in the affirmative.

'He had been in the army, was the sort of man who would carry a pistol, and who would possess a British army pistol,' said Patrick watching her. 'And anyone who went through the Great War and came out of it alive and unscathed is probably a quick thinker, one who acts instantly.'

'My thought exactly,' said the Reverend Mother. Patrick had not mentioned the third point, but she thought that Robert Newenham's experiences in the war would also cover this. Anyone who survived that terrible war would probably have their senses highly tuned to personal survival at all costs. The more she thought about that incident at the Custom House, the more she felt that there had been a deliberate intention to kill. Robert, she decided, had acted very quickly to endeavour to silence her once she had brought up the name of the infamous Captain Schulze.

Patrick was looking animated and scribbling hastily into his notebook. She did not like to interrupt him, but somehow a doubt about this earlier murder had intruded among her thoughts. Her threat to Robert Newenham today may well have been sudden and unforeseen. Who could have imagined that an elderly nun, a distant relative of his own, would suddenly bring up a name that could pose a great danger to him?

But the case of the city engineer was quite different. If James Doyle had been blackmailing him for years, and Robert's rather poverty-stricken way of life, as related by Lucy, had been due to systematic blackmail, then there must have been innumerable occasions on which he could have murdered him quietly and away from the eye of the public. An accident, such as he had tried to stage when she was in the Custom House, could have been a possibility. The two men must have been constantly in each other's company, must have visited innumerable sites where fire had rendered the old walls dangerous.

And if that list had been dropped on the night of December 11th in 1920, then it had probably been in James Doyle's hands for over two years. Why the sudden attempt at murder?

Still, it was for Patrick to investigate this death and it was her duty as a responsible citizen to impart to the police any information which could be of use to them.

And, she thought, Sam O'Mahony's name must be cleared, both for his own sake and for the sake of his mother. It was important to have some other suspects to put forward while the truth was being established. Her mind went to one of the articles pasted with such loving care into that penny copy book.

'This afternoon,' she said thoughtfully, 'I almost had a fatal accident.' Both heads turned towards her showing a flattering degree of alarm.

'I was at a meeting in the Custom House, one of those committee meetings that Mrs Murphy organized to help with fundraising for a new project of mine. Mrs Murphy thought that the reopening of the newly built Roches Stores would provide a venue and she arranged the meeting to follow on from one of the town planning meetings. After all was over, Captain Newenham conducted me over the building, even up to the top floor where goods are stored. I found myself very near the edge of an open hatch where goods are winched up from the river, and he shouted a warning, which I fear would have been too late if I had not already stepped back. In fact,' said the Reverend Mother, 'if a cat had not suddenly jumped down from the rafters and pounced on a rat close to me, I may well, in the bad light, have stepped over the edge. As it was, I stepped back and all was well.'

'And what were you talking about before this happened, Reverend Mother?' asked Patrick, eyeing her keenly.

She met his gaze. 'Oddly enough I had recalled that Captain Newenham had served in the Dorsetshire Regiment during the last war and that this had also been the regiment of Captain Schulze.'

'I see,' said Patrick quietly.

'He'll be your man,' said Dr Scher. 'Bet you fifty pounds, Patrick, he'll be your man.'

'I haven't got fifty pounds,' said Patrick with an absent-minded smile. Once again his notebook was out and he had licked the tip of his pencil, a habit which the Reverend Mother had to keep herself from condemning. He was not, she reminded herself, her pupil any longer.

'Young people today. No spirit in them,' grumbled Dr Scher and then when he saw that Patrick was not listening, he turned to his hostess. 'Who else was at your meeting, Reverend Mother? Any more ferocious murderers?'

The Reverend Mother gave him a look which she hoped

would convey her disapproval of wild exaggerations like this one, but she was interested to see what Patrick would make of another one of the committee members so she said obligingly, 'Well, Mr Browne, the acting city engineer was there. In fact, he was the focus of attention because the meeting before had been all about the rebuilding of the city hall and Mr Browne's proposal was still there, on an easel.'

She was right. Patrick immediately stopped writing, snapped a rubber band over his notebook, thrust it and the pencil back into his pocket.

'I thought that he had something up his sleeve. I thought that he might have his own proposal. He rolled up a drawing and put it away when we arrived to talk with him that time. What was it like, Reverend Mother? The one that I saw on the wall looked like a rebuilding of the old place, exactly the same as the one that had been burned down.' Patrick was always very professional, but there was an eager note of interest that his former teacher recognized. Patrick, she remembered, even as a small child, always wanted to pursue each enquiry to its utmost limits.

'For one thing, it was built at the end of the Grand Parade,' she said.

'Impossible. There isn't room,' scoffed Dr Scher while Patrick waited to hear more.

'Ah, but, there would be room,' said the Reverend Mother, 'if you roofed over the river at that place, and don't say that it can't be done when it was accomplished over two hundred years ago. Enterprising ancestors of mine were instrumental in roofing over Patrick Street and the Grand Parade itself, and, of course, the South Mall.'

'It could work,' admitted Dr Scher. A smile spread over his face after a minute. He was quite an artist, thought the Reverend Mother. He had a cherished collection of silver on which he doted and spent large sums of money on. 'Do you know,' he said after a minute, 'that's a damn fine idea. What was the building itself like?'

The Reverend Mother consulted her inner eye. 'Beautiful,' she said. 'Just like something that you would find in Venice. Baroque in style. He had painted the drawing. A blue sky and

St Fin Barre's Cathedral and the hill of Barrack Street in the background. It looked wonderful.' Even against a grey sky, it would still look pretty good, she thought.

'Mr Doyle,' said Patrick dispassionately, 'would not, I reckon, be a man to promote his assistant's idea in preference to his own.'

'Could pinch it, couldn't he?' enquired Dr Scher.

The Reverend Mother shook her head. 'He would have been too astute a man for that,' she said. 'Mr Browne is related to many of the foremost families in the city. The city engineer could not have got away with a deliberate theft of his assistant's idea. In fact, it may have rebounded to Thomas Browne's advantage. Once that sparklingly individual idea had gained public knowledge, it may have been that Mr Doyle would have been forced to adopt it and it would have been Mr Browne who got the credit and even international renown. The idea, of course, would have been enormously expensive, but that does not seem to hold up many grandiose projects in this city of ours.'

'I think I'll go and see him again,' said Patrick rising to his feet. Dr Scher followed him reluctantly as the Reverend Mother touched the bell for Sister Bernadette. She would, she thought, have to get back to her accounts and her bill paying, though there was one of those pasted-in articles that she wanted to reread.

'Patsy Mullane from the library is waiting in one of the parlours, Reverend Mother,' said Sister Bernadette when she arrived. 'I told her that you were very busy today, but she insisted on waiting. She said she doesn't mind how long that she has to wait, but she must speak to you.'

'Very well,' said the Reverend Mother with an inward sigh. 'Bring her in as soon as you have shown out Dr Scher and the inspector.'

Her visitors had not discussed whether Mrs O'Mahony's tragic death was likely to be a murder or a suicide and she was quite glad about that. She wanted time to ponder the possibilities. Was it feasible, she wondered, that the murderer of James Doyle thought that the poor woman had witnessed something, something which might not have seemed significant at the time, but which, later, she might have recalled?

Or could there be another reason for the killing of Mrs O'Mahony?

And what, she wondered, as she waited quietly for her next visitor, could Patsy Mullane, former library assistant and now a sweeper of sawdust at the English Market, have to say to the Reverend Mother at St Mary's of the Isle?

But when Sister Bernadette returned, she was alone.

'She just went, Reverend Mother. Not a sign of her anywhere. I told her that she would have to wait as you had visitors with you, that Inspector Cashman and Dr Scher were in your room with you. I offered her a cup of tea. I gave her the *Cork Examiner* to read.' Sister Bernadette's voice was getting more aggrieved by the minute.

'I expect she remembered an appointment,' said the Reverend Mother absent-mindedly. Was it, she wondered when the lay sister had taken herself off, was it the mention of the doctor or of the civic guard that had made Patsy rush away? The latter, she suspected. But if so, why?

# EIGHTEEN

W.B. Yeats:
I write it out in a verse –
McDonagh and Mac Bride
And Connolly and Pearse
Now, and in time to be,
Whenever green is worn,
Are changed, changed utterly:
A terrible beauty is born.

Eileen was feeling frozen. The damp mud slathered onto Sister Mary Immaculate's bloomers had now penetrated the stout flannel from which they had been made and they clung clammily to her skin. The remains of the old black woollen dress did nothing much to warm her. It was threadbare in places and very thin over the rest of it. It was probably about forty years old, she thought. She had no memory of her mother wearing it, so it may have belonged, like the shawl, to her grandmother. She quickened her step, longing to swing her arms, but the narrow raised path inside the tunnel was only about two feet wide, and here and there the roughly cut stones poked jagged edges out so that she had to turn sideways to get past them. She could not risk a false step which would send her tumbling onto the rails four feet below her and might result in a broken ankle. Still, she could see better now, and she went as fast as she could. But after a few minutes she looked back. Where was Sam?

He seemed to hang back, fumbling at the wall with one hand. Of course his sight was poor and his glasses might not help down here in the dark. She suppressed a feeling of impatience and waited for him.

'How long does this thing go on for?' He sounded angry and frustrated and she didn't reply. It was dangerous to talk too much. He should have the sense to know that. She felt irritated. She had risked so much for this daring rescue. She shuddered to think what Tom Hurley would say about them bringing a lorry-load of soldiers within a couple of miles of their hideout, if he ever found out. She walked on, moving as fast as she dared.

But she was steadily getting colder. Her feet and legs up to the knee, luckily, were encased in warm woollen socks and close-fitting leather boots, but her hands were like blocks of ice and she was beginning to shiver. She couldn't keep on creeping like this. She would have to take a chance. Keeping her arms tightly squeezed against her sides, she began to run along the narrow pathway that was more like a ledge, but she didn't care. The blood began to move around in her body and warmed her. She daren't look over her shoulder in case she lost her balance, but she hoped that Sam was following her example.

The tunnel, she remembered, was about nine hundred yards long. The ventilation shaft and ladder was about halfway, they had reckoned when she had first explored it. They had spent a day, last summer, herself and Aoife, lying up on the flowering grasses, hidden from sight by the whitethorn bush, and listening to the birds singing until they suddenly stopped at the approach of a train. This train that they had met at the level crossing would go out to Bandon, would stop there. The engine would go around and the train would make its way back to Cork in about an hour. But how long had they been ducking and dodging around the hedges and bushes? She should have checked the time. It couldn't have been a whole hour. Nevertheless she had an uneasy feeling.

The mouth of the tunnel was now visible – a pale grey arch. Surely that would put heart into Sam! Feeling much warmer, she slowed down and then stopped, waiting for him to catch up. She flattened herself with her back to the rough wall and looked back. For a moment, she could see nothing. It was much blacker behind her than in front. 'Oh, come on,' she whispered impatiently. What was wrong with him? 'Try to keep up with me,' she whispered when he came slowly into view. 'We'll be out soon.'

He made no answer and she thought that his breath sounded

loud in the confined darkness. Surely he couldn't be out-of-breath, crawling along so slowly? Eileen turned and went on. She didn't run, though. She had to stay with him. He was her responsibility.

And then a heart-stopping noise. It was the sound of the steam whistle which was mounted on the boiler of the train. And it was coming from in front of her. The Bandon train must be returning to Cork instead of going on to Bantry.

Eileen's first instinct was to run. Perhaps if she ran at full speed, she could beat the train. But she knew, even if she could achieve that, Sam would be left behind. He couldn't even keep up with a slow run. Desperately she looked backwards. They were nearer to the tunnel exit than the ladder shaft. It was not worth it to go back.

Soon there would be a train thundering along at full speed. All they could do was flatten themselves against the wall and hope for the best. But now other fears entered her mind. Would there be room for them? She had a strong impression that the train itself was wider than the sunken space occupied by the rails, that doors, door handles and footboards would overhang the ledge on which they were walking. She remembered when she and Aoife had peered down from their hiding place by the blackthorn bush that it had appeared as though the train filled every inch of the tunnel.

'Quick,' she said in a voice that even she heard was full of panic. 'Quick, Sam, run as fast as you can. We must get out of here before the train gets into the tunnel.'

The noise of the train was louder than ever. She could see the steam and sparks ahead of them. It was getting to the mouth of the tunnel more quickly than she had guessed it could do. It sounded its whistle, a signal to passengers to pull up the carriage windows or else their clothes and the upholstered seats would be covered with sticky black smuts. She looked over her shoulder, and her heart gave a lurch. Sam was a long way behind her, moving clumsily, banging his shoulder against the protruding rock and stopping to rub it. She could have screamed but there was no point. Her mind had suddenly remembered something.

The main ventilation shaft, the one with the well-secured

iron ladder, was too far back, but now she suddenly remembered that there were others, not well-built like the one they'd come down, but just about a foot wide, and a foot deep, really just a groove chipped out of the rock with an iron grid above it. Probably a place where a narrow ladder could be inserted if the grid needed attention.

Better than nothing, she thought, and said over her shoulder, 'Just a little further, Sam.'

And then she began to run. She heard him behind her, breathing hard as if he was doing a hundred-yard sprint. Now the pale grey of the arched end of the tunnel was stabbed with two glaring lights in the distance. Only another few seconds and it would be upon them. Should she stop and face the tunnel wall and hope for the best? But something stubborn within her insisted that she should go on.

'Quick, Sam,' she yelled. There was no point in trying to be quiet now. The whole countryside, including the soldiers, would be deafened by the noise of the train. She glanced back once – she supposed that he was trying his best, but he was lagging further and further behind.

And then she saw it from the corner of her eye. A gleam of light from overhead and she had almost missed it. The groove in the rock was slightly less shallow than she remembered.

'Sam! We must wait here. Squash against the rock!' Her voice trembled and the noise was becoming deafening. Then with one defiant shriek from the whistle, the train entered the tunnel.

Suddenly Sam was beside her. He squeezed in behind her, his body pushed into hers. The dark prison clothes would melt into the rock; at least she hoped so. She hated feeling helpless. The jagged rock pressed into her, but she forced herself not to flinch. The noise was dreadful, sickening and unbearable, as the train passed in a tornado that seemed to rock the whole tunnel. For a moment she feared that it would snatch up their bodies and carry them along in its progress. The air was boiling hot and the smoke stung her eyes. Even so, she caught a glance of the train's fireman. He had seen them. His grotesquely blackened face was turned towards them, the shovel poised mid-air, and the mouth dropped open showing strangely white teeth, the eyes wide and staring.

But then the train reached the end of the tunnel, and the noise began to fade.

'Come on, Sam. That fireman saw us. Let's move!' Sam didn't seem to be listening. He was bending down, his hands holding on to his legs, just above the knees. For a moment she thought that he was vomiting. There was a strange hooping sound coming from him.

'Sam,' she began, knowing that she sounded impatient, but it was for his safety that she was worried. 'Come on, Sam,' she said again and then realized that he was not vomiting. He was trying desperately to breathe.

'My asthma!' he choked the words out and for a moment she felt relieved. Loads of people got asthma. A girl in her class used to go up to newly tarred poles and breathe in the fumes of the shining black sticky stuff, which seemed to help her. Some people said smoking was good for it, though the smoke from the train seemed to have made him worse. Their only hope now was to get out into the countryside and to hide behind hedges and bushes until darkness fell. When and if the search was called off they could make their way to the farmhouse.

But Sam was not getting any better. His breathing was terrible. He tried to straighten up, but then went back to holding his legs again. Timidly she rubbed his back and then when that didn't seem to do anything she hit him sharply between the shoulder blades. She remembered her mother doing that to her when she had choked over a piece of stale bread.

It didn't seem to work with Sam. He moved impatiently away from her, and stretched his hands upwards against the rock face. It seemed that he was willing himself to breathe, dragging in air with sounds like the creaking of a rusty hinge, but it was no good. He made desperate croaking sounds ending with a strangely high-pitched cawing noise. And then he managed to cough, not a satisfying cough that might clear his lungs, but a harsh metallic explosion that rang through the tunnel.

'Smoke . . .' he said with difficulty, and then, with a great effort, 'can't breathe.'

'Let's get you out of here,' she said. 'You'll be fine once we get into the fresh air.'

She took his arm and endeavoured to pull him along the narrow ledge. He tried, frantically hard, gulping for air. But every yard or so, he had to stop and bend, doubled over, desperately holding his legs.

'Imagine my arm is a rope,' she said. 'Just pull yourself along, like you were climbing up a mountain. Take one step at a time.' Her mind went to Robert Louis Stevenson's book *Kidnapped*. When Davy was ill with his chest and couldn't breathe he had done something like this. 'I'll count. We'll keep going for fifty seconds and then you can stop for a rest.' They were, she reckoned, now about three-quarters of the way along the tunnel, getting nearer to its mouth. She did the sum rapidly in her head while mechanically counting aloud in a low voice. About another two hundred yards, if they were lucky, she thought optimistically. Sam did not manage the first fifty yards without stopping for another agonizing convulsion, but she got him going more quickly, drawing him along at a steady pace. It was heart-breaking to listen to him, but he was no better when he stopped, so she kept tugging him on.

'I think I can smell the air of the fields; you'll be much better now,' she said with false assurance. He had been faltering, but her words heartened him, and she picked up on the counting again. She even skipped from thirty-one to forty-two and they reached the fifty mark without a breakdown. 'Eamonn was telling me about the sea,' she said, hoping to distract him. 'He said that we would go there, one day. I've never even seen the sea. He loves a place called Ballycotton. He said the air is great up on the cliffs. It blows all the way from America. Great for bad chests, he said.' Her own heart was beating with slow violence. What if Sam collapsed completely? Could she possibly carry him? But then he moved forward and they began to make progress. Only a hundred yards, now, she told him.

They had to stop twice more, but each time she managed to get him moving again, pretending to smell the air, trying to keep his mind fixed on streams and cliffs and then, in desperation, talking about the night of the big wind, a few years before the great famine when her mother's grandmother found a five-pound note blowing across the field on the following morning. He still coughed, that hard, dry cough and he still wheezed, but the terrible crowing sound seemed to have stopped for the moment.

'Another fifty yards,' she said as much to herself as to him.

The pale grey of the tunnel entrance now had changed into a misty green. It was hard to see out, or perhaps that was just the effect of their long time in the darkness of the tunnel, but as they came nearer, she realized that it was not anything to do with her eyes.

Outside the tunnel there was a thick dense fog.

Eileen began to feel better. This was ideal. It would be impossible for any soldiers to see them. In fact, the fog would probably make them give up the chase and get into their lorry and try to negotiate their way back to the city. That was, of course, supposing that the fireman had not told what he had seen in the tunnel. She tried to put this possibility from her mind. She was sure the train hadn't stopped at the end of the tunnel. Its brakes, someone had told her, took about four hundred yards to bring it to a halt. Would they bother to stop and report the sighting of two people in the tunnel, just because they saw some soldiers in the distance in the fields? Eileen tried to put the matter from her mind, dismissing the possibility that there might be soldiers with guns standing ready for them when they emerged.

But now she was worried that Sam might not make it. Every breath that he took seemed to her terrified mind as if it might be his last. The sound was thin and high, and from time to time he had to stop and clutch at his chest. Was he having a heart attack, she wondered, with a panic-stricken memory of her grandmother's sudden death when she had been a very small child? Did people die of asthma? She didn't know.

'Only a little bit further now,' she said. Her voice sounded casual and unworried, but her own heart was thumping with acute terror. When they finally reached the end of the tunnel, a terrible paroxysm of wheezy dry coughing broke from him and he held on to the sprouting branch of an elderberry as though it were the only thing between him and death.

'Let's find somewhere for you to sit down out of the wet,' she said as cheerfully as she could manage. The ground around them was littered with pieces of rock that had been chipped away when the hillside had been tunnelled out. Most of them were an awkward shape, not worth carting away for building material, but she saw a flat, smooth piece that was half buried by the small hillock behind it. She scrabbled with her nails at it and managed to clear most of the wet moss from its surface. The fog was getting thicker and it did occur to her that even though it would help to keep them concealed, it was not the best air for Sam to breathe. There was nothing that she could do about that, though. She went back and coaxed him to stagger over to the stone and collapse onto it.

'Are you feeling any better?' she asked tentatively. He shook his head wordlessly. He had taken off his glasses and without them his eyes looked wide and frightened, she thought. And that terrified her. She hoped that he might reassure her; might say that he had been worse lots of times; that he would be all right in a minute. But he didn't and his naked eyes told another story.

Turning over the possibilities in her mind, she took a decision and, despite the danger that if she left him he might die alone there on the hillside, she knew it was her only choice.

'Sam,' she said as steadily as she could manage, 'I'm going to go and fetch Eamonn, one of the fellows that got you out of gaol, you remember him, the tall fellow wearing the clerical collar? He was a medical student and he has a box full of drugs and things that we took from a chemist shop. He'll know what to do for you. He's really good at digging out bullets and things.'

She looked at him hopefully, but he did not appear to be even listening to her; all of his attention was concentrated on the struggle to breathe.

'I'll be back as soon as I can,' she promised and left him, then, before her resolution wavered.

The fog was so thick that there was no need for concealment so she went straight across the field, walking diagonally and trusting to her instincts. The farm was on top of the hill so she could not go far wrong if she continued to climb.

The fog began to diminish the higher she got. This often happened around here. It was a valley fog; often she had stood outside the farmhouse and looked down at what appeared to be a hollow filled with soft greyish white clouds. For a moment she wondered whether she should have somehow dragged Sam up here, but dismissed it. He could barely stumble a few feet along level ground. She had done the only possible thing, she told herself, and then was cheered by the sight of the enormous old Scots Pine tree that grew outside the house of the farmer who had lent them a place belonging to his dead uncle. Now she knew exactly where she was and she walked on the inside of the hedge that lined the country lane.

From time to time she thought she heard a sound behind her, but each time she stopped, there was nothing. Probably some farm dog, absent from his duties, in pursuit of a fox, now slinking home for his supper in the furtive way that those intelligent animals showed when they knew that they were in the wrong. Some day, she thought, when all of this is over and when Ireland, all thirty-two counties of it, was free, then she would get herself a dog. By then, of course, she would be studying medicine at the university at the expense of the new state. Her mind strayed over this happy dream and although she heard a sound again she did not take any notice, but slipped through the hedge at the right moment, crossed over the empty lane and went through the gate and up the avenue to their farmhouse. The lights were on in the sitting room and in the kitchen and upstairs in most of the bedrooms. It looked, she thought, with a surge of relief, as though the others had got back safely.

She had just lifted her hand to knock on the door, when a voice spoke from behind her.

'What the hell do you think you are playing at?'

She spun around, but she knew who it was. He stood there in belted raincoat and slouch hat, all drenched with moisture. She couldn't see his face, the hat hid that, but his voice was rough with anger and she quailed for a moment. There was always something rather dangerous about Tom Hurley.

It was Aoife who opened the door and her face was terrified, her eyes not on Eileen, but on the man who stood behind her. Eileen turned. Tom Hurley had a pistol in his hand and it was pointed directly at her. She stared him down ignoring Aoife's gasp of horror.

'You'd better put that thing away,' she said. 'It might go off.'

'Get inside,' he said and the words exploded from him.

She gave a shrug. Really, she thought, why does he always have to be acting the dangerous outlaw? Her attention was taken by Eamonn who was coming down the stairs.

'Oh, Eamonn,' she said and then stopped. He had a sharp knife, dripping with water in his hand. 'Is Fred all right?' she asked.

'He's fine. We gave him some whiskey and then I dug the bullet out. He's fast asleep and snoring now.' Eamonn's tone was uneasy and his eyes, like Aoife's, were fixed upon Tom Hurley.

'Shut that door, girl.' Tom was definitely in very bad humour and Eileen could not altogether blame him. They were under his orders and they had undertaken an action without his knowledge. She hoped that he did not know about the soldiers, but his first words, when he had ushered them all into the sitting room, destroyed that wish.

'Unauthorized gaol break, betrayal of a secret house to a pack of soldiers: I could have the lot of you court-martialled and shot,' he said harshly.

'The soldiers didn't find this place, did they?' Eileen turned to Eamonn and he shook his head silently. She breathed with relief and turned back to Tom Hurley.

'I'm responsible,' she said steadily. 'It was my idea.'

'What a surprise!' he said sarcastically. The mouth of his pistol was still pointed steadily at her. 'You've got too big for your boots, young lady,' he said and glanced down at her feet, his eyes widening a little when they saw her mud-plastered bloomers which were now, she realized, drying into an odd pattern of dark grey with patches of vivid pink showing through.

'I'll pass sentence on you tomorrow morning,' he said. 'In the meantime, get up to your room and stay there.'

She stared back defiantly at him. 'You can do what you like with me,' she said, 'but there is a dying man down there in the valley.'

'Man.' His eyes went around, counting. They were all there, except for Fred. 'What man?'

'Sam O'Mahony. Eamonn, he's having a terrible attack of asthma. I think he's in a terrible way.' She hesitated for a moment and then said, 'Eamonn, his lips are a bit blue. What does that mean?'

'I'm afraid—'

'Shut up, shut up all of you. I don't want to hear another word about this. Sam O'Mahony, indeed. A man who has done his best to turn the people of Cork against our organisation. How dare you go and let him out of prison without any authorization? The sooner he is recaptured the better. And if he dies on the hillside,' finished Tom Hurley, 'well, so much the better. It will save the state the cost of the trial and of the rope to hang him.'

'And, of course, it would clear everyone else of suspicion,' shouted Eileen. It was a random shot but it went home. So he *was* there, she thought just before he grabbed her by the arm and pushed her in front of him. She felt the hard round circle of the pistol muzzle press into her back and for a second she prayed to herself: *Dear God, don't let him shoot me in the spine.* Then Tom seized her by the arm and began to pull her towards the stairs. She shrugged herself free and marched ahead of him, her head held high, but she knew that she was trembling violently and when she heard the key turn in the door, she felt nothing but relief.

'I'm taking this key with me and you don't get out of there until I say so,' he shouted, adding with a sneer in his voice, 'hope you've got a pot in there. You girls can't do it out of the window like fellows, I suppose.' And then she heard his footsteps going back down the stairs and the sound of his voice shouting orders.

A few moments later, the front door was closed with a quiet click and then she heard the chug-chug of the motorbike. She went to the window and looked out, standing in the shelter of the curtain. He didn't take the road to Cork, but turned in the direction of Ballinhassig. She wondered for a minute why he was going to the village, but then her thoughts went back to Sam and she clutched the curtain hard, in an effort not to cry. She had made such a mess of everything! Eamonn's face when she had mentioned 'blue lips' had been enough for her. She just had to get back to him. Swiftly she left the window, changed into her breeches and tweed jacket. She went over to the bed, stripping the sheets from it and knotting them together. Then she added the sheets from Aoife's bed. She soon had a serviceable rope, studded with knots, which she laid on the floor.

She knew that her actions earlier that day might mean the end of her time with the Republicans. She faced that near-certainty and knew, with a cold feeling in her spine, that it might mean, also, that she would be shot for insubordination.

And at that moment the lock of the door clicked open and Eamonn came in quietly.

'Let's go,' he said. 'I've got some ephedrine. It's great stuff. Lucky that I grabbed a bottle when we raided the chemist shop that time.'

Eileen was looking at the key in the door. 'Did he give that to you?' she asked.

Eamonn shook his head. 'It's the same lock on all of the bedroom doors,' he said casually. 'Fred and I discovered that on the first day we came here. We didn't like to tell you girls in case you might freak out or something.'

Eileen ignored this. Her mind was working fast. She wasn't going to turn down Eamonn's offer. It might mean the difference between life and death for Sam, but she knew how much the Republican movement meant to him. Quickly she tied one end of her knotted sheets' rope to the leg of Aoife's bed and threw the other end out through the open window.

'Lock the door again when I go out,' she said. 'Act dumb in the morning. No one can take responsibility, then. No one heard or saw anything. You were all in the kitchen at the back of the house and Aoife slept in Carrie's bed. No one came near me – his highness had the key, after all.'

And then she hesitated again as they reached the front door. The glorious cause meant everything to Eamonn. He was the most visionary and idealistic of them all.

'Give me the ephedrine, Eamonn. I'll give it to him. You stay here. And remember, you know nothing.'

He shook his head. 'No,' he said. 'If he has gone too far, I might just have to do a tracheotomy. I've watched one being performed and I think I'd be able to do it. I've brought a tube with me.'

She had no idea what he was talking about. She stared at him uncertainly, but then he said firmly, 'I know I'm not a qualified doctor, but I swore the Hippocratic oath to myself when I started my medical course. A sick man comes before anything else. Come on, Eileen, let's go.'

The fog seemed worse when they went out, but they both knew the way so well that they had no problems. All of those days becoming familiar with the countryside around the farmhouse – a radius of at least two miles, Tom Hurley had ordered – all of that time had been very well spent. Eileen led the way, feeling much happier, despite everything. After all Sam was a young man. Young men didn't die of something as ordinary and simple as asthma. And she had enormous faith in Eamonn. She concentrated on walking fast and leading the way as directly as possible.

But when they reached the exit of the tunnel, there was no sign of Sam.

# NINETEEN

Alan Ellis
Reporter on *Cork Examiner:*

'I had been given a special pass that afternoon showing that,
as a journalist, I could travel during the curfew hours. Major
General Edward Strickland himself signed it. He was
commanding the British 6th Division covering the city.
So I felt comparatively safe from any unwelcome attention.
Looking back, I was living in a fool's paradise because,
a few days later, the Auxiliaries shot an old man named
Guest – he was a night watchman at the Cork Distillery.
He had a pass, too. But they claimed that he had failed
to answer a challenge!'

'**M**essage for you from the gaol, inspector,' said Joe.
'The escaped prisoner, Sam O'Mahony, the one that
the Republicans sprung, he's been recaptured, he's
back behind bars.'

'What happened?' Patrick was surprised. There had been
quite a few gaol breaks masterminded by the Republicans and
they had always been very efficient affairs. Usually the prisoner
was moved to another part of the country and nothing was
heard of him again. As far as he could remember, there had
never been a recapture.

'Well, someone turned him in yesterday evening. A man in a
raincoat, hat pulled down, hard to see his face . . .' Joe was
consulting his notes. 'He walked into the police barracks in
Ballinhassig, just said, "There's an escaped prisoner lying out
in the fields beside the exit from the tunnel. He's having a bad
asthma attack so you'd better get there before he pegs out." And
then he just cleared off before they could ask him anything. Very
slow those country police, sir. Still, they managed to find Sam
O'Mahony. He was in a bad way, but when he was back behind

bars, the governor of the prison got hold of Dr Scher and he pulled him around. Oh, and –' once again Joe consulted his notes – 'Dr Scher phoned, looking for you.' I told him that you were due in shortly and he said he'd pop around and take you out to lunch. How did the interview with Captain Newenham go, sir?'

'He produced his pistol very readily, just as soon as I asked whether he owned a gun. Almost as though he expected the question. Had it there in the drawer of his desk, funny place to keep it, I thought, but perhaps, since he knew that I was coming, he had put it there to be handy. But, of course,' he added, 'the fact that he still has a pistol didn't mean that he couldn't have owned another one. Some of these country gents have a roomful of guns, so I've been told. And, apparently, pistols are often sold in pairs.'

'What did you make of him?' Joe, thought Patrick, was making progress. Six months ago he would have blurted out: 'Do you think he done it, sir?'

'A cool customer. He went through his war service in a couple of sentences. I challenged him about Captain Schulze and he said that he hardly knew him and that they had nothing whatsoever in common so that they never met.'

'So he didn't admit anything.' Joe sounded disappointed.

'Of course,' said Patrick, 'this idea that Captain Newenham supplied the list for the targeted buildings on the night of the burning down of the city, well, we'll never get the evidence for that, I'd say. The city engineer may or may not have been blackmailing him, but how can we prove it? Both men would have kept that as a secret. Thanks, Joe,' he added and waited for the constable to take the hint and leave him to think.

'There's something else, sir,' said Joe standing his ground. His face flushed and he spoke rapidly as though embarrassed by what he had to say. 'I have another piece of information for you, sir. When I was on the way back here, this boy came up to me. He'd have been about twelve years old, I'd say, no more. Very badly dressed, poor as anything. The type that would do anything for a penny. Well, anyway, sir, he told me some sort of story. It was about the bishop's chaplain, sir. It's not very nice.' Joe stopped, his face even redder than a moment before.

'Go on,' said Patrick impatiently. Joe would have to grow

a thicker skin. As a policeman he had to face all types of crime.

'Well, he said, sir . . . he alleged, I should say, he told me that Father de Courcy had picked up his sister, only a bit older than himself, that's what he said, one night, in the dark, she was standing on the quays, and he picked her up in his car. He said that his sister drowned herself when she knew that she was pregnant, but before she threw herself in the river she told her brother that Father de Courcy was the one that gave her the baby.'

'What did you say then?'

'Well, I think that I made a mess of it. I tried to get him to come back to the barracks with me, I knew that you would want to question him, but he just held out his hand and asked for half a crown.'

'You didn't give it to him, I hope.'

'No, sir,' said Joe, 'but perhaps I should have given him something, because he just shouted, "The other fellow, that fellow that's been murdered, he gave me half a crown. If it was worth half a crown to him, it's worth it to you." I tried to grab him, but he got away from me,' said Joe shamefacedly, 'the sleeve of his jacket came off in my hand and there wasn't a sign of him. He just ducked through the crowds and disappeared.'

'Never mind,' said Patrick. 'It could have happened to any of us. Just keep an eye out for him, Joe, when you are out in the streets.'

Had there been anything in that story, he wondered, after Joe had gone out? He would, he thought, have a word with the Reverend Mother. She would know all about Father de Courcy.

Of course, what the bishop's secretary did was no business of his, if the girl had been of age, but what had taken his attention immediately was the story of the man who had given half a crown for the boy's tale. Had James Doyle made use of the information in order to blackmail the priest? And if he had, did it have anything to do with the murder? The bishop's secretary, after all, had been present on that morning in the English Market.

# TWENTY

St Thomas Aquinas:
*Principiis essendi et gubernationis sunt parentes et patria,*
*quae dedi nati et nutriti*
(The most important factors in our existence are our parents
and our country, which have given us birth and nourishment)

Patsy Mullane came back to the convent the following morning a good half hour before morning school started. Sister Bernadette was rather sulky when she escorted her in and she did not press any offers of tea on her. The Reverend Mother looked at her visitor with concern. It had been less than a week since she had seen Patsy pushing her broom around at the English Market, but in those few days it almost seemed as if the woman had lost weight. And had not slept much. Her eyes were heavy and rimmed with black circles and her hands were shaking with fear or with tiredness. Perhaps she was ill. The market would have opened at eight in the morning and it was surprising that Patsy was not there.

'Are you well, Patsy?' she asked her former pupil.

'Yes, thank you, Reverend Mother.' Patsy's voice shook and for a moment she opened and then closed her mouth, as though she had forgotten what to say.

'You wanted to see me,' prompted the Reverend Mother.

'That's right. I wanted to ask you something, to tell you . . .'

'Yes?' The Reverend Mother sat back in her chair, tucked her hands into her wide sleeves and prepared to listen. Why had the woman gone out of her way to inform on Tom Hurley when most people of the city would have kept that knowledge to themselves? It was a dangerous thing to pass on information about the rebels. Could she have had any romantic interest in the young son of Mrs O'Mahony? But that was surely most unlikely. Patsy, thought the Reverend Mother looking back through the years, must be forty and she looked every day of her age. A young man with a good opinion of himself, such as Sam O'Mahony was reputed to be, would be most unlikely to be interested in her.

So why had she given information about Tom Hurley – a deed that might have her shot as a spy if the so-called Republican Army ever found out?

Patsy was finding it hard to get to the point, going over her memories of school, of how proud she was when she passed her certificate, how this had enabled her to get a position at the library and how happy she had been working there. The Reverend Mother listened patiently, her eyelids lowered, not allowing herself even one glance at the clock. The playground outside had begun to fill up with children and the shrill voices penetrated through the badly fitting window. Soon it would be time for school, but she didn't have a class to teach until the afternoon. Patsy, she thought, for everyone's sake, would have to be given the confidence to work her courage to the sticking point.

But Patsy seemed to have run out of steam. The Reverend Mother raised her eyes and said an encouraging, 'Yes', but this was answered only by an uncomfortable silence.

Then the bell for the beginning of school rang, and the sudden clang seemed to alarm Patsy and force her into action. She started, half stood up as though she were once again a pupil in the school, and then sat down again. Soon the clamour ceased and was replaced by an unnatural quiet as the children, headed by their teachers, lined up in the playground waiting to be marched inside.

Patsy turned to the Reverend Mother and said hurriedly, 'I want to enter.'

'To enter.' The Reverend Mother was startled, but did her best to keep her voice neutral. The quiet repetition of her own last two words seemed to prod Patsy into an explanation.

'I mean I want to enter the convent, to become one of the sisters, not a teacher or anything, I wouldn't have a dowry and I don't have the right sort of education, not enough of it, I mean.' Patsy stopped and looked embarrassed.

'Why do you want to enter, Patsy?'

This question, when asked of potential candidates, was usually followed by a string of protestations and frequent mention of God, but Patsy just stared at her in a frightened fashion as though she had been asked to solve a very difficult problem. The Reverend Mother decided to rephrase her question.

'What would you hope to get from joining the sisterhood, Patsy?' Here again was a great opportunity for God to come into the conversation, but Patsy did not avail herself of this.

She gulped once or twice and then said breathlessly, 'I'd be safe here.'

The Reverend Mother had been mother superior of the convent for a very long time and had received many different answers from eager postulants to this question, but she had never before heard an answer such as this.

Though the Reverend Mother did not reply, Patsy seemed to sense her surprise and she went on hurriedly, 'I mean it would be nice and peaceful. There wouldn't be any worries. That sort of thing.' Her face was flushed, red and purple and then fading back to its original pale mauve, a colour that she had acquired from working in the draughty chill of the market. Worries was an odd word to use, but perhaps no surprise. The woman did look worried. The Reverend Mother leaned towards her.

'I suppose everyone has some worries,' she said. 'Tell me what is worrying you, Patsy.' Patsy shot a frightened glance at the door so Reverend Mother got to her feet, went across and turned the key in it. 'There,' she said reassuringly, 'no one can come in and interrupt us.'

She was half sorry not to have told Sister Bernadette to fetch some tea. It might have bridged this awkward moment. Patsy was staring at her and there was indecision as well as fear in her eyes.

'You'll have to be open and honest with me, Patsy.' She spoke briskly and decisively and Patsy responded immediately to the note of authority.

'I'm frightened about that shooting last Friday in the market, Reverend Mother,' she said almost in a whisper. 'I don't want to work there any longer.'

'Frightened that it might happen to you?'

Patsy shook her head wordlessly. She looked appealingly at the Reverend Mother.

'I'd be a very good sister,' she said. 'I'm a good worker. I'm great at sweeping and scrubbing now. I'd do anything you wanted. No job is too hard for me.'

'Tell me why you are frightened, Patsy.' The Reverend Mother reached across and patted the rough hands that twisted each other. 'I can't help if I don't know the truth,' she went on.

'I'm scared that the guards will think I did it.'

'Did what?'

'The shooting.'

The Reverend Mother stared at her with perplexity. The idea of Patsy Mullane, with her heavy glasses and her shaky hands, firing a gun, seemed a very strange one. 'Why would you think that anyone will accuse you of that, Patsy?' she said soothingly.

This simple question seemed to alarm Patsy, but after a minute she answered in a shaking voice, 'I told a lie.'

'Well, that's not the end of the world,' said the Reverend Mother in bracing tones. Mrs O'Mahony's words came to her and she repeated them aloud, 'I suppose that there are times when we all tell a lie. I've told them myself.' And she smiled reassuringly.

Patsy gave her an incredulous glance and twisted her hands together again. The fingers were badly swollen with chilblains and one began to bleed.

'Don't!' said the Reverend Mother sternly. She fetched a large cotton handkerchief from the top drawer of her bureau and handed it to Patsy, who wrapped it around her hand and then stared at the blood oozing through it.

'Tell me the lie you told,' ordered the Reverend Mother. 'If it's anything to do with the events last Friday, then we must think hard, both of us.'

Patsy lifted her eyes, wide and frightened. 'I told the guards that the door to the gallery was locked,' she said.

'And it wasn't, is that it?'

Patsy shook her head.

'Well, it might be best to tell Inspector Cashman about that. He'll understand that you didn't want to show up the superintendent – I suppose he had forgotten to lock it, was that it?'

Patsy shook her head. 'No, it was me.' And then when the Reverend Mother just waited for more, she blurted out, 'I do it every day. I just open it every morning when Mr O'Donnell is seeing to the delivery carts. I . . .' And then she stopped.

'Yes, go on,' said the Reverend Mother. This, she thought, might be more serious than she had first imagined.

'You see, Mr O'Donnell has a meal up there every evening. He'd have some roast chicken and some beer or else some sausage or something like that. He buys things from the stalls, and he usually has a pint or two of beer, too. He doesn't always finish everything. He's one to light a cigarette in the middle of his meal. And then when he finishes, he just walks off, puts the keys on a hook in the weighing office, locks up the place with his own key, and there's a woman who comes in to clean his office in the morning . . .' Patsy was becoming more fluent now and the Reverend Mother nodded in an encouraging fashion. Her mind was working hard behind the bland expression.

'So I slip the keys off the hook – they stay there in the weighing office all night because of fire regulations; the super-intendent has one key to the Patrick Street side and the two beadles have the keys to the Princes Street and the Grand Parade entrance, but the gallery stays locked until later in the morning when the superintendent goes up there to count the rents and things like that.' Patsy looked anxiously across and the Reverend Mother nodded her comprehension. The quicker she could get Patsy to tell her story and encourage her to repeat it to Patrick, the better.

'And I just quickly undo the lock while he's busy with the carts and then some time later in the morning, when he's somewhere in the Grand Parade, or the St Patrick Street side of the market, I slip upstairs and, and . . . well, I . . . I eat it up,' said Patsy in a shame-faced fashion.

'And then lock the door after you,' suggested the Reverend Mother, but Patsy shook her head.

'No, the superintendent always has them in his pocket. Just as soon as he comes in from the lane, from seeing to the carters, he goes and puts them in his pocket. But there's always something he needs from upstairs during the morning and usually he sends me to get it and then I pretend to unlock the door and then lock it when I come back down.'

'But on Friday . . .'

'On Friday he was too busy with all that crowd, all the fuss.'

'So the door to the gallery stairs was unlocked at the time that the shot was fired, is that right, Patsy?'

The Reverend Mother hardly waited for the nod of confirmation before she leaned back in her chair and drew in a deep breath. In her mind, she apologised to Dr Scher. She had not taken too much notice of his talk about angles and now it had transpired that the gallery had been open after all and the shot could have been fired from there. Yes, the angle of the path of the bullet had probably told a true story.

'And the lights going out, Patsy, had that happened on other occasions . . .?'

'Sometimes,' confessed Patsy, 'they were funny, those lights, always ready to go out. The lead piping needed looking at, so Mr O'Donnell used to say. So they used to go out from time to time, and then, again, I might nip up there sometimes and turn them off myself so that Mr O'Donnell would give me his keys and tell me to see to them. He'd never be bothered going up there himself. Or if there's too many people around, I just switch off the gas before I come down the stairs. I can feel my way; I know the place so well so I can be back with my broom before anyone has a chance to light a candle.'

'But on Friday, on Friday when they went off just before the shot . . .?'

'I had nothing to do with that, Reverend Mother,' said Patsy in an alarmed fashion. 'They just went off of themselves. The pipes are very old.'

Or else the killer turned them off, thought the Reverend Mother. She gave Patsy a minute or two to relax, to enjoy the

benefit of confession, of unloading her soul of its guilt and
then she said as gently as she could, 'I think it's important
that you tell Inspector Cashman what you have just told me,
Patsy. An innocent man might well be hanged for this murder
if you do not. There is no possibility that Sam O'Mahony
could have gone up to the gallery. I saw him myself the minute
that the lights went out and he was standing beside his
mother's stall. He wasn't the one that switched them off and
as far as I can remember, the shot went off a second or so
after we were plunged into darkness.'

'Could I enter before I tell the inspector? Please, Reverend
Mother, please. I'd love to be one of the sisters. And I know
that you will keep me safe and you won't allow them to take
me off to prison, will you?' She was gazing up imploringly
and the Reverend Mother knew that she had to make some
response to that appeal.

'I'll tell you what I'll do, Patsy, we'll keep you here for a
few days. Those chilblains of yours are very bad. I'll ask Dr
Scher to come and look at them. I'll get Sister Bernadette to
phone the superintendent and tell him that you're ill. But you
must promise me to tell everything to Inspector Cashman, if
I do that. I'll stay with you, if you wish.' She looked doubt-
fully at Patsy; the woman had nodded reluctantly, but there
was still a panic-stricken look in her eyes. Did Patsy know
more than she had said, wondered the Reverend Mother? She
rang the bell for Sister Bernadette and then went out of the
door to meet her in the corridor, lowering her voice so that
her words would not travel through the door to Patsy's ears.

'Sister, I want to keep Patsy Mullane for a few days here
at the convent. She can have the St Christopher room, can't
she? Get one of the young sisters to light a fire and to make
up the bed there. Oh, and bring some tea and cake, and then
I want you to sit with Patsy for five minutes while I make a
few phone calls.'

One of the things about being Mother Superior of the
convent, she thought with a certain twinge of guilt, is that
one need not embark on explanations. The St Christopher
room was kept to offer overnight accommodation to the
parents of the lay sisters who came from the country, and

who could not afford the prices of a night's lodging in the city. Named after the patron saint of travellers, it was a small, almost cupboard-size space – in fact, it had once been a cupboard and still was used to store spare blankets whenever the weather was warm enough to do without them. It housed the hot water tank and was quite cosy. A few days in bed there would improve those septic-looking chilblains and Patsy could do with a rest, lying in a warm room and eating regular meals.

She would also be safe there, thought the Reverend Mother gravely, as she went back into her room.

Once Sister Bernadette arrived with the tea tray, she went down the corridor and lifting the phone gave the number of the police barracks. Patrick was there and promised to come as soon as he could, his earnest voice said, and she thanked him before putting down the receiver. She looked through the window on her way back up the corridor and saw Dr Scher coming out of the gardener's shed. Mr Cotter, she thought, distracted from her reflections about the murder. He still resolutely refused to go into hospital and Dr Scher was of the opinion that he was just as well off where he was and was no danger to others. He, Dr Scher, would visit him often and give medicine to ensure he was as comfortable as possible. 'I'll get him into hospital when the end is near,' he had said, and she had confidence in his judgement. She went to the back door now and waited for him.

'You're very good,' she said warmly. 'I'm sure it's a great consolation to Mr Cotter to have you visit. I was going to ask you whether I should hire a boy to help him – the boy could have meals in the kitchen, but perhaps that would not be enough to keep him safe. I wouldn't like to expose anyone to the infection.'

'I'd leave him alone,' said Dr Scher. 'He has only a few weeks to go. We'll get him into hospital soon. He's getting weaker by the day. He says he enjoys doing the spring pruning of the shrubs and the potatoes are already planted and that, with the soil so cold, there won't be anything else much to be done before the summer.'

'And, by the summer . . .?'

'He'll be in the ground himself, by then, I'd say,' said Dr Scher.

'I see.' The Reverend Mother tried to tell herself that it would be a happy release, that there was nothing more that she could do or could have done. Nevertheless, she felt guilty. With difficulty, she shifted her mind back to her other problem.

'I'd like you to have a look at Patsy Mullane,' she said. 'She has very infected-looking chilblains and I'm going to keep her here for a few days. Sister Bernadette is with her at the moment and Patrick is on his way over as she wants to talk to him.'

There was a gleam of interest in his eye, but he didn't question her.

'I'll tell you what, I'll just pop up and see Sister Mary Assumpta and then I need to go into the kitchen and make sure that Sister Imelda's cut has healed and perhaps by then you'll have Patsy in bed and I can have a look at her. If she has bad chilblains on her hands, then she probably has worse on her feet. I'll give her a good check-up, don't you worry.'

And then he was mounting the stairs without waiting for a reply and the Reverend Mother went back into her room. Patsy, she noticed, had not touched the cake, but she had swallowed a cup of tea. No sooner had she taken her customary seat at her desk than the doorbell rang and she despatched Sister Bernadette. A minute later Patrick was in the room.

'I came straight away,' he said as she thanked him and then he looked across at her visitor.

'Would you like me to stay, or to go away, Patsy?' She guessed what the answer would be.

'No, no, please stay, please, you tell him all about it, Reverend Mother. You know what I want to say.'

'I don't think that is a good idea, Patsy. You are an intelligent woman. Just be sensible now and talk to the inspector. You need to tell him the story of that Friday morning, starting from the time when the market opened to the carters and the stallholders at eight o'clock. Would you like a piece of paper and a pen and ink, inspector? Please do sit at my desk and I will sit over here beside you, Patsy.'

Duly prompted, Patrick sat down and began to write, probably filling in the date, the time, and the full name and occupation of the former librarian. Patsy stopped twisting her hands and wrapped them again in the large, bloodstained handkerchief. She seemed calmed by Patrick's detachment.

'You arrived at the English Market just before eight on Friday morning,' prompted the Reverend Mother and Patsy obediently began her story, hesitating a little when she came to her reason for leaving the door to the gallery open, and substituting the words 'tidying up' for her more frank avowal earlier on. She insisted she had nothing to do with the lights going out.

Patrick wrote busily, read it over to himself in silence and then looked up. 'You have been most helpful, Miss Mullane,' he said and Patsy blushed slightly at his respectful tone. 'I must just ask you one question, just for form's sake – if I don't, I'll get into terrible trouble,' he added with a smile. Patsy gave a nervous giggle.

'I just must ask you whether anyone asked you to leave the gallery door open last Friday morning.'

Patsy shook her head. 'No, no one.'

Patrick wrote for a moment and then lifted his head. 'And another question, if you don't mind. Did you ever do this before?'

This was a more difficult question, but after a few moments' delay, it was answered. 'A few times.' Patsy's voice was hesitant and Patrick glanced at the Reverend Mother and then back at his sheet.

'Shall I put "most days"?' he suggested and she nodded.

'And did you see anyone go up there, at any stage of the morning?'

'No . . . no one.' There had been, thought the Reverend Mother, again a slight hesitation in Patsy's voice. Patrick must have heard it also, because he looked up quickly and then said, 'Are you quite sure? It's very easy to forget something when what happened next was so shocking and so terrible. Just think very carefully. It might have been something you hardly noticed . . .'

'I would have noticed someone going to the door because I'd have been afraid that they would tell Mr O'Donnell that the door was unlocked.' Patsy sounded rather belligerent and once again the Reverend Mother wondered whether she was telling the truth. Patsy had a look on her face as though she had suddenly thought of something. But then she shook her head resolutely. 'No, no one,' she said.

Patrick left a few moments of silence before thanking her again and then reading through her evidence and requesting her to sign on the bottom of the page. Patsy looked from one to the other hesitantly when she had done this, and then came a knock at the door.

'Ah, that is Sister Bernadette. She'll take you up to a nice warm bed and when you are tucked up, Dr Scher will come in and see if he can do anything for those chilblains of yours,' said the Reverend Mother. No more, she was sure, could be got out of Patsy just now, but perhaps she would visit her later on in the day, or in the evening, when there might be more to divulge.

'I'm glad that you are keeping her,' said Patrick when the door had closed behind them and Patsy's footsteps were heard echoing on the wooden floor of the corridor, making quite a noise compared with the sheepskin slippers that the lay sisters wore. In answer to her look of enquiry, he said, 'She may have seen someone. Perhaps she even saw Tom Hurley, himself, go up the stairs. She could be in danger,' he added and the Reverend Mother nodded slowly and thoughtfully.

'While she spoke, I was thinking of Mrs O'Mahony,' she said. 'I still don't think her death was a suicide. What if she saw someone go up – perhaps not that or she would have mentioned it immediately. She would be as brave as a lion when it came to her son's danger and would have jumped to his defence even if it were the bishop himself that she had seen. But afterwards, perhaps even on the following morning, she might have thought it over, realized that someone was missing just before the lights went out, mentioned something, perhaps asked someone a question, perhaps merely looked speculatively at someone and the murderer took fright. What do you think, Patrick?'

'Are you thinking about Tom Hurley, Reverend Mother?'

'I'm thinking of everyone who had a reason to wish James Doyle dead,' said the Reverend Mother, enunciating her words with care. He might, she thought, be right about Tom Hurley, but she did not want to hazard an opinion on this. It was too easy in this divided city to heap the responsibility for every crime on to the backs of the rebel army. There might be many reasons for the killing of James Doyle and some of these could be a private affair, a matter concerned with the safety or the reputation of an individual not connected with any of the Republicans. She thought about Robert Newenham, short of money, possibly blackmailed by the city engineer. And of Thomas Browne, whose splendid plan for the rebuilding of the city hall had been sidelined by the late James Doyle, and of the others in the city who had suffered from his vainglorious pursuit of his own wealth and reputation, his ignoring of the plight of poor people whose homes and whose places of work had been burned out on that terrible night, and who had never managed to go back to the living that they had been making before.

She looked across at him. 'You appear worried,' she observed.

'Just something that Joe told me. A boy came up to him in the street . . .'

She listened attentively as he told the story, but shook her head when he reached his conclusion. 'I've heard nothing about him,' she said.

'In any case, this business of the gallery being unlocked has changed everything,' he said thoughtfully. 'This makes it almost certain that the murder was committed by a man who was there before the lights went out and who had slipped away before they were relit. In other words, Tom Hurley. This looks to have all the hallmarks of a Republican assassination.'

'You may be right,' said the Reverend Mother and then said no more.

She had, she decided, a moral duty to get Sam out of prison if, as it seemed, he had not committed the murder, and if Patrick felt that Tom Hurley was guilty then there would, she hoped, be little point in detaining Sam for too long.

But was it the correct explanation? She believed not. When he left, she took from her drawer the copy books sent to her by Mrs O'Mahony and went through Sam's articles for the *Cork Examiner* very carefully again. And then she paused over the one where she had previously turned down the corner of the page.

Yes, she thought. Of course. Everything fitted.

# TWENTY-ONE

St Thomas Aquinas:
*Lex est quoddam dictamen practicae rationis*
(The law can be said to be the dictate of natural reason)

'I had a visitor last night, someone you know, Reverend Mother,' said Dr Scher. He had well timed his visits to Sister Assumpta and to Patsy Mullane, she thought, concealing a smile as she invited him to come in to her room and sit by the fire. The bell had just rung for the end of the school day when the Reverend Mother met him coming down the stairs. Sister Bernadette had accompanied him and now, all smiles, waited for Reverend Mother to invite him into her room before promising some tea and cake.

'A visitor?' The Reverend Mother waited until the door was closed before putting her question.

'Yes, a visitor. It was quite late when she came. My house-keeper didn't recognize her for a moment. All dressed up, she was. Very neat little hat, jacket, short skirt, nice stockings and shoes. Pretty girl. Of course, as soon as I saw the big grey eyes, I knew who it was . . .'

'Eileen!' exclaimed the Reverend Mother.

'That's right.' He laughed quietly to himself, and she half-smiled. They both, she knew, were remembering the time when she had asked him to extract a bullet from Eileen's arm and to shelter her from pursuit. 'She had a copy of the *Evening Echo* with her,' he went on, 'and she had it open at the page where there was an account of Sam O'Mahony's escape and recapture. At the bottom of it was a line that said he had been found in the throes – that was their word – of an asthma attack and that I had been called to the scene by Inspector Cashman.'

'Is Sam all right?' asked the Reverend Mother. She was conscious of a feeling of responsibility towards the dead mother of the young man. Prison, she thought, must be very hard on an asthmatic. She would have to move quickly.

'It was touch and go,' admitted Dr Scher, 'but I pulled him around. I've made them change his cell, move him up to the top floor where he can get more air. I told her that, told her all about it, and in return she told me the story of the gaol break. It was Eileen and her friends who released him,' he added.

He waited for a moment looking at her expectantly and then said in shocked tones, 'Don't smile, Reverend Mother. Surely you don't condone a pack of youngsters going into a gaol – one of them dressed as a woman and one as a priest, if you please – and then taking the prisoner away on the back of a motorbike. They nearly got away with it, too, but Sam had this asthma attack. Eileen left him in order to fetch one of those medical students, but in the meantime someone walked into the police station at Ballinhassig and informed on him. So Sam must have been secretly a member of the Republicans, all along,' he finished.

The Reverend Mother knit her brows. She was conscious of feelings of surprise. This did not fit in with what she had understood from her readings of his column on the *Cork Examiner*, and it did not fit in with her solution to the murder of the city engineer. But if he were not, then why was Eileen involved? She asked the last question aloud.

'She didn't tell me anything,' said Dr Scher. 'Well, she wouldn't, would she? She asked me to ask you if she could come to see you this evening. She's back living with her mother and she's found a job in the Lee Printing Works, run by a man called Langford, I think. They are just down the road from me – in Stable Lane, just off the South Terrace. There are rumours that they print a lot of Republican stuff, but they do other things too, leaflets for shops, posters, anything really. Probably the authorities turn a blind eye to their other activities. Though it's suspicious that she found a job so quickly in a city of unemployment, so in all probability, she got the job through her Republican connections. Anyway, I promised to drop into the printing works and to leave her a note if you were happy to see her. She said that she knew of the time and

the place that would suit you.' Dr Scher peered at her
inquisitively.

'I'm always pleased to see any of my past pupils,' said the
Reverend Mother sedately. 'Please tell her that I would be
delighted to see her this evening. A printing works is an interesting position for her. I hope she gets the chance to put her
ideas down on paper.' Thomas Aquinas, she thought, was in
favour of people arriving slowly at the discovery of the truth.
Had she rushed ahead in her solution to the murder? And then
she turned her mind from Eileen and thought about Sam and
about Patsy. No, she thought, I'm sure that I'm right. And I
can't afford to wait any longer.

'And now, on a different matter, Dr Scher,' she resumed.
'I'm getting increasingly worried about our gardener, Mr Cotter.
I don't think that he is able to carry on any longer. I think that
he should be in hospital under supervision.'

Dr Scher sighed. 'I wish that I could convince him of this.
He keeps saying that he is fine. First it was a matter of getting
the seed potatoes into the ground and now it's a matter of
earthing them up, or some such expression. He says that he
can just as easily die in his shed as in hospital.'

'I don't agree,' said the Reverend Mother crisply. 'He would
cause a great upset to whoever finds him if he were to die in
that shed in our garden. He should be in hospital where he
can be looked after properly. He's coughing very badly. The
matter worries me, Dr Scher. I am responsible for the adults
and the children of this convent and, although I understand
what you say about the germs not spreading easily in the
fresh air, nevertheless, I don't suppose that it is out of the
question. I'm afraid that I have made up my mind that, for
the good of the community, it would be better if he were
under supervision and in hospital.'

She drank her tea meditatively, keeping her eyes hooded and
fixed on her cup. She could sense him looking at her, perhaps
reproachfully, but she had made up her mind. She had no right
to allow others to run a risk just for a little false sentimentality
about a dying man. The living needed to be protected, also.

'How is Sam, now?' she asked briskly as she saw him open
his mouth, probably to argue.

This distracted him as she had meant it to do. His mind switched to another case.

'He has pulled around well,' he said. 'I'll go in and see him every morning, try to keep up his spirits. He is very depressed, very upset about his mother. Thinks he made a mess of his escape and he knows that he won't get another chance. He has been banned from having visitors now.'

'And Patsy?' she asked.

'Chilblains much better, but she's not keen to get up. Looked frightened when I suggested that she might. I suggested that she might have a walk around the garden but she begged me not to make her. She seemed to be terrified at the very idea.'

'Terrified.' The Reverend Mother considered the matter for the moment and then nodded her head.

'Let her stay where she is for another day or so,' she decreed. 'She could do with a rest and she's quite safe where she is on the top floor of the convent. No one can get at her there. And now, Dr Scher, how quickly can you get an ambulance to transfer Mr Cotter to hospital? You may use our phone, if you wish. Now would be best. Things are quiet now and the children won't be involved. And tell Mr Cotter that I shall visit him in hospital,' she added as he drained his cup and got to his feet. He was slightly shocked at her harshness, she thought, but she ignored his expression. Her whole life consisted of weighing up priorities. She had little room for sentimentality.

The Reverend Mother went out punctually at nine o'clock of the evening in order to lock the convent chapel. This was a duty which she had taken upon herself so that the other sisters could enjoy their two hours of recreation that followed the last service and ended with their bedtime. She had always enjoyed the walk through the shrubbery in the quiet evening air and tonight was exceptionally pleasant with neither fog nor rain. She cast a glance towards the direction of the gardener's shed. It was well hidden from the nuns' garden, probably built like that in order that it would not disturb their privacy, but she knew that now it was empty. She would, she thought, have to ask Dr Scher's advice about having it thoroughly

fumigated before engaging another gardener. Mr Cotter had
worked well for the time that he had been in position, and of
course as a boy he had lived in the country so that he knew
something about growing things and had doubled the size of
the beds, but perhaps, this time, she would endeavour to find
someone who specialized in fruit and vegetables. Increasingly
the convent was having to feed children as well as the nuns
and a lot of those useless evergreen shrubs and stiff-stemmed
roses, and certainly the carefully mowed lawn, could be
grubbed up so that gradually the whole garden could be planted
with edible produce. She thought of the children eating fresh
peas and the image distracted her from her sadness about
Mr Cotter.

Eileen was already in the chapel. She was sitting on the
back seat, just near to the doorway, long legs crossed and one
high-heeled shoe dangling from a toe over the worn tiles of
the middle aisle. She was dressed as Dr Scher had described
her and the Reverend Mother gave a nod of approval.

'You're looking well, Eileen,' she said.

'I collected my money for the last three articles on the *Cork
Examiner* and bought these. They're second-hand, but they
got me a job.' Eileen stood up, smoothing down her skirt and
glancing down at herself with an air of approval.

'A job,' echoed the Reverend Mother. Eileen could, or need
not, respond to the inferred question. 'Let's go into the vestry.
I need to make sure that all is well there before I lock up.'

Father Toomey had left his stole and alb lying around as
usual after the evening service, but the Reverend Mother
ignored these. She had more important affairs on her mind
than tidying up after the priest. She sat on a chair and looked
up at the girl.

'How are you, Eileen?' she asked affectionately. By the
light of the candle she could see the girl's face flush.

'I'm back with my mam, Reverend Mother,' she said and
then, almost defiantly, 'I'm still a patriot, but I've decided to
leave the Republican army. I've got a job now in the Lee
Printing Works.'

She waited. Eileen was never at a loss for words. There
would be more to come.

'Did Dr Scher tell you about us rescuing Sam?' Eileen perched on the corner of a low cupboard and examined her shoe. 'Well, it all went wrong.' And then the whole story poured out, a mixture of bravado, a few giggles, a lot of self-blame, and then huge, biting resentment. The Reverend Mother listened gravely. Eileen, she reminded herself, was still only seventeen years old and she had the usual adolescent mood swings.

'And I will never, ever forgive Tom Hurley,' she finished. 'He betrayed Sam. And he betrayed me, too. I believed in the cause, but now I can't shut my eyes any more to the fact that a lot of the time it is just sheer murder that is going on, like shooting a man because he was a Protestant.'

'Was Sam a member of the Republican Party?' This, thought the Reverend Mother, was most unlikely if Tom Hurley was the one who had informed the police. She was not surprised when Eileen shook her head vigorously. She even giggled.

'No, not in a hundred years. He's dead against violence. Sam was the one that convinced me of how terrible it was to kill people just because you disagreed with their views.'

'But you and your fellow members felt that you should rescue Sam?'

'Well, you see I knew him,' said Eileen looking embarrassed. 'I met him because he criticized something that I wrote. I went to have it out with him and we, sort of, well, we made friends.'

'I see,' said the Reverend Mother. 'You were always a very good friend, Eileen.'

'And a very bad enemy.' The words flashed from the girl. She sat on one of the altar boys' stools. 'I can't go to the police myself, Reverend Mother. My name is probably down as a terrorist, or something; I would be arrested as soon as I went in through the door, but you could give a message from me, couldn't you?'

'Tell me what you have on your mind, Eileen.'

'Sam didn't do this murder, Reverend Mother, but I know who did and I want the right man arrested for it.'

'You know, or you guess?'

'I know,' said Eileen defiantly. 'It was Tom Hurley. He told me, told us all, that he was there. He knew all about the gun landing on Sam O'Mahony's foot, he knew about it before there was anything in the papers or before anyone had a chance to tell what happened. He said that it couldn't have been better, that Sam was an enemy of our party and there was enough evidence to hang him and to stop the police looking any further.'

'I see,' said the Reverend Mother thoughtfully. 'I was there myself, of course.'

'Tom Hurley told me that, too. He said that he saw you. Did you see him, a thin man, in a belted raincoat? You wouldn't have seen his face, I'd say. He wears one of those slouch hats, one size too big for him and always keeps it pulled down to one side, hiding most of his face. He would have been by the candle stall. He brought back some candles for us on the morning when the city engineer was shot.'

'I saw him,' said the Reverend Mother. 'But he had gone by the time that the lights went on again. Miss Mullane from the library, do you remember her? Well, she went up and turned them on and then everyone saw the dead body and they saw Sam with the pistol in his hand. He threw it into the fountain and when I next looked at Mr Skiddy's soap and candle stall, the man in the raincoat had vanished.'

'There you are,' said Eileen with satisfaction. 'That was Tom Hurley. I'm sure that he killed the city engineer.'

'Why do you think that he did that?'

Eileen shrugged. 'He's always killing people; it would be nothing to him,' she said with a simplicity that slightly took the Reverend Mother aback.

'And you don't mind the thought that he might go to gaol, might hang for the murder?'

'I care a million times more for Sam than I do for him, and in any case,' said Eileen, confidently, 'the police will never catch him. Tom Hurley is as slippery as an eel. He turned Sam in because he wanted to get them off his back, but now he's gone, to Tipperary, someone said. We have a different man in charge of the Cork units now.'

The Reverend Mother studied her carefully. 'Are you thinking of marrying that young man, Eileen?' she asked.

Eileen flushed a rosy colour. 'I'm not thinking of marrying anyone, Reverend Mother. I'm a modern girl. I want to have a career, to be a journalist, or an author or something like that. Get myself some more education, perhaps and go to be a doctor.'

'But you must have felt something for this young man to have gone to such trouble and risk your friends' lives as well as your own.'

'That's a matter of justice.' Eileen looked at her defiantly and the Reverend Mother nodded her head respectfully.

'I see,' she said. Eileen, she thought, had probably fallen out of love by now, but would be too stubborn to admit it. She thought back to the time when she was seventeen, wandering on the cliffs of Ballycotton by the ocean, dazed by love, and then, quite suddenly, it was gone, replaced by a cold dislike of the man concerned.

'And you would like me to talk to Inspector Cashman about this.'

Eileen looked a little uncomfortable but then nodded. 'Sam has to be got out of gaol,' she said, 'but I hate being a traitor . . .'

'We'll leave it to Inspector Cashman to deal with this matter.' The Reverend Mother got to her feet. 'Well, Eileen, I think that you've made the right decision. Your mother will be pleased to have you at home again. She's a very good mother and did a lot for you. You were the most advanced child that ever came into our school and it was all due to your mother's care for you.'

'I know. I've made a mess of everything.' Eileen looked rather downcast.

'Well, you've many years ahead of you. Sometimes I, even at my age, make a mess of things, but then I know by now that I just have to start all over again and do it right the next time.' The Reverend Mother made her voice sound bracing and encouraging. She blew out the candles and locked the door when they were both outside.

'Keep in touch,' she said, waiting until the girl had slipped away. And then she walked swiftly towards the convent door.

Once back in her room, she thoughtfully evaluated what

Eileen had said. No, she thought, I'm afraid that it changes nothing. She would still have to do what she had promised herself to do.

St Thomas Aquinas, she remembered, had said that the law was just a matter of common sense.

She did not, she reflected, appear to have any choice in the matter which she had to reveal. The innocent had to be protected and the guilty prevented from doing harm.

# TWENTY-TWO

St Thomas Aquinas:
*Utrum Deus possit facere quod praeterita non fuerint.*
(Whether God has the power to obliterate the past)

'Sister Bernadette, could you telephone Dr Scher and ask him what time he means to visit Mr Cotter? I would like to meet him at the hospital.' The Reverend Mother did not even raise her eyes from her desk when she said this and Sister Bernadette instantly went off without questioning.

When she had gone, the Reverend Mother read, for the tenth time, that article by Sam O'Mahony. A very well-written piece, poignant, too. But terrible consequences had followed it. Apart from its initial result where it may or may not have influenced events, it had, she was sure, caused the death of the city engineer and probably the death of Mrs O'Mahony; had caused the arrest and probable sentence of death on the writer himself, and had put others such as Patsy Mullane in severe danger.

*The pen is mightier than the sword.*

Who was it who had said that? She had often quoted it to her senior English class and they had looked back at her with a lack of interest – all except Eileen who had argued vigorously that nothing ever changed unless the pen was followed by the sword – but now, thought the Reverend Mother, looking down at her desk again, she could say wholeheartedly that the pen was certainly as dangerous as the sword. If Sam had not written that article, and, she acknowledged, it had taken quite a bit of courage to write such a piece in this rebel city; but if he had not written it, he might be at liberty and his mother might be alive and vigorously selling her tripe and drisheen in the English Market.

'Dr Scher said that he would be at the hospital at three o'clock, Reverend Mother.'

The Reverend Mother fished out her watch from the depths

of her pocket and clicked it open. It was just half past one. Morning school was over and the community had finished their midday meal. The afternoon lay ahead of her, free of appointments and duties that could be postponed to the evening hours.

'Thank you, Sister Bernadette,' she said. 'And could you please tell Sister Mary Immaculate that I am going out now to visit Mr Cotter in hospital.'

'Yes, Reverend Mother.' Not even by a glance at the clock did Sister Bernadette betray her surprise. 'Will I call for a taxi?'

'No, thank you, sister. I shall walk.' Carefully she put away in her drawer the copy books into which Mrs O'Mahony had so lovingly pasted the articles written by her son. Perhaps Sam would like to have them as a memorial to his mother's love and pride in him.

And then as soon as Sister Bernadette was back in the kitchen she went to the phone and gave the number for the police barracks.

The day had fulfilled the promise of the evening before and for once the sun was out when she set off, walking along the quays. There was a strong wind from the south and the usual smell of the river was diluted by the breeze. Coming up from the sea, she thought, and a sudden wave of nostalgia came over her, as her firmly anchored veil blew out behind her, almost like a sail. She had not seen the sea for more than fifty years, had not been in a boat for longer than that. Her whole life since she was seventeen years old had been spent in the centre of this city built upon a marsh, and suddenly she felt dispirited. There was so much evil lurking beneath the cheerful scene of rippling water and bobbing ships unloading on the quays, an evil that ran below the surface, just as the stinking sewage ran below the drains beside the pavement, ready to well up from time to time. Perhaps she was getting old, perhaps she should retire. Her cousin Lucy had phoned earlier to say that she had heard on the grapevine that Robert Newenham was thinking of joining a cousin of his in South Africa and for a moment she envied him the adventure of seeing new worlds and living under a warm sun. A better ending than he deserved, perhaps, but Cork would be a safer place without a man like that.

'It's the Reverend Mother!' There was a shrill outcry and some barefooted seven-year-olds immediately joined her, forming an escort until she reached George's Quay. She sent them back, then, but her mood had lightened. She had pointed out to them that one of the ships had come from Canada bearing logs that would be turned into newspapers like the *Cork Examiner*, and she had promised that she would bring a globe into their classroom on Monday in order to show them where Canada was, had offered a sweet for anyone who could describe the flag of Canada on that day, and had explained how giant machines would chew up the logs into a sort of sawdust and would mix the wood pulp with some sort of glue and then roll out the stuff and let it to dry and then there would be sheets and sheets of paper. She left them excitedly planning to ask for some sawdust from the nearby sawmill so that they could make their own paper with it.

A smile on her lips, she made her way down the quay and then down South Terrace and knocked on the door of Dr Scher's house. She was sick of her own company. She could do with a comfortable drive in his battered old Humber instead of a long walk uphill to the barracks.

Patrick was at his desk when they arrived. He welcomed them with his usual courtesy, and then sat back and looked across his desk at the Reverend Mother. 'You've thought of something, something of significance, haven't you?' he said quietly. 'Do you think that you have identified the murderer?'

'Identifying the murderer of a man who appeared to be so universally disliked such as the civil engineer, Mr James Doyle, was a challenging task,' began the Reverend Mother thoughtfully. She leaned back in her chair and looked across at Patrick. 'It was, of course, relatively easy to find someone who might have been his murderer. There were so many possibilities. So many people feared or disliked the late city engineer, or bore him a grudge. I think that there was almost no doubt that he was blackmailing Robert Newenham. And again, there was little doubt in my mind that Robert Newenham would not scruple to kill. He had fought in a terrible war where human life was held in very low esteem. And he was, to my knowledge, a member of a family who were addicted to blood sports. I had my own rather worrying experience of him. So, of course, he was always a possibility. But somehow, I didn't think it was likely that he would have committed murder so openly. I'll come back to this point in a minute, if I may.' She paused for a moment and then said, 'And then, of course, I felt also that those who were left without a job or even a home after the burning down of Cork were possibilities. Most people who lost possessions, jobs or houses on that night probably thought that they would be speedily compensated and all would be made good, once the British government accepted responsibility and paid for rebuilding.'

She stopped as Dr Scher gave a short laugh and then said hastily, 'Sorry, Reverend Mother, just past the days of believing in fairy tales.'

'But that,' continued the Reverend Mother, addressing herself to Patrick, 'as we know, that did not happen. Perhaps as Dr Scher says, we were naïve to expect it. The money was spent, and continued to be spent, on some rather vainglorious schemes, while those who had been thrown out of work, who had lost their shops and shelter on that night, continued to suffer. Much of that could be laid at the door of the city engineer who failed to rebuild the library and the small buildings in the lanes which had been burned out.

'So from amongst those dispossessed people, I pondered over the possibility of Michael Skiddy and of Patsy, both of whom were present and both of whom had suffered greatly by Mr Doyle's action, or inaction.

'And then, of course, there was Thomas Browne, whose grand vision for the future of the city hall had been suppressed by the dead man. If that had been agreed upon, then Thomas Browne's name would have become well-known. And if it had been built, then his future and his fame would have been assured. Would that have been a motive for murder? It depends, does it not, on how important it would have been for Thomas Browne to gain fame and fortune?'

Both men looked thoughtful now, Patrick more than Dr Scher, she considered and she looked at him enquiringly.

'As you know, I had some sort of report about the bishop's secretary, but let's leave that for the moment. I would prefer to hear what you have to say, Reverend Mother. You have a better knowledge of most of those people than I have.'

She nodded gravely before continuing. 'But somehow when we think about those names, Captain Newenham, Mr Browne, the bishop's secretary, Father de Courcy, all those who clustered around James Doyle, it just seemed as if those men had too much to lose by committing this murder in such an open fashion. Why was it done at a time when there were a hundred witnesses? That's what I asked myself.

'And then, of course, there was Sam O'Mahony. His motive would, naturally, be revenge, and sometimes the thought of an injustice can grow in the mind, can obliterate almost all reason until it becomes an overpowering impulse and unbalances the mind. But somehow, I did not think that Sam's mind was unbalanced. I did not think, having looked at the blank astonishment on his face on that Friday morning when the city engineer was killed, somehow I did not think that he had been the one to fire that fatal shot. I accepted his explanation that the gun had been dropped on his foot. By accident? Or by malice?

'Malice, of course, was another possibility. Sam had not made himself popular with some of his articles. I have read them all carefully and have concluded that he was a young man who did not hesitate to speak out. Yes, he did speak out against the corruption amongst those who are now in power, but he spoke out also against the Republicans, against their wanton taking of life, against the evil of those so-called tit-for-tat murders.'

'Terrible risk to take, murdering someone in the open, in front of half Cork,' said Dr Scher thoughtfully and the Reverend Mother swung around to face him.

'Exactly,' she said emphatically. 'For all those around on that morning, including the bishop's secretary, for Thomas Browne, for Michael Skiddy, this certainly would have been a huge risk. Even for Robert Newenham, who had previously killed, but only as licensed by society, there would have been an unnecessary danger in this. And although all of these people may have had a smouldering resentment, why not do it somewhere else? On a quiet night in a back street, or perhaps, even better, on an unquiet night when guns rang from street to street and onlookers fled from the bullets. I suggest that a hatred towards James Doyle would not have been enough for such a drastic action in full public view. But there was someone else there, someone who had few scruples, someone who could justify his action, who would be approved by his associates, or by most of them, anyway,' she amended with a quick thought of Eileen, 'someone, who was trained in assassination, who could act quickly, disappear fast and have a network of escape channels to fall back on.'

'Tom Hurley,' breathed Patrick.

The Reverend Mother nodded. 'He fits the bill exactly,' she said with a rare digression into slang. 'Publicly, the Republicans had condemned the city engineer as guilty of corruption, and as leader of the anti-Sinn Fein party; privately Tom Hurley hated him because his own father had suffered from the ridiculous delay in rebuilding the library where he had been caretaker and then, of course, after the library was burned down, he was given a week's wages and had been unemployed afterwards.'

'He died six months later, Tom Hurley's father,' said Dr Scher. 'He was bone thin. I remember his death. One of those people who just seemed to give up. The place he lived in, in Maylor Street, was burned down and that hit him badly, too.'

Another death, thought the Reverend Mother wearily and then she stirred herself. There was one death which she could now, perhaps, prevent. She had to make her case and she went steadily through the evidence.

'Of course Tom Hurley was trained in guerrilla warfare, he would have learned to move fast, to escape quickly, taking advantage of the fear which these military organisations generated among ordinary people. And there was an additional reason why he should be considered as a suspect on that morning, and that was the fact that the gun was dropped at Sam O'Mahony's feet.'

'Sam was not in favour of the Republicans, was he, judging by some of his articles?' Dr Scher put the question while Patrick nodded quietly.

'That's right,' continued the Reverend Mother. 'Sam O'Mahony had written many articles criticizing the Republicans for their violence and so, in the mind of Tom Hurley, he would be judged to be worthy of death. By shooting the civic engineer from the gallery, then dropping the pistol down next to where Sam was standing it would appear that two enemies had been disposed of with one shot. Even some of Tom Hurley's associates, I believe, strongly suspected that he had been the killer.' Her mind went to Eileen's impassioned outburst.

'But you don't, do you? I know by the way you are talking that you have something else up your sleeve,' said Dr Scher. 'Though I can't for the life of me see who is left,' he added. Then he said suddenly in horrified tones, 'Not Patsy Mullane, don't tell me that Patsy Mullane is our killer!'

'What made you feel that Tom Hurley was not the murderer, Reverend Mother?' asked Patrick respectfully.

'It was the murder of Mrs O'Mahony. And I was fairly sure in my own mind that it was murder. She was not the sort of woman who would put that almost unbearable burden onto her son at the moment of his greatest need. The letter, with its opening words: "I can't go on" could have been abandoned as she began to feel ill. And when I heard that there had been an egg shell, I immediately thought of the possibility that the rat poison had been put in there, easily done with a large darning needle to puncture the shell. A smear of egg white would close it up again. And this was where I decided that Tom Hurley was not the murderer. Why should he bother to kill Mrs O'Mahony? He had made good his escape and was hidden away in a Republican safe house. Why such an elaborate and secret method, rather than a bullet and a quick escape? No, Mrs O'Mahony, I felt was murdered because the killer had reason to believe that she might have noticed them on that morning. It may be that she did, or it may be that she did not, but it would be enough for the doubt to arise. Killing,' said the Reverend Mother bleakly, 'is, perhaps, like all other sins, much easier after the first time that you have done it.

The murderer certainly did not hesitate. But this time there was no gun involved. And I had to ask myself why? Even though the revolver used to kill James Doyle was in the hands of the police, people like Robert Newenham, Thomas Browne, Tom Hurley, all of these would have easy access to other weapons, sporting guns or even knives. Rat poison is the weapon of the poor and the present of an egg is the gift of the poor, a gift from someone who has little to give.

'And, Patrick, Patsy's evidence that the door to the gallery was, in fact, unlocked at the time of the murder, and that she had been in the habit of popping up there every morning in order to eat a little of Mr O'Donnell's leftovers that he kept in his office, well, that did change matters, didn't it? It makes perfect sense of Dr Scher's evidence that the shot was fired at an angle from above the victim, whereas before, as the bullet had carved a steep pathway, it had looked as though it may have been shot by someone considerably taller than the victim, someone like Robert Newenham.'

'But now you no longer think that he is guilty?'

'No,' said the Reverend Mother. She looked from one face to another. 'No,' she repeated. 'I have changed my mind about this. You see, Patrick, I think you were actually investigating the wrong crime. I am convinced,' she went on, 'that the true victim was Sam O'Mahony. The man who planned murder was resolved that Sam would suffer the pangs, not just of death, but of death by hanging, by strangulation, that he would know the long agony of months in prison, of the waiting for the trail, of seeing the judge's black cap, of hearing the terrible words: "to be hanged by the neck until you are dead", and then of being taken out and strangled slowly, and none of us knows what that feels like, though a father or mother could perhaps imagine . . .'

'A father! You're talking about young Frank Cotter,' exclaimed Dr Scher.

'That's right,' said the Reverend Mother gravely. 'I'm afraid, Dr Scher, when you told Mr Cotter that he had only a few months to live, you passed a death sentence, not just for him, but for the city engineer, and for Mrs O'Mahony, also, though not, if we can take action immediately, for Sam O'Mahony.'

She got to her feet decisively, 'You told me that you are due to visit him at three o'clock today so I think that we should go now, if you will be so kind as to come with us, Patrick.' She paused for a moment and then said quietly, 'There will be no need to arrest him, will there? You can delay matters, can't you? Dr Scher will tell you that the man has not long to go. He will soon be appearing in front of the supreme judge.'

Dr Scher drove them to the Union Hospital. When they came into the hallway, the Reverend Mother dropped back and stood with Patrick. They waited quietly while the matron had a whispered conversation with Dr Scher and then followed him, not into a large ward, as she had feared, but to a small room at the side.

Mr Cotter was asleep when they came in. He was wearing a pair of striped pyjamas and had been shaved. He had a look of great weariness about his drawn face and his breath rattled and whistled in his lungs like a steam engine. Dr Scher bent down and put a finger on his wrist and then withdrew it after a minute. He drew his stethoscope from his pocket and held the round disc to the man's chest, slipping it inside the pyjama jacket without waking him. He left it there for a couple of minutes and then straightened and looked at the Reverend Mother, slightly shaking his head.

For a moment the Reverend Mother panicked. Had she delayed too long and would the valuable information be lost because of her hesitation, perhaps even cowardice? Dr Scher was beckoning to her and she followed him from the side ward to where Patrick stood silently waiting.

'I have to talk to him,' she said when they were in the corridor. 'It's most important. He has the evidence that will free Sam O'Mahony. Otherwise it's all guesswork and a good lawyer might demolish the whole matter as conjecture. Is he, is he in a coma?'

'No, just very weak. Not long to go. I was wrong and you were right. Death could come at any minute now. He's gone downhill more quickly than I expected.'

'I must speak with him,' she repeated resolutely.

He nodded. 'Wait here for a few minutes,' he said. He

opened his case, looked inside and then went back into the room. She stayed gazing out of the window. A single rhododendron, stuck into a symmetrically oval bed, flowered unhappily in the centre of a well-scalped lawn, isolated from all shade and all companionship of bushes and trees. She let her eyes rest on it as she thought through the morning of the death of the city engineer. No assassination after all, but a simple murder for private reasons. But not so simple, a complex scheme, evolved by a man almost driven mad by unhappiness. She was sad for him, but the living mattered more. Sam O'Mahony had a lifetime ahead of him. He had to be cleared of that charge of murder. She faced Dr Scher when he came back, his face grave.

'You can talk to him, now,' he said.

'Come with me, both of you,' she said. She opened her own attaché case and took out a piece of paper which she had written out the evening before. She glanced through it, then slowed her usual rapid reading speed to meticulous checking. Yes, she thought, as she replaced the sheet within her case and followed Dr Scher, yes, it covered everything.

Mr Cotter was sitting, propped up by pillows and his wasted hands, still slightly ingrained with soil, rested on the starched linen sheet. A nurse was with him and as they came in, she said in a murmur to Dr Scher, 'I'll fetch the priest. He's just hearing confessions in the hospital chapel.'

'Let the man have his cup of tea, first,' said Dr Scher in a hearty way. 'Mr Cotter isn't in a rush, are you? And here's the Reverend Mother to pay him a visit. She'll have him out weeding his potatoes before you know where you are.'

The nurse gave a dutiful smile while the gardener turned his eyes on the Reverend Mother. She did not waste any time. Charity was good, but a community could not exist without justice for its members. The matter would have to be handled carefully. From the look in the nurse's and Dr Scher's eyes, there was no time to waste.

'I was very sorry to hear from Dr Scher about the death of your son,' she began.

That startled him. A slight, very slight, tinge of colour came into his cheeks and he looked at her.

'What was his name?' she asked gently. It was good to remind herself of what had happened to that boy.

'Frank.'

'And he was your only child,' she said.

He nodded, but did not reply. His eyes were on her.

'And he was accused of killing the former RIC policeman.'

'That's right.' He had a defiant look and his bloodless lips were compressed, but he did not, as he had done with Dr Scher a few weeks ago, protest the boy's innocence of the crime.

The Reverend Mother allowed a few seconds of silence to ensue. He had not mentioned the hanging and neither would she. Her concern now was for another boy, another deeply loved son.

'The man, the RIC man, had collected his bicycle from your shop. You had repaired it.' She guessed that from the article. It had passed over this quickly, dwelling more on the poignancy of a man cycling out on the Lee Road, fishing rod strapped to his bicycle, sitting on the banks of the river, fishing peacefully on a sunlit afternoon, and then the assassin's bullet. Nevertheless, Sam had mentioned it.

'Frank was a patriot,' said his father, getting the words out with difficulty as he gasped for breath. 'He thought that he was doing this for Ireland.'

'You felt that Sam O'Mahony's article in the *Cork Examiner* stirred up feeling against your son; was perhaps instrumental in the verdict of guilty that was passed on him?'

He seemed about to deny it. She could see how thoughts flitted across his face, but then with an exhausted sigh, he said, 'Yes.'

'And then there was that terrible accident when the burned-out house next door to you tumbled down and smashed your premises, destroying the building and your tools and everything that had helped you to make a livelihood.'

This brought a flush of anger to his cheeks. 'The place should have been rebuilt in a few weeks after the fire,' he said bitterly, his voice rough and hoarse. 'Too busy with all the big buildings on Patrick Street. No interest in poor people in the lanes.' He choked and coughed agonisingly and the Reverend Mother held her breath. Dr Scher took a syringe from his case and injected something and then held a glass of water to the man's lips.

'You were understandably bitter against the city engineer,' said the Reverend Mother. Her voice was calm and she kept it clear of any shadow of reproach. 'And you felt,' she continued, 'very much more bitterly, that Sam O'Mahony had been responsible for the conviction of your son.' She would not ask whether the murder of James Doyle and the attempt to get Sam O'Mahony hanged had been an impulse on the morning or whether this had been planned. The visit of the city engineer to the English Market had probably been trumpeted in the *Cork Examiner* days before. In any case, during this very late spring Mr Cotter would have been in and out of the market to buy his cabbage and carrot seedlings, his onion sets, and, of course, the all-important seed potatoes. She had seen the stall herself on that morning when she had gone to buy him the present of buttered eggs. No, looking at the sunken eyes and hearing the stentorian breathing, the Reverend Mother knew that there was little time left. She had witnessed death too often to be under any illusion. The most important thing was to ensure Sam's release from prison. She took from her attaché case the statement that she had penned yesterday evening and began to read aloud: 'I, Augustin Cotter, acknowledge that I fired the bullet that killed James Doyle, city engineer, and that I dropped the gun at the feet of Sam O'Mahony in order that he might be suspected of the crime . . .'

# TWENTY-THREE

St Thomas Aquinas:
*Ubi amor, ibi oculus.*
(Where there is love, there is insight)

'I've come to say thank you to you, Reverend Mother. Inspector Cashman said that you always believed in me.'

That was well put, thought the Reverend Mother. Patrick was acquiring diplomacy. She had no desire that her role in the solution to the murder of James Doyle would be made public. Aloud she said, 'How are you, Sam?'

He didn't look well, she thought. His skin had a greyish tinge and there were black circles under his eyes. He had lost weight, also. He didn't answer her conventional question.

'I wanted to ask you about the death of my mother,' he said abruptly.

She bowed her head, taking refuge in the conventional nun-like pose, eyelids lowered, hands tucked into sleeves, veil and wimple shielding her face as she thought hard. There had been no mention of the death of Mrs O'Mahony in the confession that she had written out for Mr Cotter. She had asked him about it after he signed the confession, but it seemed to be a step too far for him. He had merely closed his eyes and lain very still. It was, she thought, a deed too evil for him to acknowledge before witnesses; she hoped afterwards that he had been able to acknowledge it to the priest who heard his deathbed confession.

But now Mrs O'Mahony's son had come to her and had asked for the truth and she thought he deserved to know her thoughts on the subject. Patrick, as a policeman, could not speculate, but what she said to this unhappy young man, was, she thought, between God and herself. She raised her head and looked at him intently.

'How old are you?' she asked.

He looked startled. 'Twenty-one,' he said and then in a slightly childlike way, he added, 'and a half.'

'And in all of the years that you knew your mother, have you ever known her to take the easy way out? Did she ever say, "What's the use?" Did she ever lie on in bed, instead of going to the slaughter houses, preparing her tripe and drisheen, being at her stall every morning, no matter what the weather was like, no matter what she felt like?'

'No,' he said. He flushed in a conscience-stricken way. 'I should have been more help to her,' he said.

'You were the light of her life,' said the Reverend Mother. 'Don't underestimate that. We all need a beacon towards which we strive.' She was not given to poetical outbursts, but she felt a need to comfort this young man. 'If your mother had committed suicide after that light was extinguished, then I might have believed it,' she continued calmly, 'but not while you were still there, not while you needed her strength, not while there was anything left that she could do for you.' Even stand, like Mary, Mother of God, at the foot of the scaffold, she said to herself.

Mrs O'Mahony, she thought, had tried one approach with her, had tried to make her bear false witness, but when that had failed, she would have then turned her mind to that morning, to an endeavour to pinpoint the real murderer.

'She may have been asking questions around the market, she may even have questioned the man himself,' she said aloud.

'Do you think that she suspected him?' Sam clenched one hand into a fist.

'No, I don't. There were lots of people who bore a grudge against the civic authorities, and perhaps against James Doyle in particular, as he was known to be corrupt. There was no real reason why she should pick out a man who was a humble gardener. No, I don't think that she suspected him. If she had, she would not have accepted an egg from him, but I do think that she was asking questions, was enquiring about anyone who might have been near to the gallery steps just before the shot was fired.' Mrs O'Mahony would have remembered about Patsy's little habit of popping upstairs with the superintendent's keys. The door to the staircase was quite near to the drisheen and tripe stall.

'An egg?' There was an expression of puzzlement in his eyes.

'I gave him six buttered eggs,' said the Reverend Mother sadly. 'I don't think that he had much appetite, much will to live by this stage. He gave one of them to your mother, I think. People were giving her small presents, some little gifts of sympathy. There were still some traces of the rat poison in the shell. She fried it for her supper with some of her drisheen.'

She thought he might weep, but he didn't. Colour flamed into his face and his fist clenched so tightly that she could see the knuckles whiten.

'It's a good job that he is dead and buried,' he said explosively and then stopped.

'Evil had entered his soul,' said the Reverend Mother bleakly. 'He had brooded on his revenge for too long.'

'And all about an article that I wrote.'

'Why did you write it?' she asked gently. It was time to divert him from his mother's terrible ending.

'I didn't intend anything against Frank Cotter,' he said impatiently. 'He had been arrested and charged by the time that I wrote it.'

'But not convicted,' said the Reverend Mother.

'He hadn't a hope of being found not guilty. He was a member of the Republicans, he had been seen cycling up the Lee Road on that afternoon, he had been known to possess a gun, had been suspected strongly of being involved in the murder of another former policeman, another RIC man. In any case, I never even mentioned his name. My article had nothing to do with his conviction.'

Nevertheless, thought the Reverend Mother, it had been published in the *Cork Examiner* and it was well-known that Cork people read every word of the *Cork Examiner*. No jury would have been unaware of that article, she guessed.

'And what are you going to do now, Sam?' she asked.

'Going to England,' he said briefly. 'I'm off on the ferry to Holyhead tomorrow. I'll get a job in London. The editor of the *Cork Examiner* has promised to write me a good reference.'

'And Eileen?' she queried.

She saw his face darken. 'She won't hear of it,' he said. 'She's wedded to all those ridiculous notions. Working for those printing works on the South Terrace. They publish all those IRA pamphlets.' His face darkened and he said, 'I could write quite a story about that fellow who runs it, that fellow that Eileen thinks is such a marvellous person, he's been involved in—'

'Don't,' said the Reverend Mother.

She rose to her feet and held out her hand.

'Well, I must say goodbye now, Sam, and I will pray for you and for the soul of your mother.' She thought of giving him some advice about Eileen, she thought of quoting the girl's favourite poet, William Butler Yeats, who had said so poignantly, "Tread softly, because you tread on my dreams," but in the end she did neither, just shook him by the hand and wished him the best of luck in his new life in London.

Eileen, she thought, would tread a different road.